# The Vampire and the Case of the Secretive Siren

Heather G. Harris & Jilleen Dolbeare

Published by Hellhound Press Limited

Copyright © 2024 by Heather G. Harris and Jilleen Dolbeare

All rights reserved.

No portion of this book may be reproduced in any form without written permission from the publisher or author, except as permitted by U.S. copyright law.

Published by Hellhound Press Limited.

Cover design by Christian Bentulan (No AI utilised).

## Jill's Dedication

I dedicate this book to the great state of Alaska. Alaska's beauty and its people have given me enough inspiration to fill hundreds of books! Even though I wasn't born here, I'll carry Alaska in my soul wherever I go. Also, to my family for putting up with me. Last but not least, to the bestest co-writer on earth, thanks for all the fun!

## Heather's Dedication

I dedicate this book to my Patreons – thank you for your faith in me. Thank you to my husband who does so much to support me. And finally thanks to Jill!

# Content Warnings

Please see the full content warnings on Heather's website if you are concerned about triggers.

All of Heather's books have occasional poor language and scenes of violence.

*Please note that all of Heather's works are written in British English with British phrases, spellings and grammar being utilised throughout.*

*If you think you have found a typo, please do let Heather know here.*

# Foreword

If you'd like to hear the latest gossip, bargains and new releases from us, then please join our newsletters!

If you'd like some lovely FREE BOOKS then join Heather's newsletter by signing up at her website, and you can get a couple of free stories, as well as pictures of her dog and other helpful things.

If you like free Audiobooks, then do subscribe to Heather's brand new YouTube channel https://www.youtube.com/@HeatherGHarrisAuth or where you can listen to all her audiobooks for free!

Jill will also give you FREE BOOKS, but she will send you cat images instead! Sign up to Jill's Newsletter on her website.

# Chapter 1

Fluffy and I burst into the Nomo's office, panting. 'We came as fast as we could! What's the emergency?'

'There's been a break-in. Let's move!' Gunnar barked. As we jogged out to the Nomo's vehicle, he threw Fluffy's K-9 vest to me. I caught it and hastily dressed my dog in his bulletproof jacket.

We leapt in the SUV and the car roared forward. 'Where's the break-in?' I asked as we careened around the corner.

'Do you remember the Grimes brothers?'

How could I forget them? They were the town's unofficial moonshiners. Portlock was a 'damp' town, one that didn't allow the sale of alcohol, but you could pay to have it shipped in. That concession was controlled through the Nomo's – the supernatural police's – office. People supplemented legitimate alcohol with the Grimes brothers' significantly less legal moonshine.

Since the brothers followed most of the rules and didn't sell to people who'd been banned from buying alcohol, they were allowed to conduct business just outside the town limits but still within the protection of Portlock's magical barrier.

Gunnar was one of their customers, and if I hadn't recently sworn off alcohol (again), I'd have considered it too, because the akpik 'shine they'd given to me had been phenomenal. Top-drawer stuff. Plus, my dad would have been horrified to think his daughter was drinking moonshine, which was definitely a reason to buy it.

'Yes, I remember,' I confirmed. 'I've met Larry Grimes. A break-in at their house?' The brothers appeared to live in a rundown, corrugated tin shed – but they were illusion witches and their real home was beautiful. Hiding their house was not only convenient; it also kept demanding riffraff from finding them outside working hours.

'No, their shop.' Gunnar was throwing his vehicle around at terrifying speed. I clung to the seat and told myself that I was an undead vampire; the chances were that even in a car accident I'd be fine.

We left the town limits and started up the mountain, and the road changed from paved to gravel. I was being shaken more than a James Bond Martini cocktail.

Gunnar was concentrating on driving so I fell silent. The last time we'd responded to a break-in, Mrs Wright, the oldest member of the community, had claimed that the old evil haunting Portlock had returned. We'd found a fresh cairn with a creepy doll on top of it, and a few days later the freakish toy had been replaced with a murdered vampire. Kivuk's back had been snapped and he'd been laid over the cairn with a stake in his heart.

No one knew what had happened, but the townsfolk were muttering uneasily about the beast beyond the barrier. I swallowed hard as I wondered what this break-in would bring us. I wiped my suddenly clammy hands on my trousers.

Gunnar noticed my unease and connected the dots. 'Not that kind of break-in,' he reassured me. 'A real one; someone stealing moonshine from their store. I'm hoping the perpetrators are still hanging around. The alarm is silent, so they might not realise they've been discovered.'

'We can hope,' I said faintly. I was actually hoping that the perpetrators were long gone, not because a confrontation scared me but because I really enjoyed unravelling the whodunit. I loved getting my Sherlock Holmes on. If the thieves were there when we rocked up, it would be a waste of a good mystery. Unfortunately, in the couple of months since I'd solved a murder case there had been depressingly few mysteries to dig into. Fender benders, assaults, drunk and disorderly – but nothing fun to sink my fangs into.

Gunnar pulled onto a road I hadn't been on before. It was in better condition and my bones gave a happy sigh as they stopped rattling. In the distance, there was an old-fashioned log cabin with a sod roof and a large sign that said Trading Post. One of the huge front windows was smashed and a light was flaring through the darkness. Bingo.

I frowned at the name. Obviously, I'd heard of trading posts, but they weren't something we had back in the UK where you pretty much always paid with cold hard cash, unless you lived in a hippy commune. 'It's a trading post?' I asked. 'I thought the brothers just sold moonshine?'

Gunnar nodded. 'They do, but they have a few things in the store. For some of the locals, this is the easiest place to get milk, bread, eggs and snacks, without braving the long, bumpy ride into town.' Having just braved that long, bumpy ride, I could understand that. Portlock believed in potholes; they were obviously a test of a driver's character.

We parked up and Gunnar drew his gun as we left the vehicle. We waited a moment but couldn't see any movement in the store, and I felt a thrill of excitement; the perpetrators were probably gone! I mentally rubbed my hands together with glee. Not that I wanted to *encourage* crime or anything, but now we'd have something to solve.

One of the large front windows had been smashed in, and the glass door had a long crack that had been fixed with silver duct tape that had obviously been in situ for a while. That damage hadn't been done by our would-be robbers. If the door was any indication of how the Grimes brothers dealt with repairs, I wondered how long it would take them to buy a new window. No amount of duct tape was going to fix that bad boy.

Gunnar opened the door and the bell chimed. There was one occupant in the room. 'Dammit Lenny!' my boss groused as he lowered his gun. 'I told you to stay home until I'd checked it out!'

'It's my store,' Lenny bitched. 'I'll come here when I want.'

'And what if you'd been met with an enraged drunken shifter?'

Lenny smiled grimly. 'Then he'd suddenly be seeing his worst nightmare come to life, brother.' His hands danced in front of him and a moment later flames appeared around us.

Fear consumed me, and suddenly I saw Virginia and Jim coiled together in one last chargrilled embrace. 'Fuck!' I swore loudly, looking around for a fire extinguisher.

Before I could properly enter the dark embrace of panic, I realised that the flames had no heat. As quickly as the illusory fire had come, it wavered and disappeared. 'For example,' Lenny said, looking at me curiously, 'the lady was afraid of fire – though it was fire *within* and I didn't quite know how to replicate that in an illusion.'

I glared at him. He'd somehow trawled through my head and looked for my fears. My fangs snicked down and Lenny held up his hands. 'Whoa! Calm down. Just making a point, little lady. No offence meant. I didn't see nothing in your head, just a little of your heart.'

'Is that supposed to be an apology?' Vulnerability was making me aggressive.

'Well, no. I don't suppose it was. I'm sorry, lady.' He sounded sincere. 'I was just making a point to this here mountain of a man that I'm not without my defences.'

'Neither am I.' I bared my fangs threateningly.

'Bunny,' Gunnar said softly, 'take a breath. Step outside if you need to.' His voice held no censure.

I took a deep breath, tried to subdue my fear and my fangs retreated. Lenny squinted at me. 'So, *you're* Bunny. You made an impression on Larry.'

'You've made one on me.' My grim tone indicated that it hadn't been a good one.

He guffawed. 'Who is this handsome fella?' he asked, kneeling down to pet Fluffy.

'He's a trained police dog, so watch your fingers,' Gunnar warned. When Lenny snatched back his hand, he smirked. Fluffy yipped and his tongue lolled out in a doggy grin. He thought it was funny, too.

'See if I save any of my finest akpik for you, Nomo,' Lenny said grumpily.

'So, tell us what happened?' Gunnar got back into work mode. 'The perps were gone when you arrived?'

'Yeah. Come this way, I've got some evidence for you. I arrived just after they left, so it took no time at all to find them on camera. You'll soon catch these teenage brats,' he said with satisfaction.

Teenage brats? Dammit: it didn't look like there was going to be much of a thrill in this hunt after all.

# Chapter 2

Lenny led us through the store. It wasn't very big, but it had been divided into two parts. The front section had a counter, a few shelves of groceries and items you'd find in most convenience stores, while the back held a large glass-fronted refrigerated section full of moonshine with a small section dedicated to juice, milk, and soft drinks.

The door to the back room behind the refrigerated section had a handwritten sign that said 'Staff Only' in barely legible scrawl. This room was full of boxes and had another refrigerated section. There was a large door, presumably for bringing in stock, which appeared to have been the criminals' point of ingress. It was wedged shut, but it had been clearly forced open because the lock was busted.

Gunnar tugged on nitrile gloves and passed me a pair. With no apparent effort, he moved the large rock with which Lenny had wedged shut the broken door. Lenny grimaced; the rock might be heavy for an illusion witch but apparently it was a mere pebble for a demigod.

I stood by Gunnar as he examined both the front and back of the door. 'See these gouges here and how the wood has splintered?' he murmured. I nodded, looking at the marks running parallel to each other. 'What do you think?' he asked.

I eyed the marks. 'Shifter? Bear maybe?'

He beamed and clapped me lightly on the shoulder. 'Got it in one! We're looking for a bear shifter all right.' He moved the boulder back into place to give the room some semblance of being secured, even if it was as illusory as Lenny's magic. 'What was taken?' he asked Lenny.

'A couple of cases of moonshine, some snacks and the little cash we keep up front.'

'Why do you think it was teenagers?'

'We might be backwards backwoods, Gunnar, but we do have security cameras!'

'Of course you do,' Gunnar said soothingly. 'You mind showing us?'

'Sure.' Lenny led us to a tiny office just off the back room. It was little more than a store cupboard and contained only a desk, ancient-looking computer, an old-fashioned TV, and a VHS tape machine.

Gunnar slid me an incredulous look and I stifled a grin. Lenny may have had security cameras but the setup was ancient, possibly older than Mrs Wright. 'Lenny,' my boss asked carefully, 'when exactly did you install your surveillance?'

Lenny looked thoughtful and scratched at his scraggy white beard. 'Ninety-four, I reckon? Sometime around there.' Not older than three-thousand-year-old Mrs Wright, but definitely older than me.

I could see the amusement lurking in Gunnar's eyes. 'I see. I gather the footage isn't real clear?'

'Clear enough to see it's teenagers,' Lenny snapped and folded his arms indignantly.

'Sure, sure. That's great. You show us how it works.'

The store owner huffed and unfolded his arms. We waited patiently whilst he booted up the machine and rewound the tape. I hadn't seen a VHS tape since I was a kid when I'd recorded the whole of *House*. I'd asked Mum and Dad for a video recorder because I knew that my nanny loved the series and we sometimes watched a couple of episodes before we knuckled down to do homework. The memory made me feel nostalgic, and I winced a little at the sudden ache in my heart.

The TV flickered on and I focused on the job at hand. The cameras showed four split screens – no doubt this had been a high-end system back in the nineties. One camera faced the front door and the counter; one had a view of the back area including the back door; one covered outside the front door, and one covered the outside at the back.

The thieves approached from the woods at the back of the building. There were three of them and they were jostling each other, as if they were already a bit drunk or egging each other on. The perps were three teenage lads with short hair; they were skinny and scrawny, not quite grown into their lanky frames.

Lenny was right: although it was hard to identify them from the atrociously grainy footage, it was clear that they were somewhere between fourteen and eighteen years old. As we expected, when they reached the back of the shop one of them shifted into bear form. He clawed at the back door, wrenched it open and destroyed the lock.

I watched them move into the back room. Once inside, the bear waddled to the front of the shop and used his claws to rip open the cash box, which crumpled like a tin can. He seemed off-balance and fell over more than once – and at one point he crashed through the front window. Ouch. He picked himself up and climbed back in, not caring about the glass that had shattered all around him.

The other kids, still in human form, hauled out a couple of crates of moonshine. The bear shifted back into a boy and helped himself to a pile of snacks, eating as he went. I wondered if they'd been indulging in other substances besides alcohol; considering the voracious way he tore into the packets and dropped crisps everywhere, I'd bet good money the bear shifter had the munchies.

After grabbing a few more packets of crisps, he shifted back into bear form and lumbered back out on four legs, dropping the packets on the way. Why had he shifted just then? He'd lost all of the snacks he'd stolen.

We watched the boys move back into the woods. A minute or so later, Lenny rumbled up and parked at the rear of the shop. He went in through the busted door and walked around to check out the damage.

Gunnar and I watched the footage three times. On the fourth time, he sighed. 'I'm pretty sure I know who the bear shifter is.' He looked at Lenny. 'You want to press charges?'

Lenny tugged his beard. 'Naw – I was a young idiot once too. Just make 'em say sorry and pay for the damage and loss of stock. I'll total a figure up. But scare 'em so they don't come knocking again.'

'You got it,' the Nomo promised. 'Is it all right if we take the footage, Len?'

'Fill your boots.'

'Great. We'll photograph the crime scene then we'll get out of your hair.'

Gunnar gestured for me to follow him and we went back to the car for the crime-scene kit. We pulled on booties over our shoes – even Fluffy had some little booties that he absolutely despised – then returned to the shop with the camera, the kit and Gunnar's notebook.

I suppressed a smirk as Fluffy tried to kick off his boots with every step. 'Leave them on,' I ordered in a low voice, 'and focus on what you can find.'

He gave an answering bark; though the look he gave me was baleful, he stopped trying to kick off his footwear.

I started in the main shop and set out cones next to signs of damage or theft. Putting one next to the crisps on the floor made my tummy rumble; in my haste to get into work, I hadn't had any breakfast. I'd have to grab something later because it wouldn't do to have some of those blood cravings that everyone kept warning me about. I prided myself on my professionalism; suddenly gnawing on a neighbour would be a no-no.

Fluffy gave a low yip and I went to see what he'd found. On the glass of the front window where the bear had climbed in and out was a small hank of fur. I had no idea if the shifter's DNA would be the same in bear form as it was in human form, but we could surely do something with it. I took some photos, then carefully bagged and tagged it.

Gunnar worked the back room and secured the videotape, and between the two of us we documented the scene quickly and efficiently. I gave a small proud smile; I'd come a long way since I'd landed in Portlock two months earlier. Securing and documenting the scene was becoming like second nature to me and Gunnar, and we worked together like a well-oiled machine.

Our perpetrators had better enjoy their snacks and 'shine because soon they'd be behind bars. And

Gunnar's wife Sigrid loved cooking gruel for the prisoners' breakfasts.

# Chapter 3

As we bounced our way back down the mountain, I asked impatiently, 'So tell me. Who is the bear shifter?'

'I'm thinking it's the oldest son of Mads Arctos. I don't know the kid's first name but I've seen him around town with his dad.'

'The name Mads doesn't inspire trust,' I said drily. 'Does he have anger issues?'

Gunnar grimaced. 'Like you wouldn't believe.'

Great. I didn't bother asking whether being named Mads had given him rage problems, or if he was named Mads *because* of his rage problems; either way, he was still an angry bear. Wondering about the chicken or the egg in this instance would probably still leave me carved up like a turkey. 'Are we heading to the Arctos residence next?' I asked.

Gunnar was quiet for a moment. 'Well, as I said, Mads has rage issues, so arresting his son is gonna be real tricky.'

'Are you worried for us or for his son?' I asked.

He chuckled. 'A bit of both.'

'So we're not just going knocking?'

'Not without appropriate backup. We'll pick up Stan first.'

Oh boy. Stan Ahmaogak was a polar-bear shifter and the leader of the land-shifters in Portlock. He could handle a raging brown-bear shifter – but he also had a teensy-weensy crush on me and was pursuing me relentlessly. We'd got off to a rocky start when he'd drunk his way under a table at my 'Welcome to Portlock' party, but, after a lot of apologies and chai lattes, I'd finally agreed to a real date one day. I'd tried to make it easier on myself by making it a double date; my co-worker Sidnee and her boyfriend Chris had gamely agreed to be my wingmen.

During the last couple of months Chris had set me up with a few of his buddies, but something hadn't quite been right about any of them. Maybe I still wasn't ready. The evenings had been pleasant but I hadn't felt any urge to repeat them. It was different with Stan because I'd really grown to like him. He'd popped into the Nomo's office a few times to bring me my favourite chai latte and have a quick chat. If it were not for the expression in his eyes when he thought I wasn't looking, I'd have said we were close to becoming friends. Sometimes, though, he looked at me like I was lunch and he wanted to eat me up.

We were having our long-awaited double date that night. Maybe this case would run on too long and I wouldn't be able to make it. A girl could dream.

'You really think we need him?' I asked plaintively.

Gunnar slid me an amused look; he'd noticed Stan bringing me drinks. 'I do. Why don't you call him when we get back in cell range and see if we can pick him up? We'll get it over and done, like ripping off a Band-Aid.'

I sighed but hauled out my phone and dialled. 'Bunny,' Stan answered warmly. 'To what do I owe the pleasure?' He was practically purring at me. Did polar bears purr? I didn't ask; implying he was some sort of pussycat would not be well received.

'Business, I'm afraid,' I said briskly. 'We need your help with a shifter. Can we pick you up?'

'Sure.' Suddenly his tone was businesslike and all hints of flirtation were gone. 'If you meet me at the South Harbour, that would be best.'

'You got it. We'll see you in ten.' I hung up.

Stan fished for a living and he must have just got in. I relayed the information to Gunnar and he turned towards the South Harbour.

We had found Eric Walker's body at the North Harbour, and sometimes I could still see the bloody scene. He had been sliced and diced and, because he had died in the middle of shifting, his body was a twisted horror. I hadn't had to return to North Harbour since then, for which I was grateful, but at some point I'd have to do the brave thing and face my fears. Vampires weren't supposed to be upset by corpses since we were walking ones.

Stan was striding up to the car park when we pulled in, fishing gear slung over his shoulder. We parked next to his truck Bessie – yes, he was the type to name his truck – and he slung the fishing gear into his vehicle. He closed and locked it, then climbed into the back seat of our SUV next to my dog.

'Hey Fluff,' he greeted, ruffling the top of my dog's head. Fluffy gave him a friendly bark hello. 'So where are we going?' Stan asked as we pulled away,

'We need your help with Mads Arctos. His son is being stupid.' Gunnar explained briefly what had happened at the trading post.

'You wanna go and poke at Mads, huh? Talk about poking the bear.'

'We gotta go where the evidence points us, and it's pointing to Mads' kid. Any suggestions about handling the situation?'

Stan blew out a breath. 'Yeah, let me do the talking and stay back. Things'll probably get furry before we get Mads to listen.'

'What's the kid's name?' I asked.

'Russ – Russell.' Stan frowned. 'He's a good kid, responsible. I'm pretty surprised he'd do anything like this. I hope you're mistaken.'

'I don't think we are,' Gunnar said. 'The footage is grainy, but I'm ninety percent sure it's him.'

Stan grimaced. 'That's not looking good for Russ, then. His mum is going to be steamed. Better worry more about her than Mads.'

Gunnar was a mountain of a man, not brown-bear or polar-bear huge but immensely strong. Sidnee had told me he was a demigod and I was pretty sure she was telling the truth; though there was a faint chance she was yanking my chain. Still, if she'd told me Gunnar was half-giant, I'd have believed her because the man had *stature*. Whatever he was, he wasn't a vampire; unlike me, he didn't need extra speed and strength to get him out of the way of a raging bear. At least, I didn't think he did – I hadn't seen him run yet. He was more a stand-your-ground type; in a battle, he'd be the one holding the line until the last swing of his axe.

'Just remember we need to ask Mads some questions then we need to talk to Russell,' Gunnar reminded Stan.

'Yeah, I know. I'll make sure Mads is still coherent when I'm done with him.' Stan's tone was grim. He clearly thought a brawl was inevitable.

We pulled up at the house and he got out. 'Stay back,' he instructed tersely, looking at me with real concern. *That* was the real reason I wasn't eager to date him, no matter how good he looked in his jeans. Whilst I appreciated his concern, he'd best look after his *own* back. I could look after mine – even if he still didn't realise it.

# Chapter 4

We hung back as Stan had instructed, and I checked out the house whilst he rolled his shoulders and strolled up the path. It was a modest but well-cared-for family home with a neatly maintained front garden.

Stan knocked and a woman answered who I assumed was Mads' wife. She looked motherly and was wearing an apron, as if we'd caught her mid-baking. She had shoulder-length red hair streaked with grey and appeared to be in her mid-forties, although the signs of age were deceptive in a lot of supernats.

As we edged closer, I heard Stan diplomatically explaining our suspicions about Russ. Mrs Mads' lips tightened before she disappeared from view. With my sharp hearing, I heard her calling for her son, 'Russell

Michael Arctos!' He was definitely in trouble; he'd just got the full-name shout.

There was a ruckus in the background followed by an exasperated shout of 'Mads, no!' Next, a gigantic brown bear came flying out of the door, barrelled into Stan and knocked him clear off his feet.

Even as he flew through the air, Stan was shifting. I might have taken the time to admire the snow-white fur of his polar-bear form, but he and Mads were already grappling and ferocious growls were rending the air.

Despite my fear that they'd tear each other apart, I soon registered that despite the threatening growls the bears weren't using their claws or teeth. This was the bear equivalent of WWF: a lot of grappling, noise, and show, but no real threat of violence. Even so, Gunnar and I stepped back a little more and kept the SUV between us and the hulking beasts. One of them could hurt us by accident if they rolled into us; they were *heavy*.

Mrs Arctos came out into the garden, ran down the front steps and picked up a garden hose. She turned it on, aimed it at both bears and set a stream of water flying at them. Stunned, they separated and turned to face their new foe.

She was livid. 'Mads Arctos, you shift back now or you are sleeping in the garage for a *week*!'

The brown bear backed off instantly and shifted back into human form looking a bit sheepish. Mads was a burly man with a fine coating of black hair *everywhere*. Didn't they know about waxing here? I averted my eyes from his naked form, wishing I could burn the image from my eidetic memory, but I knew Mads' physique would be imprinted on my mind forever. I grimaced; Mrs Arctos might have been a lucky woman, but I really wished I hadn't seen his schlong, no matter how impressive it was.

'You too, Stan Ahmaogak!' she barked.

As Stan shifted, I looked away and kept my eyes squeezed tight; if I was going to see Stan's naked form, I didn't want it to be in circumstances like this. Besides, it was cold out; it might not be a fair environment in which to judge his prospects.

I heard Gunnar go to the back of the Nomo vehicle and rummage around to find some clothes. A moment later he murmured reassuringly, 'He's dressed. You can open your eyes now.'

Dressed was an overstatement: Stan had pulled on tight navy shorts that revealed that he seemed to be doing okay, cold weather or no. A smile played at his lips as he saw me take in his incredibly muscular form. His abs game was strong, and his midsection was so sculpted that I bet Michelangelo had asked him for tips. I gulped and tore my eyes away.

'What are you going to threaten *me* with, April?' Stan asked Mads' wife with a cocky grin. 'You can't banish me to my own couch.'

She smiled playfully then hosed him down again. I burst out laughing. Well, that was one way to handle him. Stan spluttered but quit talking. It was nice to see that she wasn't afraid of him in the slightest; he might be her leader, but she didn't fear him. He went up a little more in my estimation.

Hands on hips, April turned to her husband. 'If Russ *did* break into the Trading Post, you need to be mad at him, not at Stan, not at the Nomo.'

Mads hung his head a little as he took the dressing down. 'All right, love. Sorry.'

Gunnar and I looked at each other in surprise: she had the big tough man wrapped tightly round her finger. I wondered if she could give me advice – ten top tips to tame tough, testosterone-filled-men.

April bellowed into the house, 'Russell Michael Arctos, get down here this minute! I've called you twice already – don't make me shout a third time!' Her voice snapped out like a whip and the threat was heavy in the air. For all Mads had his cool nickname, we could tell who was the boss in this family.

A tall, gangly boy appeared. He had his mother's ginger hair and a smattering of freckles across his pale skin. 'What, Mom? I was in the middle of a game,' he whined.

Mrs Arctos grabbed her son by the shoulder and pulled him out of the house. His eyes widened as he caught sight of the Nomo and Stan. 'Did you break into the Trading Post?' she demanded.

Russell stared at us and gaped, but a moment later he widened his eyes in faux innocence. I didn't buy it for a second and apparently neither did his mother. Before he could open his mouth, she laid into him again. 'You better answer truthfully, Russell, or the video games, the computer and your phone – all of them – are going in the trash!'

*Ooof*. April Arctos was a heavyweight and she wasn't messing around. Russell hesitated another moment and licked his lips, then his shoulders slumped in defeat. He hung his head and told the truth to his toes. 'Yeah. We did.'

His mother looked apoplectic; her lips were pressed so tightly together; it was a wonder they didn't disappear entirely. 'You are going to pay it all back. Every. Single. Dime. And until that is done, you're grounded from your computer, your phone, and your friends. Do you hear me?'

'I thought we were supposed to be afraid of Mads,' I whispered to Gunnar.

'Me too,' he whispered back,

April levelled a glare at us both. 'What else do you need to know, Nomo?' she demanded.

'Who were the other two boys?' Gunnar asked.

Russ looked like he was going to bolt, but his mom put a firm hand on his shoulder and squeezed. 'Tell him.'

'They'll call me a snitch!'

'That's better than what I'll call you if you don't give me their names *right now!*' she snarled.

Russell huffed a breath and gave up. 'Whatever. It was Jake and Sky.'

'Jake and Sky what?' Gunnar asked. 'Give me their full names, son. Let's not have any confusion.'

Russ mumbled a bit, but a nudge from his mom cleared up his vocal problem. 'Jacob Olsen and Skylark Riverdream.' He rattled off their addresses.

'Thanks. When we get the bill from the Grimes' brothers, we'll let you know,' Gunnar said.

'Why did you do it?' April exploded. 'What were you thinking?'

Russ shrugged. 'I guess I wasn't thinking too clearly. We just wanted some booze and none of us had any at home.'

His mother looked like she was having a nuclear-level meltdown. She was taking deep breaths and trying to count to ten, her lips moving soundlessly as she tried to calm herself.

'Are you going to take me to jail?' the boy sounded hopeful as he looked up at Gunnar.

'The Grimes haven't decided if they are pressing charges,' Gunnar fibbed. 'I suggest an apology might help, as well as paying for the things you took and the damage to the store. With all that, you *might* just avoid my cell.'

Russell looked even sicker; he'd probably been hoping that we'd take him away because his mother looked fit to kill him.

His dad looked weirdly proud that his weedy son was finally striking out on his own. It might not be necessarily the best way but Mads seemed relieved that his son was finally growing a set and living his own life.

I doubted Russell would be having much more freedom by the time April was done with them. She was spitting fury. In a way it was nice to see, because my mum had never cared enough about me to get this irate; I'd always felt that I was a constant source of disappointment to her. April's anger was a sign of love, though I doubted Russell would see it that way.

Now it was time to track down Jake and Skylark and see what they said. Russell had cracked faster than a walnut being smashed with a hammer, so I kind of hoped the other boys would pose more of a challenge.

# Chapter 5

We drove to the car park where Stan's truck was waiting. 'I'll pick you up for dinner at 3am,' he said as he climbed out of the car.

'Oh, it's fine. I'll walk,' I said hastily.

'The moon's high,' he told me gruffly. 'I'll pick you up. See you then.'

I sighed as he closed our SUV door and climbed into his own truck. I liked Stan but his behaviour was a mite too controlling for my taste. I was just finding and embracing my own independence; I didn't want to be with someone who would seek to curtail it.

'I think April should lead the shifters,' I said to Gunnar. 'She had Stan and Mads quivering in their boots.' Fluffy barked agreement, tongue lolling with amusement.

Gunnar laughed. 'Yeah, she's something else, all right.'

'What kind of a name is Skylark?' I asked. Since my name was Bunny, my tongue was firmly in my cheek.

The Nomo laughed. 'I've heard the kid's parents were hippies – their family name is Riverdream. They're often out and about on protests, though they're always peaceful and I've never arrested any of them. Their other kids are called Peregrine and Kestrel.'

And I thought Elizabeth Octavia Barrington was bad. If my name was Skylark Riverdream, I'd be acting up, too. 'Protests?' I asked.

'Some folks will protest anything, but most disturbances here are about the barrier tax.'

I'd seen the tax on my paycheck, and the amount deducted had been a bit eye-watering. 'What's the barrier tax for?' I asked, 'I mean, obviously it funds the barrier, but why is it so expensive?'

'We pay the elemental witches to run it. That causes some bad feeling between the witches and the others

– some feel like the witches are profiting from the community's fears.'

'Well, the fears aren't baseless, are they?' I shivered as I remembered Kivuk's broken body and the look of horror on his twisted face.

'No, I don't reckon they are,' Gunnar admitted. 'But some folks don't believe in the beast beyond the barrier, and they think we're paying through the nose for nothing. The beast – whatever it is – has been dormant for years. Frankly, we all thought that it was dead and there was even some talk about lowering the barrier.'

'But it's not dead?'

'Doesn't seem so. Seems like it was hibernating and something – or some*one* – woke it right up.'

I shivered again and licked my suddenly dry lips. I didn't want to talk about the monsters anymore so I cast around for a change of subject. 'Which of the kids are we heading to first, Jacob or Skylark?'

'Skylark. I don't know Jacob's family so well and the Riverdreams are on the way to his house.' Gunnar turned down a street not far from the Arctos' family's place and pulled up in front of a dark-green, split-level house. There weren't any cars in the driveway and Gunnar grimaced. 'Nobody home, I reckon.' Even so, we got out and walked up to the door.

He pressed the doorbell and a dog barked inside, but we couldn't hear anyone approaching the door. After a second ring of the bell and some more frantic barking, no one appeared so we left.

It only took a few minutes to arrive at Jake's house. The three boys didn't live far from each other, a trifecta of trouble. Jake's home was a white bungalow; it was similar to mine, so it was likely to be borough housing. That meant one of Jake's parents probably worked for the borough.

We left Fluffy in the car and knocked briskly. A tiny girl opened the door; she had jam all over her mouth and a good amount of it in her blonde hair. Gunnar squatted down so he didn't tower over her. 'Hey, little lady, is your mama home?'

She nodded but continued to stare at us as she absent-mindedly smeared jammy fingers into her hair. 'Would you go get your mama please?' Gunnar added.

She toddled off. We waited by the open doorway for a while but no one came. Gunnar looked at me. I shrugged and called out, 'Hello? Mr or Mrs Olsen? It's the Nomo's office.'

A distant, 'Just a moment!' drifted out and a tired-looking woman came to the door. Even though Gunnar didn't know the family, it was clear that she recognised him. She looked at him in surprise then tried to smooth her hair, which was coming out of its ponytail in a thousand directions. I guessed Jam Kid got her neatness from her mum.

'Nomo! What can I do for you?'

'Is Jake around?' Gunnar asked.

She frowned. 'I don't know. Why? Is he in trouble?'

'I'm sorry to say that he is, ma'am. He and his two buddies, Russell Arctos and Skylark Riverdream, apparently broke into the Trading Post, stole some moonshine, snacks, and cash, broke the door and a window.'

She looked stunned then closed her eyes and pinched the bridge of her nose. 'You have got to be kidding me,' she muttered under her breath. She opened her eyes. 'Just a minute, Nomo. I'll go and see if he's here.'

There was a baby crying in the distance and I felt bad for Mrs Olsen. She looked overworked and stressed.

She came back several minutes later but without her son in tow. 'He's not here.' She looked scared. 'What will happen to him?'

'We need to talk to him, then he and the other boys will have to pay back the Grimes brothers. They haven't pressed charges yet but if they do, we'll talk about what that will look like. It'd be best to get an apology to them and pay them back before the court gets involved. We've got Jake on CCTV and a witness corroborated his presence.' Gunnar gave her a card with our numbers on it and asked her to call when her son returned.

She nodded, but her hand was trembling as she took the card. I smiled at her; trying to offer whatever comfort I could, though it wasn't a lot. Her kid was out doing who knows what, possibly with Skylark. For their sakes, I hoped that we didn't get another call out: one break-in was a foolish teenage decision, two were charges and juvenile detention.

That was a two-for-two strike out since neither kid was home. Never mind: it was only a matter of time before we tracked them both down and threw the book at them. I hoped they weren't smart enough to duck.

# Chapter 6

The rest of my workday – I still called it that, even though I worked through the night – was quiet, so Gunnar and I went to the gun range to practise shooting. He had officially assigned me a gun, figuring that was a better idea rather than just tossing me one in the heat of battle. So far he'd done that twice – and I'd only been in town two months.

My weapon looked enormous; apparently it was a .44, which I'd learned was related to the ammo size. Gunnar promised it shot big bullets to stop big brutes, bears, and beasts. He was joking about that last one – at least, I hoped he was.

The gun range was a covered area, well-lit through the night hours for those community members who were nocturnal. It was summer at the moment, so it was light most of the time; when I'd moved here, I'd been daydreaming about the two months of darkness in winter, but I'd forgotten that in summer it was almost always daylight.

We were at the pistol range, which I guessed was different from the shotgun and rifle ranges; Gunnar had promised we'd get to those in time. For now, he wanted to get me comfortable around guns. I came from the United Kingdom where even the police weren't armed; the only people who shot with any regularity were the aristocracy. Apparently clay-pigeon or real-game shooting was the done thing in the stately homes of England, but to my mother's despair I'd never climbed into that particular social circle. Lords, ladies, and kings weren't really my thing, but give me shots with a side of drum and bass, and I was golden. Maybe these days murder, mayhem, and magic were my forte. I had taken to my new life like a duck to water and I was truly proud of myself. New Bunny was coming along a treat. I was even trying to get over my fear of guns. Though that was very much a work in progress.

'Okay, let's look at your weapon,' Gunnar said gruffly.

I pulled out the case and opened it gingerly, staring at the thing inside like it was a spider. Man, I hated spiders.

Gunnar sighed noisily. 'This will go faster if you pick it up.'

'Ummm.' I stared at the gun then grasped the handle with my forefinger and thumb and lifted it from its foam bed. I *felt* Gunnar roll his eyes at me.

He took the gun, clicked a button and the middle bit that held the bullets – the cylinder – popped open. 'Look inside,' he ordered. 'It isn't loaded.'

I looked. He was right: the chambers were empty.

'I want you to learn the revolver because it has fewer moving parts and it's easier for a beginner. See this round thing? That's the revolving drum that feeds the shells into position for firing. First thing is loading it. You push this...' he pointed to a small knob next to the drum '...and this...' another knob '...and the cylinder pops out for loading.' He made me practise a few times until the movements at least felt normal, even if they weren't comfortable.

'Good. Now let's put the ammo in.' Gunnar held up the bullets for me to see that the pointy end went in first. I gave him a flat look; I knew *that* much. He gave me an unrepentant grin. 'These here are bear rounds. When you shoot, the gun's gonna give a bit of a kick. Hold on real tight. I'll show you how to grip it properly in a moment.'

I nodded and finished loading under his supervision. When I was done, I clicked the cylinder back in place. I felt pleased; I'd be a pro in no time.

'Now, this model has something called a double-action trigger,' Gunnar said. I nodded even though I had no idea what that meant. My face must have given that away because he explained, 'It means you can cock the gun and shoot, but you don't have to. You can just press through the tension of the trigger and it will arm itself. That's quicker when you're in a hurry.'

I nodded again. Quicker sounded good.

'I'll demonstrate.' Gunnar drew back the curved deal at the back of the gun. 'This is called cocking. This is the hammer. Now the gun is armed, and when I squeeze the trigger it will fire.' He released the cocking mechanism and set the gun down. 'Put on your ear protection and I'll show you what I mean.' He covered his own ears, checked that my ear protection was fitted properly then picked up the gun, cocked it, pointed it, and shot at the target. Bullseye.

He set the gun down and pointed to my ear defenders. I lifted one cup so I could listen to him. 'I don't have to cock this gun – I can squeeze through the double action. You can tell because it gives a slight click then the tension will be higher when you squeeze through.'

We settled our ear defenders back in place and he shot again, this time without pulling the curved deal at the back of the gun. Bullseye again. Neat. He put down the gun and said, 'Your turn. We'll try both ways. Just remember, don't put your finger on the trigger until you're ready to shoot – and never point it at something you aren't planning to shoot. Got it?'

I nodded. Gun safety was a big deal, and I didn't want him to think I wasn't taking this seriously. I put my ear protection back on and ran through the steps in my mind then picked up the revolver, cocked it and placed my hands around it like Gunnar had showed me.

I aimed at the target and squeezed the trigger. *Bam* – the gun slammed into my hand and bucked so hard I barely held on to it. I squealed, 'Jeez!' and hurriedly set it back down. That thing had a life of its own! It had kicked worse than a pissed-off donkey.

'You okay?" Gunnar asked.

I pulled off the ear defenders. 'Yeah. I wasn't expecting that.'

'It has a decent kick. Those are big rounds. I could have warned you more, but it's one of those "learn by doing" things.' He studied my face. 'Are you ready to try without cocking?'

'Sure,' I said with a calmness I wasn't feeling. Fake it till you make it, right?

I put my ear protection back on and picked up the gun. This time, I knew to hold on tighter. I drew the trigger back and felt the extra give, the slight click and then the higher tension. I squeezed through it and – *bam*.

This time I compensated for the kick and held onto the gun's grip tightly. Too hard, way too hard; the handle crumpled in my iron-strong vampiric grip. 'Oh shit!' I stared at the twisted hunk of metal.

Gunnar looked at the ruined grip for a moment before bursting into laughter. 'A little less firm next time,' he chuckled. 'You did well, though. You hit the target.'

I looked: I had hit it just on the edge but even so I grinned and gave Gunnar a high five.

'You'll make an excellent shooter someday! Once we get you another gun, Calamity Jane. Here, practise with mine.'

We shot the rest of the rounds then reloaded and went through two more sequences. By the end, I was hitting the target about seventy-five percent of the time. Gunnar said that I had the basics down and just needed more practice. I felt chuffed but tried to keep my grin to a modest smile; grinning like a loon didn't exactly say 'law and order'.

Back at the station, I called the Riverdreams' house. Gunnar was sitting in the waiting area and his eyebrows shot up when my call was answered. I quickly explained the issue to Mrs Riverdream and started to ask her to bring Skylark in, but Gunnar tapped his watch and shook his head. I asked them to come in tomorrow and she gruffly agreed.

'Why not get them in now?' I asked Gunnar plaintively. 'Skylark will talk to the others and they'll all get their stories straight!'

Gunnar smiled. 'Whilst I appreciate your zeal, Bunny, it's the end of our shift and this isn't even a crime where charges are going to be brought. We're just trying to shake these kids up so they don't fall by the wayside. And you? You're trying to get out of your date!'

My mouth dropped open. Dammit, I was. How had he known that?

He laughed. 'You're on your own. If you want to cancel then do, but you don't get to blame me. I'd never hear the end of it. Sigrid thinks you and Stan will make a cute couple.'

I groaned aloud.

'Off you go.' He waved me away. 'Have a nice date.'

Shoot me now.

# Chapter 7

My house had burned to a shell two months earlier and I'd been sofa-surfing ever since. The previous week I'd finally received the keys to my new home. To say I was grateful was a gross understatement.

This house had the same floor plan as the others supplied by the borough, although it was a little newer than my previous one. It was a bungalow with two bedrooms, a large laundry/bathroom, and an open-plan living room and kitchen. The colour scheme was a light, soothing blue and white. It had immediately felt like home.

I had nothing to take with me but Fluffy's bowls, a few clothes, and some toiletries. A single tote, and we were moved; if I hadn't been so excited, it would have been depressing. Luckily the home came with some furniture, so I had a bed and a sofa once more.

'Home sweet home,' I called to Fluffy as we walked in. I gave him some fresh water then hopped in the shower to start getting ready for dinner. I didn't want to go too dressy because we were only going to the Garden of Eat'n, so I slung on clean jeans, a silver top that hung just right, and a pair of incredibly high heels. I decided I might as well wear my skyscrapers since Stan was picking me up and I wouldn't have to walk far. I swiped on a little make-up; regretfully there was no time for fake eyelashes or painting my nails.

When the doorbell rang, I'd already swilled down my cup of blood and I was good to go. 'Don't wait up!' I joked to Fluffy and he let out a growl. He was absolutely waiting up. He had already eaten, been outside to the toilet, and was relaxing on the sofa in front of the TV.

I grabbed a small clutch purse that could hold my phone and opened the door to Stan. He'd made a real effort; like me, he was wearing jeans but he'd paired them with a shirt and smart shoes. His brown hair was brushed and styled with some sort of gel. 'Hi!' I chirped. 'You look great.'

'That's my line,' he replied, his eyes dark with admiration. 'You look beautiful.'

I felt my cheeks warm. 'Thanks. Let's go. I hate being late.' I stepped out and locked the door.

'No problem.' He opened the car door for me. We chatted lightly during the short drive to the diner then Stan parked up and insisted on holding the door for me again.

Sidnee beamed as I walked in and waved me over. She was wearing a dusky-pink top that complemented her skin tone perfectly, and she'd piled her hair in an elaborate updo. Chris was sporting a shirt and some lovely smelling aftershave – we'd all made an effort.

Chris stood up as we arrived and the men shook hands and did some shoulder clapping. I slid into the booth opposite Sidnee and next to Stan. 'Chris is arranging for us to take a trip to Anchorage to see *Hamilton*!' my friend burst out, almost bouncing in her seat.

I grinned. 'That will be so much fun. I love the theatre. I haven't seen *Hamilton* but I've heard great things.'

'It's supposed to be great.' Chris gazed soppily at Sidnee. 'A weekend away is just what we need.' The way he looked at her made me squirm a little as if I were intruding on a private moment. He had plans for the weekend, and they totally involved naughty underwear. I'd have to check Sidnee was prepared because I wasn't sure she was a naughty-underwear girl, and I might need to do some educating. Then again, she might surprise me. It's always the quiet ones.

'I hope you're feeling game,' Sidnee said to me with a grin.

'Game for what?' I asked cautiously.

'It's karaoke night!'

My jaw dropped. 'But it's a damp town! You can't do karaoke sober. Karaoke should be illegal without alcohol!'

Stan laughed. 'I bet you'll smash it. From what I remember of the "Welcome to Portlock Party", which admittedly isn't much, you have a great set of lungs.'

I winced. 'I sang?'

'Ooooh, yeah,' Sidnee said with relish. 'Taylor Swift's "Lover".'

Stan's smile widened. 'You danced, too.'

'Stop teasing her,' Chris rebuked him. 'You didn't dance.' He paused and a smile tugged at his lips. 'Well, not the *whole* time. That was when you fell into a table and knocked a whole tray of drinks over.' He smirked.

I groaned and dropped my head into my hands. The others started to laugh at my expense. I sat up and rolled my eyes good-naturedly. 'You guys suck. What is this, gang up on Bunny day?'

Stan leaned forward. 'I've been dying to ask, how did you come by the name Bunny?'

'I once tried to speak in nothing but rabbit puns and jokes for a whole day. My friends nicknamed me Bunny. It stuck.' I shrugged.

Chris mock-frowned at me. 'Wait a second – someone is telling fibs! You told me it was because of your overwhelming love of carrot cake.'

'That too.'

Stan was laughing. 'Do you tell a different story every time?'

'Of course not!' I protested, eyes wide. 'Not *every* time. I re-use the really good ones. Government experimentation is my favourite!'

Chris's smile faded. 'What's the real reason?'

I winked. 'That'll die with me. Now, what are we drinking?'

Stan slid a hipflask out of his pocket. 'Order a Coke, and we can add a hint of moonshine.'

'Nice!' I laughed. '*Now* I can do karaoke!'

Sidnee clapped her hands. 'I'm on shift later so I've got to take it easy, but I'll cheer you all on. Besides, I don't need a drink to have fun!'

'No, you don't,' Chris agreed with an adoring expression. 'You're fun all the time. Now, it's time to let our hair down.' He reached over, started pulling bobby pins out of her hair and her beautiful locks came tumbling down.

She mock huffed at him. 'Do you know how long it took me to get it that perfect?'

'It's better this way,' he murmured. 'It reminds me of the other night in the water,' he winked.

She blushed and I made a mental note to tease her about it in the morning. It looked like she wouldn't need any underwear advice from me. It definitely *was* always the quiet ones!

When my Coke arrived, Stan doctored it with a generous glug of 'shine and did the same to his own drink. The night was looking up: it was time to say bye-bye to Teetotal Bunny, and hello to Belting Out Songs Bunny.

# Chapter 8

My head was pounding. Ugh: I loved moonshine but it did *not* love me. Blearily, I checked the time. Barely 11am – I never slept well when I'd had a drink, but that was ridiculous. Five hours sleep was *not* enough.

I rolled over and tried to go back to sleep but my throbbing head wasn't helping matters. Muttering a few choice swear words, I got up and stumbled to the shower, then dressed in fresh PJs and a dressing gown. A cup of blood and the pain would go, then I could mooch on the sofa before work.

My work schedule was far from Dolly Parton's nine to five; usually I went in during the late afternoon or early evening and stayed through the night until 2am or 3am. Much of the town was the same; Portlock's core hours were wildly different to a normal – or pedestrian – town. Shops, cafes and even the funeral home opened much longer to cater for both the day and night crowds. As a consequence, employees worked day and night shifts so a lot of the day crowd had also adapted to nocturnal hours. Portlock was at its quietest in the morning when most of its supernatural denizens were sleeping.

Being a vampire, I preferred being around at night, though I had my charmed necklace that allowed me to walk in the daylight without combusting into the fire of a thousand suns. I'd recently had its spell renewed, but even so I still felt a little edgy having the sun burn down on me. That happened a lot during the Alaskan summer; at the moment we were only having five hours of darkness.

Fluffy lifted his head and looked at me as I chugged warm blood. 'My head hurts,' I complained, and his tongue lolled out in a doggy grin.

Stan had walked me home; he'd drunk too much to drive his truck but he'd insisted on making sure I reached home safely. It was sweet if a little misguided because he was three sheets to the wind. I doubted he'd have been much use if someone had attacked me.

There had been a moment on my doorstep when tension had hung in the air ... but then I'd realised that what was curling in my tummy was dread, not excitement. I'd turned away, unlocked my door and given him a jaunty wave as I stepped inside. Then I'd slammed the door shut in his face. It wasn't my finest moment but, sexy as he was, I had absolutely zero desire to do tonsil hockey with him. Something about it all felt *wrong*; there was no spark between us, not from my end, at least.

I flicked on the TV and lost myself in some truly terrible daytime dramas where the shock reveal was that the baby wasn't the husband's. As I watched, intrusive memories flashed back, like when Stan had sung 'You Give Love a Bad Name' by Bon Jovi, or when Chris and Sidnee had soppily duetted 'We Found Love' by Rhianna. Groaning, I remembered singing 'I Am Woman' by Helen Reddy. Stake me now.

At some point, sleep took me again, and when I woke it was 4pm. I had a crick in my neck and it was only an hour before I was on shift. Fuck! I flew around the house getting dressed in my work clothes and packing a hasty lunch for later. By the time I was ready, the crick in my neck was all gone: vampire healing was the best.

My mind skittered to Virginia cutting into me with my kitchen knife and I pushed it away. I didn't need that now. *La la la*. I'd deal with the trauma another day.

'Let's go!' I said to Fluffy. My new home was two blocks further away from the heart of the town, but it didn't make that much difference. Anyway, I was just grateful to have a home again.

We double-timed it to work and arrived five minutes before the Riverdreams were due in for an interview. Sidnee was at the front desk, yawning. 'Ready for bed?' I grinned.

'You bet! I slept before our night out, but it's made for a long day. I've been daydreaming about bed. Luckily it's been a total graveyard shift. Gunnar swung in about half an hour ago.'

The door pinged and a mother and son walked in: the Riverdreams. I wasn't sure what to expect from the supposedly 'hippy' family, but they looked normal. I was a little disappointed – I'd been hoping for flared jeans, long hair, and patchouli oil, maybe some flowers in the hair. Sadly, all of those things were absent. What a let-down.

Skylark was visibly sullen, and his mother looked stressed. 'Cordelia and Skylark Riverdream,' she said briskly. 'Here for an interview.'

Sidnee smiled. 'Take a seat. The Nomo will be with you in a moment.'

'I'll tell him you're here,' I offered.

I knocked once on the doorjamb of Gunnar's office. 'Hey, boss, Skylark and his mum are here.'

He pushed away from his desk. 'Let's see what the kid has to say.'

# Chapter 9

Skylark had his mother's mousy hair and brown eyes, but he lacked her sunny disposition. She kept smiling through her stress and trying to assure us that it was all a mistake – though the smile vanished when we showed her the CCTV footage and she recognised her son. Looking wounded, she rounded on him. 'You swore to me you didn't do it!'

The boy sank further into his chair and wouldn't meet her eyes. He shrugged. 'Whatever.'

'Sky! This is a huge deal. You damaged the Grimes' property – you *stole* from them!' Cordelia's eyes were wide. She turned to us. 'We'll pay for the damage, of course, and for the stolen items.' She started to wring her hands. 'Are they going to press charges?'

'They're thinking on it,' Gunnar lied. He levelled a hard look at Skylark. 'You best be apologising.'

'You bet your bottom dollar he'll be apologising!' his mother snapped.

Nothing she said seemed to impact on him; he appeared nonchalant about committing a crime and being caught, and when I caught his eyes I couldn't see a hint of remorse. If he wasn't careful, he'd slide down a slippery slope to something bad.

Gunnar and I talked to Cordelia while Skylark pretty much ignored the discussion. His mother needed to get some tips from April Arctos. Throughout the whole interview the boy was sullen, uncooperative, and annoyingly close-lipped. We gave up after a frustrating half an hour. I hoped the experience would scare him enough that he'd turn over a new leaf, but I wouldn't have bet on it.

Gunnar escorted them out. When he came back, he said, 'That kid will be back here someday.'

I nodded grimly. 'Yeah. I don't think he's learnt his lesson.'

'I'll see if I can't get Calliope or Soapy to keep an eye on him.'

'Skylark's a siren?'

'As far as I know he's not a siren, but he's definitely a water-based shifter so he's in the siren group. Sidnee confirmed it.'

Sidnee had clocked off while we were interviewing so I went to sit at the front desk. After five minutes, I took a call from Jake's mum and we set an appointment for them to come in an hour later. That made us three for three. Damn: this mystery had been wrapped up with a bow far too early and easily for my liking.

I was filling out the paperwork when Gunnar called me back to his office. 'I have a question for you and I need you to really think on it.'

'Okay.' My mind went a million places and my heart flopped lazily in my chest, my vampiric version of it speeding up. Was I in trouble?

He leaned back into his chair, his keen eyes watching me. 'Would you be interested in becoming an official investigator?'

My mind went blank. 'What do you mean?'

'I'm an elected official. I've worked in law enforcement for years but I never took any official training to become a detective. After the murder, I realised that you have a gift for this stuff – I don't think we'd have caught our murderer without you. I want to send you to the academy to train you up.'

'Like a police academy?'

'Just like.'

'Oh!' I gasped, completely taken aback. I had been daydreaming about just this sort of scenario – who hasn't dreamed about being Rizzoli or Isles?

'The next class isn't for a few months. You have four or five weeks to think about it before I need to get you enrolled.'

I grinned. 'I would *love* that!' To become a proper part of the Nomo's team would be a dream come true – I'd always wanted to be a detective!

Gunnar grinned. 'I thought you would.' He opened a desk drawer. 'We're a small supernat town, but the Nomo's office has been woefully undermanned for quite some time. Sidnee loves the paperwork and she isn't interested in being on the ground, whereas you seem to thrive on it. You need proper training, but you've learned a heck of a lot on the job these last two months so I have no hesitation in offering this to you now.' He lifted out a brand-new shiny Nomo badge with a number two on it.

I gaped. 'Seriously?'

'Seriously.'

'Thank you! I swear I won't let you down.'

'I know you won't,' he said gruffly. 'One day you'll take my place as Nomo, Officer Bunny. If you want it.'

I felt my throat close with emotion; nobody had ever showed such faith in me, not ever. 'Thanks, Gunnar, that means a lot to me. You've been grooming me for the badge this whole time, haven't you?' He winked as I secured the badge on my shirt.

Before things could get too sappy, the Olsens showed up. Jake was dark haired, slight and very, very sorry. Stress was rolling off him in waves and he cried as he confessed to breaking into the Grimes' store. 'I'm so sorry. I don't know what we were thinking!' He was wringing his hands. His mom started to cry and his dad comforted her; he seemed incapable of speech.

Jake was their oldest son and there was a ten-year gap between him and his three younger siblings, the youngest of which were three-year-old twins. Jake seemed like he had a sensible head on his shoulders, but he'd been swept up in mob mentality and the need to be cool. He'd made a stupid decision and he was contrite.

I felt bad for all of them. Teenagers in groups without adult supervision had been making bad decisions since the beginning of time; I know I had. It was a miracle I'd survived long enough to be killed in my early twenties.

Jake promised to pay back every penny, and I believed him. Unlike with the other two boys, Gunnar reassured him that charges weren't being brought against him. After the family had gone, we completed the paperwork and reported back to the Grimes. With the kids apologising and agreeing to pay for the damage, the case was officially closed.

I didn't know it then, but that was the start of something *far* bigger.

# Chapter 10

The next day Fluffy and I walked to work. As was my habit, I touched the daylight charm around my neck before I stepped out to reassure myself that it was there. The charm sat next to the triskele that my nana had given me when I was sixteen. She'd promised that it would protect me and that she'd be beside me as long as I wore it. Though the latter might be true, the former was clearly not since I was now the walking undead.

I held the triskele for a moment and thought of my grandmother, of her kind, worn face and her cheeky eyes that had sparkled with mischief. She had loved cake in the afternoon and had a ridiculous fondness for eating fish sticks. She'd loved gardening and I'd often found her digging around in the earth. A wave of sadness washed over me: I missed her. If she could see me now, what would she think of me, Officer Bunny, a vampire, more than four thousand miles from home?

She'd be proud, I told myself firmly. I tucked the triskele and the daylight charm under my shirt. Connor had told me the charm was rare and expensive so it was better not to advertise it, though my daylight walking probably did that anyway.

Fluffy nudged into me and I looked down at him. 'Sorry, I was a million miles away.' As I patted him, his head snapped abruptly to the left and he barked three times in warning. I followed his gaze and saw a familiar figure: Connor MacKenzie.

My heart did its weak flip-flop and my stupid fangs dropped down. I closed my eyes and swore under my breath; I still had little control over them and it was so embarrassing. I was the worst vampire ever.

I begged the fangs silently to go back to where they belonged but they ignored me. I didn't understand why they'd dropped down because it wasn't like I thought that Connor was a threat to me. Behind him was another man I didn't recognise dressed all in black and giving off strong fuck-off vibes. He was scanning the area constantly and it made me nervous.

Connor gave me one of his slow smiles that made my insides tighten. 'Hey, Bunny. How you doing?'

I'd been avoiding him since the fire. He had taken care of me – and, more importantly, my dog – without hesitation, and that kind of caring scared me. Plus, I was very attracted to him and I thought that he felt the same.

I wasn't ready to date but seeing Chris and Sidnee's closeness had brought a pang to my heart: I wanted that closeness, those little touches and shared glances, the inside jokes. I'd been alone a long time; even with my parents I'd felt alone. I wanted to change that.

I gave Connor a tight-lipped smile to hide my traitorous fangs. 'I'm good. How are you?' It was awkward keeping my lips closed as I was speaking and I sounded lispy. Ugh: I was such a dork.

'I'm heading your way. Mind if I walk with you?' Connor asked.

Fluffy looked perfectly content with the situation; he was a traitor, too. 'Yeah sure. Who's he?' I looked over my shoulder at the chap walking a few steps behind us.

'My second, Juan. He watches my back when I might be otherwise distracted.'

I stopped. 'Do I distract you?'

His blue eyes met mine, and they were hot and dark. 'Yes,' he replied simply.

I licked my lips and fell silent; I had no idea what to say. Why had I asked that damn question? I forced my feet to take a few more steps.

Connor cleared his throat. 'Your liaison said you passed all your courses and moved to once-a-month meetings. Congratulations.'

'Thanks.'

'And I see more congratulations are in order.'

'Huh?'

He reached out and lightly tapped the badge on my shirt.

'Oh yeah. That.'

'That,' he replied, his tone teasing. 'Congratulations, Officer Barrington.'

I grinned, flashing a fang. 'Thanks. Officer Bunny doesn't work so well, does it?'

'It has a certain ring to it.' His smile faded and he jerked his head at Juan, indicating he should give us more space. Juan stepped back a little further so we at least had the illusion of privacy, though with his vamp hearing he could undoubtedly hear every word. 'I sought you out this morning because I received some correspondence from London,' Connor said.

Oh fuck: the vampire king had found me. Could he force me back? My face must have shown my panic because Connor touched my shoulder. I realised I was panting.

'Oh hey! It's okay, Bunny,' he reassured me. 'It was from your parents. Sorry, I should have led with that.'

I breathed out harshly. 'My *parents*?'

'Yes. A vampire called John Brown arranged the contact, and he also sent a note.'

John? There was only one vampire named John that I knew, the John who had helped me escape from London. I'd never caught his surname. 'What did he say?'

Connor's eyebrows rose; I suppose it was telling that I'd asked for John's message before my parents'. 'He said, "Franklin was paid by a witch".'

He studied me while I processed that information. Franklin was my sadistic sire and he'd been paid fifty thousand pounds to turn me into a vampire – by a *witch*? Why on earth would a witch want to turn me? I hadn't even known any witches before I came to Portlock! Was it an enemy of my father's? Dad was the vampire king's business partner so he must know other supernats; he couldn't be as ignorant of the supernat world as I had been.

Connor continued, 'The message from your parents was a request that you get in touch with them. Obviously, I haven't given them – or anyone else – your contact details. You told me before that your emails were compromised and that you were avoiding the Vampire King of Europe. You'd obviously travelled a long way to get here, and you told me that your sire got paid to turn you. I'm assuming that was the Franklin that John Brown was referring too?'

I nodded. My throat was tight and I couldn't get any words out.

Connor frowned. 'Why would a witch pay someone to turn you? And not just anyone – I know a little about the royal families, and Franklin is Octavius's son.'

'Octavius?'

'The Vampire King of Europe,' Connor said absently as he continued to think about it.

My mind was stuck on his name. My middle name was *Octavia*: had I been named after my dad's business partner? The thought made me feel a little sick.

Oblivious to my inner turmoil, Connor went on, 'What Franklin did was strictly against vampire law so approaching him to do it was a really risky move. The witch must be someone he knows.'

'How do I find out which witches he knows?'

Connor exhaled. 'Find out from here in Alaska? I have no idea.'

'I'm not going back to London!' The words burst from me. I wasn't leaving, not even to solve my own murder.

His eyes softened. 'No one's going to make you. You got turned without permission, so you're allowed to leave the zone where you were turned. You're here now, and you're safe,' he promised fiercely. 'Gunnar did the paperwork. Even if Octavius himself came knocking, he'd go home empty handed. You hear me? He has no jurisdiction here.'

Tears filled my eyes and the relief made my knees weak. As they buckled a little, Connor wrapped his arms around me. 'Hey, you're okay,' he murmured. 'I'm sorry, I should have reassured you sooner.'

'It's alright.' I managed a watery smile. 'I know now.' The whole time I'd been in Portlock, I'd had a constant nagging worry that someone would track me down and drag me back. But if I believed Connor – and I did – then that wasn't going to happen. I felt like someone had lifted a huge weight off me.

I dried my tears, straightened and pushed him away. 'I'm okay, honestly. Thanks.' He let me go but he was still watching me with concern.

Should I contact my parents? I knew their numbers and I could ring either of them any time – but did

I want to? Part of me was worried that they would pass anything I said onto Octavius, but if Connor had promised I was safe, did it really matter?

My relationship with my parents was – complicated. I loved them and they loved me in their own way, but they weren't warm or nurturing. Their idea of good parenting was paying for the finest nannies and most expensive schools.

'I'll think about calling them,' I said finally. I looked around for Fluffy and found that he was getting his belly rubbed by Juan. My dog had also tried to give us some privacy. 'We'd better move or I'll be late for work.'

Connor winked. 'It's okay, if you're late for work, we can say that you were consulting with a council member.'

Abruptly I realised my fangs had retracted at some point. 'Hey! My fangs have gone!'

'And this is cause for celebration?' Connor looked amused.

'The stupid wankers poke out anytime they want. I can't control them.'

Laughter twinkled in his eyes. 'You're a new vampire, Bunny. Cut yourself some slack. It takes a little time, but you'll master it just like you've mastered everything else that's been thrown at you so far. I have faith in you.'

I wished that didn't make my heart feel full to bursting but it did. 'Thanks.'

He gave me a crooked, breathtakingly handsome smile. 'Anytime.'

As he delivered me to the Nomo's office, Connor took my hand, bowed low and pressed a kiss to the back of it. A jolt ran through me strong enough to draw a gasp from my lips. Before I could say anything, he flashed me another of his brilliant smiles and walked away.

I watched him leave, partly because my brain had frozen at his kiss and partly because – well, he looked great in jeans.

# Chapter 11

Gunnar and I handled the liquor shipment between us; it took an hour to get all the alcohol handed out, then the office relaxed back into its usual calm. I settled at my desk to do the paperwork from the liquor consignment; it was mainly filing, which wasn't a great love of mine, but needs must. Just because I was now an officer, I wasn't going to make Sidnee do my paperwork.

The phone rang. 'Nomo office. Officer Barrington speaking.'

'It's Gertrude. You tell Gunnar that I saw a Keelut in my yard.'

I'd met precisely one Gertrude in Portlock, and I had no idea what a Keelut was. 'Please hold,' I said firmly, subjecting her to some easy-listening music that was anything but easy to listen to. I knocked on

Gunnar's door. 'I've got Gertrude on the phone. She didn't identify herself any more than that. She says she saw a Keelut in her yard.'

He blinked. 'I sure hope not.' He stood up and came to the front desk with me and put the phone on speaker. 'Gertrude? It's Gunnar.'

'I do *not* appreciate being put on hold by that—'

'A Keelut?' Gunnar interrupted. 'Are you sure it wasn't just Remmy?'

She harrumphed. 'I know what that prick of a fox-shifter looks like in all his forms. This wasn't him. I'm telling you, it was a Keelut. One of my chickens died yesterday – that may well have been that prick Remmy – but the Keelut dug up the grave and was munching on Mary!' Her voice was affronted. 'I shot at him but missed.'

'Gertrude!' Gunnar's voice was sharp. 'I've told you about shooting at Remmy.'

'And I'm telling you it *wasn't* Remmy. Its eyes were red, Gunnar. I didn't mistake that. It's a Keelut. Death haunts Portlock.' She hung up.

Gunnar ran a hand through his hair. 'That's all we need,' he muttered. He hesitated for a moment then picked up the phone.

'Gunnar,' Liv's voice purred out. 'What a pleasure to hear from you.'

'I've had a Keelut sighting. I need you to check the barrier for holes or tears.'

Liv sighed. 'You never just call to say hey, you know?'

'Liv.' His voice was full of warning.

'All right, I'll look into it. Or my witches will.' She hung up.

'What's a Keelut?' I asked, mostly to get Gunnar's mind off Liv.

'A hairless, black-dog creature,' he said shortly.

'Well, that's not so bad.'

'It's a bad omen, a bringer and eater of death.'

'Oh! Do we believe in omens?'

'Does a bear shit in the woods?'

'I've never seen it happen, but the presence of bear poop would suggest so,' I quipped.

A glimmer of a smile worked its way across his face. 'Indeed.'

'We believe in omens and portents?'

Gunnar nodded slowly. 'Bad things are coming to Portlock.'

The phone rang again and my scalp prickled as I answered, 'Nomo office. Officer Barrington speaking.'

'We need the Nomo right now!' the male voice said urgently.

'What is the nature of your issue?' I grabbed a pad and picked up my pen.

The caller ignored my request. 'North Harbour. Now!' He hung up. Rude.

North Harbour? That was where Eric's body had been found, but we'd caught his killers so it was unlikely there would be another dead body, right? It'd be fiiiine. The Keelut was a total coincidence.

I looked at Gunnar. 'We have a call to go to North Harbour immediately. They didn't identify themselves or say what was happening,' I groused. 'Would a *little* information have killed them?'

Gunnar was already moving. 'We prepare for the worst.' His tone was grim. I knew that he was thinking that whatever we were going to had been foreshadowed by the freaky black-dog creature.

I knew the drill by now, so I grabbed Fluffy's K-9 vest and my gun, and we jumped into the Nomo's vehicle. The wheels squealed as we raced out of the car park, sirens blaring, all the way to the harbour. We were there less than ten minutes after I'd received the call; now *that* was service.

We parked up and I put the vest on Fluffy. A small crowd had gathered and most of them were standing on the wooden deck staring into the water. Were we about to find a dead body floating there? A small, macabre part of me was excited by the chance to solve another mystery; the Grimes' break-in had been too easy.

Gunnar's bulk easily cleared a path through the crowd, and Fluffy and I followed. When we reached the end of the pier, I had to scoot around my boss to see what was what. Floating in the water were what appeared to be plastic-wrapped bags. Drugs? That wasn't so bad. The Keelut was wrong: this wasn't death – this was a good time! I glared at the assembled crowd. The situation hadn't been *that* time sensitive, so the caller could have taken the time to give us some freaking details. 'Whoever called it in, next time give us more information. We could have brought Sidnee with us and saved some time!' I bitched. No one met my eyes.

Using my initiative, I pulled out my mobile and rang Sidnee. 'Hey, it's Bunny.'

'I know,' she sassed. 'Caller ID told me that much.' She stifled a yawn. 'What's up?'

'There's a bunch of bags floating in North Harbour. Can you help us get them out and maybe do an underwater search for more?'

'You thinking drugs?'

'It looks like it,' I confirmed.

'I'll be twenty minutes,' she promised. 'I'm at Chris's so it's a bit further.'

'You drive slower than my nana did,' I teased her.

'Better to be slow and safe,' she retorted primly. 'See you soon.' She hung up.

Gunnar was putting out tape, sealing off the dock and moving everyone back. 'Sidnee is on her way,' I told him.

'Good work.'

'Thanks. I'll start taking statements from the crowd.'

He beamed at me like a proud parent. I took out my pad and moved amongst the gathering taking names, addresses and brief statements, all of which could be summarised as: *I didn't see anything* and *What's in those bags?* How did they think I'd know when I'd been on the scene less time than they had?

But it wouldn't be long until I found out.

# Chapter 12

Once I'd collected the statements, we walked to a different dock where several boats were moored. Gunnar pointed at a sleek blue-and-silver boat that looked fast. 'This is a twenty-six-foot ACB with double Yamaha 150 engines. It flies.' I could see he was proud of the boat, so I smiled like I knew what the heck he was talking about.

The boat had the Nomo shield – a distinctive sun, tree, wave, and moon – emblazoned on the side. It had a closed area on top so you could stay out of the elements while you steered the boat. 'Do you get seasick?' Gunnar asked suddenly.

'I'm not sure, to be honest. I've never been on the water properly – I've been to yacht parties but they were anchored up. When we went on Stan's boat, that was my first time on a fishing boat.'

'Well, I guess we're about to find out. Vampires might not even get seasick. Do you swim?'

'I can absolutely swim,' I said confidently. Whether I *wanted* to, what with the protective water dragon lurking in the waters, was a different thing.

'Good enough. What about Fluffy?' Gunnar asked.

Fluffy barked an affirmative and gave a happy wag. 'I guess he's confident he can swim too.' It was difficult to translate Dog, but that was what I figured Fluffy meant.

The boat lurched as I climbed on board and I had to suppress a surprised squeal. *Squealing does not behove an officer of the law,* I told myself firmly. New Bunny did not squeal – unless she was really surprised. No one could hold in a squeal in those circumstances, and it was important not to hold myself to unrealistic standards.

Fluffy jumped on board next, wagged his tail and sniffed everywhere. Lucky him: he wasn't perturbed by the boat's motion. I went inside the 'house'. It wasn't as big as the one on Stan's boat but it had a similar set up: two captain-type chairs up front with a lot of electronic stuff, a steering area, a small table with a bench, and a tiny closed-off area which I assumed contained a toilet. There was also a small sink and stove. It was very compact, like a doll's house. I smirked; I was sure Gunnar wouldn't enjoy that comparison. Under the bow was a small area that could be used to sleep or store things, and Fluffy crawled in it to explore.

'Here, put this on.' Gunnar handed me a vest. 'This is your personal flotation device or PFD.'

I clicked it on; it reminded me of the ones you saw in aeroplane safety videos because it was narrow and didn't restrict my movements in the slightest. Rather than luminous yellow, this vest was red and black so at least I didn't look like a little yellow Minion to add insult to injury.

'It's so thin. It doesn't look like it'd do much. How do I activate it?' I asked nervously.

Gunnar smiled. 'Don't worry, it has inbuilt sensors. If you go into the water, it'll activate.'

I shivered a little. What if *my* sensor was faulty? I mean, I could swim so I'd be fine, but even so... I surreptitiously searched for the pull-tabs like the flight attendants always described. Nothing. Damn.

'And this one is for you.' Gunnar held up an even stranger contraption for Fluffy then put it on him. It consisted of a collar that connected with a strap between his front legs to a piece that encircled his torso. It was red and black, with bright yellow handles on the top so we could lift him from the water if he went over.

Fluffy stood patiently as Gunnar fitted it; he was such a good boy. I was also really proud to note that he wasn't desperately thin anymore and Gunnar only had to take the harness in a notch. Since everything my boss had for a police dog used to fit Killer, his German shepherd, it was a sign that Fluffy was nearly back to fighting fit.

My boy barked and turned round and round, trying to view his PFD, but then he got distracted and chased his tail instead. Gunnar gave him a friendly pat, then started checking the boat's electrics and flicking on switches. Finally, he turned a key and started the engines.

'Aren't we waiting for Sidnee?' I asked.

'Don't worry, she'll be here before we're ready to leave.' He went on deck and pulled a couple of long-handled nets from where they were stored along the sides of the boat.

On top of the cabin was a smaller rubber boat. When I looked at it curiously, Gunnar grunted, 'Skiff.' He set the nets up in cups around the back near the door, then checked something on both engines and opened a couple of compartments to check their contents.

He was correct: by the time he'd finished, Sidnee had arrived. 'Hi!' she exclaimed, jumping on board.

Gunnar waved at her. Although I didn't hear any instructions, she immediately started unhooking ropes and pulling in these bulbous black rubber things that protected the side of the boat from hitting the dock. Once unhooked, the boat moved slowly from its mooring until we'd cleared the area. Then Gunnar gave the engine some oomph, and we zoomed over to where the bags were.

Once there, Gunnar told me to use a net to pull up the bags floating on the surface. I could handle that. Meanwhile, Sidnee had started to strip off her clothes. 'I'll go see what sank!' she said cheerily.

I caught her perfect dive over the edge before she surfaced and smiled at me. The first time she'd done that, I'd noted the dark, bluish-grey colour on her back that faded to a lighter shade on her front, and her hair in a Mohawk of jellyfish-like tendrils – but I hadn't seen her shark teeth. Combined with her solid black eyes, they were a little terrifying – even though she was my best friend.

She waved her webbed hand, fins appeared down her forearms, and she dived down, flicking me with water off her fluke. I wiped it off my face and glared in her general direction, sure she was laughing at me somewhere underwater.

I continued scooping up the bags. As I reached down, suddenly I was confronted by a huge, bright, golden eye. I suppressed my yowl of surprise – officers didn't yowl – but I still threw myself backwards. Firmly telling myself to get a grip, I inched back to the edge of the boat and looked over. It was just our friendly sea dragon protector, nothing to be afraid of, but when I peered cautiously into the water, it was gone. So much for longing for more mystery and excitement.

It took Gunnar and me about thirty minutes to collect all the bags that were bobbing in the sea. As we waited for Sidnee, I was itching to dig into them to see what they held. My money was on cocaine; the tightly wrapped bags looked just how cocaine was depicted in the movies.

Sidnee's head popped up ten minutes later. She threw a large mesh bag on deck, then disappeared. She did this three more times then retrieved a final bag and launched it and herself on deck, shifting into human form before she landed fin first. I handed her a towel and her clothes. 'Thanks!' she beamed at me and quickly dressed.

When she was decent, she explained what she'd seen. 'Those bags were all on the bottom in a small sea cave. I think something – or someone – got into them, and that's why some of them were floating free.

The rest were well-anchored for a pick up. Only a sea animal, someone in my siren group or an experienced deep-sea diver could get down that deep.'

'Hmm.' Gunnar looked out over the water. 'I think we've got all the bags. They're all sealed, so nothing has leaked into the water. Let's head to land and see what we've got. Thanks, Sidnee. Good work.'

She grinned. 'Nah, thank *you*, Gunnar. You know I love an excuse to swim.'

'Plus time-and-a-half for off-shift work,' he pointed out drily.

Her smile widened. 'That too!'

I picked up one of the mesh bags and my eyebrows shot up: it must have weighed fifty kilos but Sidnee had flipped it in like it was a packet of sweets. I hadn't realised how strong she was, and I wondered if that strength extended to her human form. I'd learned that asking such questions was considered rude in supernat towns, so I was still pretty ignorant of the strengths and weaknesses of the town's supernaturals. Maybe I could find a book, or maybe the course

Gunnar was sending me on would fill in the details. I brightened: that would be awesome.

When we'd pulled up to the dock and moored the boat, we hauled the bags to the Nomo vehicle and headed to the office. Sidnee followed in her own car.

'What do you think is in the bags?' I asked Gunnar.

'Don't know until we open one,' he said placidly.

'I think it's cocaine.'

Gunnar raised an eyebrow. 'Why cocaine?'

'They look like those bags you see in the movies.'

He threw a glance at me long enough for me to see the twinkle in his eyes. 'All drugs in movies, whether marijuana, heroin, or cocaine, look the same. For all we know these contain cash – or someone's baseball-card collection. Don't jump to conclusions. We'll know soon enough.'

I felt like 'don't jump to conclusions' was Gunnar's motto. It was a good one, but the problem was that I *liked* jumping to a conclusion. Maybe I could hop to one instead.

We pulled into the car park behind our office and unloaded the bags into the evidence room.

Then Gunnar carefully unwrapped one of the plastic-wrapped packages, and we all leaned forward to see what it contained.

# Chapter 13

Gunnar cut through and removed the white plastic. The package underneath was charcoal grey; it was a container with a lid. He lifted it. 'Whoa,' he said in surprise.

'What is it?' I asked.

He hefted the lid and spun it. 'It's super-light. Here.' He tossed it to me.

I caught it; it weighed nothing. If it hadn't been solid beneath my fingers, I wouldn't have known I was holding anything. I tossed it to Sidnee. 'That's weird,' I frowned. 'It should weigh *something*. It was like holding air.'

'That's crazy,' Sidnee agreed, setting the lid back down on the evidence table.

'Some sort of magic on the box,' Gunnar postulated. He pulled out a bag made of iridescent material from the strange, ultra-light box. When he used his box cutter to open it, the blade skimmed over the material and didn't damage it in the slightest. Huh.

He opened his drawer and took out some scissors but had the same result: the scissors wouldn't cut the material. He examined the bag but couldn't find an opening or even a seam. But Gunnar wasn't going to be bested by a bag; he was determined to get into it.

He dug around in another drawer, brought out a lighter and held it to the bag. It took several seconds, but finally the material melted slightly. He grinned triumphantly and continued until a hole appeared. When he tipped the contents of the bag onto the lid I'd put back on the desk, a crystalline powder poured out. The tiny crystals were a bright, hot-pink. I'd never seen anything like them. Not cocaine, then.

Fluffy sniffed the air then whined and put his tail between his legs as he retreated from the substance. Sidnee stroked him. 'It's okay, Fluff-Ball,' she murmured.

'What is it?' I asked, staring at the pink powder.

Gunnar appeared equally stumped. 'No idea.' His eyes seemed to glaze over, his hand slowly moved forward until he touched the pink substance, almost stroking the drugs.

'Hey, should you touch it?' I asked. Not that long ago we'd arrested Shirley for growing poisons in her garden and some of them had worked on contact with skin.

Gunnar didn't respond immediately and I jostled his arm lightly. He looked at me but his eyes were unfocused for a moment before they finally sharpened.

'Drugs need to be ingested in some way,' he pointed out slowly. Nevertheless, he removed his fingers. 'It was ice-cold,' Gunnar said with faint surprise. He turned back to the drugs and the same glazed expression took over him as he reached for the drugs once again.

I pulled the bag sharply away before he could touch it. He looked at me for a moment with outrage on his face, before blinking and visibly coming back to himself. Something freaky was at play.

'Well, the box is freakily light and the bag can't be opened, and then when you do open it, there's some sort of compulsion to touch it. You said yourself there must be a ward or something on it,' I said grimly. 'This isn't drugs, it's magic.'

Gunnar grimaced but didn't disagree. He placed the bag back in the container, gently poured the powder back in and replaced the lid. I noticed he was careful this time not to look at it for too long. 'Would you get the packing tape from the back room?' he asked me.

'Sure.' As I went into the back room and found the tape, I heard a rumble like thunder. Fluffy let out a panicked howl.

'BUNNY!' Sidnee screamed.

# Chapter 14

I ran back to the evidence room. Gunnar was lying on the floor, eyes open, head lolling on his chest. 'Oh my God!' I rushed around and checked his pulse. It was steady. 'Gunnar, can you hear me?'

He said nothing. His chest was rising and falling, but his eyes were rolling like he was watching something we couldn't see. He was breathing, but not responding otherwise.

'Shit!' I muttered. 'Get some gloves on,' I barked to Sidnee. 'And don't touch that fucking stuff!'

I hastily checked to make sure there wasn't any of the powder still on the desk, then ran to the restroom to get some wet towels. I needed to clean Gunnar's hands to remove as much of the substance as I could. I pulled on nitrile gloves then carefully wiped each of his fingers.

'Shall we call an ambulance or just drive him to the hospital?' I asked Sidnee.

She was staring at Gunnar, eyes wide with fear, and for a moment she looked impossibly young and lost. 'Sidnee!' I called again. 'I need you. Focus!' I tried to snap my fingers in her face but with the gloves on no sound came. 'Sidnee!' I shouted again.

She blinked. 'He can't die.' She sounded lost, paralysed.

'He won't,' I promised. 'But we must get him help. I need you to help me take him to the hospital. It'll be quicker to drive, right?'

She nodded slowly. 'Yes.'

'Sidnee, are you back with me?'

She licked her lips. 'Get Gunnar to hospital.'

'That's it. Can you help me do it?'

She nodded robotically, then grabbed him in a fireman's lift and carried him out of the Nomo's office. I guess that answered my question about whether she carried her strength through to her human form.

Sidnee slung Gunnar into the back seat of the SUV and hastily buckled him in. She retrieved the keys from his pocket and switched on the engine. Fluffy jumped in and we set off. Sidnee had driven me to a few places before, and she was a slow, careful driver to the point of being annoying. Not today: today she took hairpin corners at breakneck speed and I broke my own rule that officers shouldn't squeal.

'Take it easy,' I urged, white knuckled. 'If we overturn the car, we won't be helping Gunnar.' She shot me a scornful look that looked strange on her usually smiling face, then ignored me.

We got to the hospital in what I suspected was record time. Sidnee didn't bother parking the car, just abandoned it outside. 'You'd better stay here,' I murmured to Fluffy. 'No dogs in the hospital, except maybe therapy dogs, and we don't have a vest for that yet. Guard the car. I'll be back soon.' Ears down and unhappy, he laid down to wait for us.

Sidnee lifted Gunnar again but this time she staggered a little under his weight. Now the adrenaline and panic were fading, her strength was leaving her.

I'd heard tales of mothers lifting cars when their kids were in danger; maybe this was a similar situation.

I took one of his arms and between us we walked him into the hospital. 'We need HELP!' Sidnee screamed. 'It's the Nomo!'

Hospital staff descended on us, a trolley was wheeled over, and the staff lay him down. He was still unresponsive, eyes roving everywhere.

'What happened?' a nurse barked. I recognised her petite form and no-nonsense demeanour: It was Martha Wakefield, wife of Frank, the drunken bear shifter.

'We found an unknown substance and Gunnar touched it. He said it was cold. Twenty seconds later, he was out like a light. He may have hit his head going down, but he's been like this ever since.' I gestured to his eyes.

'Was the substance magical?'

'We think so. The box it was in was really light – it had to be magically contained somehow.'

'All right, we'll take it from here. Don't move.' She pushed Gunnar's trolley towards a ward marked 'Magical Maladies'.

I slumped. Well, he was in the right place; now I just had to call Sigrid. Maybe I could do something else instead like poke my eyes out with a hot iron. That would be preferable.

With a grimace, I pulled out my phone. A difficult task doesn't get easier because you put it on hold. I hit dial.

# Chapter 15

When Sigrid arrived, Sidnee collapsed into her arms with a wail. 'He'll be fine,' Sigrid assured her. 'He's tougher than old boots.' She looked at me. 'Has the doctor come out?'

I shook my head. 'No. We haven't been told anything, though Martha said someone would be by with an update in—' I checked my watch '—ten minutes ago.' I huffed; waiting was *not* my strong suit.

Sigrid sat. Pulling Sidnee down next to her, she laced their hands together. 'He'll be fine,' she repeated, though I wondered if she was reassuring us or herself.

Sidnee got out her phone with her free hand. 'I'm texting Chris.' I tried to ignore the small ache her words brought me. I had no one to text, no one to come and hold *my* hand. Not that I needed my hand holding. I was *fine*. I wasn't the one who'd been knocked out.

A doctor approached us a few minutes later. 'Gunnar Johansen?' We all nodded. 'You did the right thing bringing him in when you did. His organs were shutting down. I've never seen anything like it.'

Sigrid gave a low moan and the doctor continued hastily, 'He's going to be absolutely fine. We stopped the progression of the— whatever this was. A steady stream of potions will reverse the damage. He'll be in hospital for a few days but he *will* be fine. He's coming around now, though he's not quite himself yet.'

'What do you mean?' I asked.

The doctor shrugged. 'He's a little high.'

'Can we see him? Sigrid asked, and I appreciated the 'we'.

'Yes. He's been settled into a bed on the ward – one of the nurses will tell you which one.' He gave us a brief nod and left us to it.

Martha touched my elbow, making me jump. 'Sorry,' she murmured. 'He's over here, if you want to see him.'

We all stood up then I bit my lip and sat back down. 'You should go first,' I said to Sigrid, 'I'll wait.'

'Nonsense.' She pulled me up. 'He'll want to see you. Come on.'

Gunnar apparently warranted his own private room; being the Nomo had some perks. He was hooked up to all manner of machines, but everything was beeping with a reassuring rhythm. When we walked in his eyes were tightly closed, but then they opened. They were severely bloodshot, the blue depths seemed darker and his pupils were enlarged. He gave a low groan.

Sigrid rushed to him. 'Gunnar? Can you hear me?'

He gave a happy smile. 'Sig, my beautiful Sig. You have flowers in your nose.' He reached out a clumsy hand to swipe at it.

She smiled. 'Do I, love?'

'In your ears now. Why would you want a flower in your ear? You won't be able to hear anything.'

'That would be a problem,' she agreed lightly.

'You're so beautiful, even with flowers growing out of your orifices.'

Sigrid grinned. 'I love you, Bambam.'

He gave her a dopey smile. 'Bambam loves you soooo much.'

I fully regretted following Sigrid into the hospital room. She slid me and Sidnee a look. 'Gunnar. Goon. Gun. Bang Bang, Bambam. It evolved over time.'

'Sure.' Sidnee grinned. 'You don't need to explain yourself to me and Bunny. You just look after Bambam here.'

Sigrid groaned. 'Never mention that name again.'

Sidnee sighed. 'You never let me have any fun.'

'Well, you can come over here and have flowers growing out of your orifices, if you like,' Sigrid said drily.

Sidnee snickered. 'I'm good.' And she was. Now that she'd seen with her own eyes that Gunnar was okay, something dark that had been lurking inside her eased back. The sunny Sidnee I knew was front and centre again.

Gunnar started singing 'We Go Together' from *Grease*, but obviously didn't know the words. 'We go together like rama-lama-lama ka drunken lama-ding-dong, remember forever, as shoo-bop, sha-spammy-wammy, hamm de lamb.' He got distracted. 'Mmm. Lamb. I love your cooking, Sig.' He licked his lips then promptly fell asleep and started snoring louder than I'd ever heard anyone snore before.

'At least the singing has stopped,' Sidnee muttered.

'I think this is worse,' I replied. 'We really should have filmed him.' I sighed; it was a missed chance probably never to be repeated.

'Not. A. Word.' Sigrid mock-glared at us.

I mimed zipping it. The truth was, I was almost giddy with relief. Gunnar was going to be okay. He could sing *Grease* as much as he wanted as long as he was going to be okay.

# Chapter 16

After giving an ear-splitting snore, Gunnar woke himself up and looked around blearily. He spoke slowly and deliberately, like he had to concentrate to make the sounds. 'Wh-where's the os-bos-box?'

'I sealed it,' I promised. 'It's on the desk back at the office, and the office is locked up.'

'G-gggoood.' He struggled to sit up.

'Lie down, you silly oaf,' Sigrid chastened, pushing his shoulder gently back down. 'You've been really ill. That crazy stuff knocked you on your butt. You need to take it easy.'

She wasn't wrong: he'd barely touched the drug and certainly hadn't ingested it, but it had literally knocked him out cold. What *was* that stuff? Whatever it was, it was potent as fuck – and deadly. If it was this strong and could affect supernaturals in this way, the people who had made it would be looking for it.

Questions swirled in my brain. Who in their right mind would manufacture something this deadly? What did they want to do with it? Who did they plan to use it on – and why? One thing was for sure: only bad people would make this shit, bad people who would undoubtedly do bad things to get it back.

'We need to send that stuff off for testing,' I said. 'Do we have a lab that knows about supernaturals?'

'We have a lab with a few friendlies in the know,' Gunnar confirmed.

'You'll find the details in the address book in the top drawer in his desk,' Sigrid added.

Gunnar glared. 'I'll sort it out.'

Her eyes narrowed. 'You will *not*. The doctor said you're going to be in here a couple of days on a strict potion regime. This was serious, Gunnar. You nearly *died*.'

Some of the fire left his eyes and he squeezed her hand. 'I'm sorry I scared you.' She nodded tightly.

I cleared my throat. 'I need to send it to a lab so I'll pack it up like it was before, make sure it's sealed tighter than a millionaire's wallet.'

'Good idea.' Gunnar nodded.

I could send one of the bags that was already taped shut after I'd found a few layers of plastic to put around it. The mesh bags with the other packages were still safely sealed, but we should find a more secure place to keep them; this stuff had to be dangerous to keep around and not just because of what it did. 'Where shall I store the rest?' I asked.

Gunnar grimaced. 'The only place I can think of is in one of the holding cells. We don't have a safe that's large enough.' We had a gun safe where Gunnar stored weapons but there wasn't room for large, bulky packages.

'Okay.' I stood. 'I'll get on it.'

Sidnee's phone beeped. 'I'll go, too. Chris is here to take me home.'

'Bunny,' Gunnar called, 'keep in touch. Any questions, just give me a ring.'

I nodded, but I'd seen the warning look in Sigrid's eyes; I'd keep any contacts to an absolute minimum. 'Sure. Speak soon.'

Sidnee and I went back outside. Chris was leaning against the abandoned Nomo SUV and Fluffy was barking at him loudly and repeatedly for daring to lounge on *his* property. Sidnee flew to her boyfriend and he wrapped his arms around her. 'Are you okay? What's up with Gunnar?' he asked.

'Some pink drugs,' she sniffed. 'Crazy dangerous.'

'What? *Drugs*? In Portlock?'

'Yep. We found a *huge* stash of drugs in the water tonight. Gunnar opened one of the packages and touched the damned stuff, and it nearly killed him. His organs were shutting down.'

Chris looked surprised. 'I didn't think anything could fell that man!'

'Apparently bright-pink crystals can,' she grumped.

'Do you know who put them in the bay?'

I shrugged. 'Not a clue. And now our chief investigator is out of action, it looks like I'm up. I just wish it didn't feel like amateur hour.'

Sidnee jostled me. 'You'll have the suspects in custody in no time!'

I gave a half-smile. 'I'll do my best.'

'Take me home,' Sidnee murmured to Chris as a yawn cracked her face.

'You got it.'

She chucked me the SUV's keys and hopped into Chris's car. I waved them off. I didn't need witnesses for what was going to follow. I had a British driving licence and I could drive; I could even drive a manual car. And really – how hard could it be to remember to drive on the *opposite* side of the road?

# Chapter 17

It is freaking *hard* to drive on the other side of the road. Every time I relaxed enough to enjoy myself, I found myself on the wrong side of the tarmac. I had to concentrate hard the whole time; thank goodness for my memory or in my panic I'd never have found my way back to the office.

I'd told Fluffy all about Gunnar's medical issues and that he'd be bedbound for a few days, mostly to talk it through for myself. It helped to set it all out. Whatever the drug was, I needed to track down who was making and distributing it, and I didn't have Gunnar to rely on. I needed to think this through, but first I needed to get that shit secured.

I parked behind the Nomo's office, opened the back door and locked it after I'd gone inside. It took a solid half-hour to move all the bags into an empty cell and lock them down. The jail was the most secure part of the building; you could try to break in if you were determined to, but we'd probably catch you before you got through the reinforced concrete and the steel bars, and certainly before you got away. We also had CCTV monitoring the space that Sigrid often watched remotely. Since she was also going to be out of action, I spent an hour learning how to get the footage sent through to my phone. Technology was never easy. Luckily, Gunnar's drawer had the password for the security company written on a Post-It. We'd have to talk about *his* security after all of this.

Now that I was certain I could monitor the drugs no matter where I was, I packaged up the remaining box to ship it to the lab. I'd need our new pilot to do a special run but I figured the expense was worth it; this shit was deadly and we needed results yesterday.

I called the new pilot who had replaced Jim. Edgy Kum'agyak was interesting, though I'd only met him briefly during the last drinks run. He was a one-armed bald-eagle shifter who couldn't fly any more under his own power. I knew that shifters regenerated from their injuries, but maybe growing new limbs was a step too far. It would be rude to ask.

Edgy's plane was adapted for his disability; one arm or not, he could still get his time in the sky. He answered on the first ring. 'Yo!'

'This is Officer Barrington of the Nomo's office.' I felt a surge of pride; I was going to be the best damned Nomo ever. 'I have an important package that needs to be couriered to Anchorage. Can you tell me when you can make a flight?'

'No time like the present,' he said cheerfully. Despite his native name, he spoke with a bit of an Australian twang.

'Great. Can you pick it up from the Nomo's office? We're a little understaffed at the moment.'

'Far out. I'll be by in ten and underway in thirty.' He sounded thrilled at the excuse for a flight.

'Fantastic. Thank you so much, Mr Kum'agyak.'

'Call me Edgy.'

'Right, okay, er, Edgy. I'll arrange pick-up at Anchorage airport. See you shortly.' I hung up then arranged a courier on the other side to take the package directly to the lab in the city. I marked the package: *For the Attention of Anthony Brown*; Brown was Gunnar's contact at the lab who knew about the supernat world.

Edgy strolled in ten minutes later. He was skinny, with long brown hair and bloodshot dark eyes. His clothes were rumpled, his hair unbrushed, and he smelled faintly of wacky baccy. Hmm. 'Here for the package as requested, ma'am.' He mock-saluted me with his remaining hand.

'I appreciate your promptness.' I passed him the package. 'Your last name sounds local but the accent?'

'I'm Alaskan born and raised, Sugpiaq or Alutiiq.' He shrugged. At my blank look he explained, 'Alutiiq is the Russian version, same tribe. In my teen years I had a yen for the sun so I travelled a bit. Easy enough when you're an eagle.' His tone was full of nostalgia. 'I found Australia on my travels and I stayed there a long time. A *long* time. When I lost my arm, I came back home. Mum wanted to fuss. I've stayed ever since.'

'Don't you still have a yen for the sun?'

'Well, it's all right here just now.' He was right; annoyingly, we were in a sunny summer period where there was only a handful of night hours.

It was probably rude to ask how long it had been since he'd lost his arm, but the skin on the stump still looked red and angry so I guessed it had been fairly recent. Another hint of weed danced on the air and I hesitated. 'Look, don't take this the wrong way, but you smoke marijuana, right?'

'Medicinal.' He winked. 'Helps with the old phantom pains. But don't worry, I haven't had any this morning – these are yesterday's clothes. I'm good to fly.'

Yesterday's clothes? He wasn't going to win any cleanliness awards anytime soon. Still, it was a relief that he was okay to fly. 'Okay. I was just wondering if you could tell me the details of your drug dealer?'

He grinned. 'I can tell by your accent that you're from our former colonising mistress, England. Here in Alaska, marijuana is legal. I buy it from the store.'

Bugger: there went that idea. I was back to square one. How the heck was I supposed to find a drug dealer in this town?

# Chapter 18

I spent the next hour trawling through social media and was surprised by how many of the residents had accounts. None of them mentioned being supernat, of course, but even so...

I focused on the teenagers. Remembering my hunch that Russell Arctos had been high when he broke into the Grimes' place, I pored through his socials as well as Skylark's and Jacob's, hoping to find something concrete so I could talk to them about drug use. They didn't have missing limbs and they were kids, so the likelihood of them buying marijuana at the store was zero. If they'd been high then they had a dealer and I had somewhere to start. Hopefully.

I had no idea if this was what Gunnar would be doing. Maybe he'd already know a few nefarious types. I chewed my nail. I could call him but Sigrid's warning glare had put me off. He needed rest.

I'd try it my way for now; if I was at a dead end by the end of my shift, then I'd call him tomorrow. Feeling better now that I had a course of action, I went back to the socials. It wasn't long before I hit paydirt on Skylark's page. *Hitting the ΘΥ tonight! Can't wait to see how strong I get!*

I stared at the symbols. Were they Greek? Either way, Skylark was taking something, and I didn't think it was marijuana.

The desk's phone rang. 'Nomo, Bunny speaking,' I answered. Dammit! I should have said Officer Barrington!

'I want you to arrest Skylark Riverdream,' the woman on the line said firmly.

My eyebrows shot up. I'd manifested a lead! 'I'm sorry, who is this?'

'April Arctos. That little reprobate gave my son something and now he won't shift out of his bear form. He's high as a kite. Skylark is a menace. Arrest him!'

I thought of the weird symbols on Skylark's post and my stomach clenched. 'Please take him to the hospital to get him checked out.' I rolled back my memory, visualising the doctor who had dealt with Gunnar and given us the feedback in the waiting room. 'Ask to speak to Dr Etok.'

That stunned her into silence for a moment. 'Oh my god, the *hospital*? Is he in danger?' In a split second her voice went from raging mother bear to scared mother dove.

'I'm not a healthcare professional and I don't know what he's taken, but others have suffered an adverse reaction from a new drug. I strongly suggest you have him checked out. Now.'

'I'll call back later.'

'Great. Please ask the hospital to take a blood sample to send for analysis and confirm that we can have the results.'

'Will do.' She hung up without any further pleasantries. I didn't blame her.

My gut said this was more than a little wacky baccy. Skylark's comment about 'how strong he'd be' made me wonder if the drug they'd taken was specifically for supernats. The fact that Russell was stuck in bear form...

I didn't know if the drug Russell had been given was the same one that Gunnar had touched, but my gut said that it was a strong possibility. If Skylark was dishing out this new drug, hopefully I could find something else on his socials. I went back to the screen and scrolled back through his feed. Something caught my eye: *Russ is hilarious on fisheye!* followed by lots of laughing-face emojis.

I now had a symbol and a name: fisheye. Not the sexiest name for a drug, but we were in a fishing town. Did the name and brand suggest that this drug was manufactured here? The chances seemed good, but maybe I was reaching; maybe fisheye was just a local name for it. Druggies all had different names for their favourite hit, right?

I printed out Skylark's socials and contemplated my next move. It was nearly 5am; I'd stayed longer than usual, but that seemed only right since Gunnar wasn't here to man things. He usually hung on until Sidnee came in so I guessed I'd better do the same thing. We all pulled long hours, and Sigrid helped out as needed; Gunnar preferred that *someone* be available in case of emergencies. Sidnee wouldn't be too long, and though I needed to go home and sleep I could keep going a little while longer.

It had been a crazy day and all that anxiety over Gunnar was making me crash hard – not to mention that going out drinking late and waking early hadn't exactly set me up for the day.

I was undead on my feet, and I prayed Sidnee would stumble in soon.

# Chapter 19

Sidnee gently woke me. 'Go home, Bunny. I've got it now.'

I yawned and nodded. 'Thanks.'

'See you on the flip side.'

Fluffy and I walked home, taking turns to yawn the whole way. When we got there, it was lights out right away. I slept like the dead and awoke refreshed; it was only 3pm, but I was ready to face the day and kick ass. First tasks: check in with Sidnee and get the office keys, then question Skylark Riverdream.

I started to get dressed. In my haste to get to bed, I'd chucked yesterday's jeans on the floor. When I picked them up, their weight made me blink. I rooted around in the pocket and winced: I'd brought the bloody office keys home with me! I gave a head thunk and let out a groan. Dammit. I was off to a terrible start at being the sole officer at the Nomo's.

Fluffy and I jogged towards the office – but as we approached the building I started to sprint. The front door had been kicked in and was hanging off its hinges.

Connor, Juan, and Stan were talking quietly outside. I ignored them and ran inside. 'Sidnee!' I breathed again when I saw her sitting at her desk. 'What happened?'

She looked pale but she dredged up a smile. 'Oh, you know, a little attempted armed robbery.' She waved her hand. 'Nothing to worry about.'

'The drugs?'

She grinned. 'You took the keys with you so I couldn't have let them in if I'd tried. I hit the alarm and the others came running.' She sighed. 'The bastards ran away before these guys arrived though.'

'You're okay?'

'Totally fine,' she assured me. 'A little shaken, but okay.'

'How many of them were there?'

'Two. One of them was silent, the other barked out orders at me. Something about the way he spoke and moved make me think he's ex-military.'

'Were they armed?'

'Yeah, but I flashed my teeth and they took off.' She gave a wobbly smile. 'I guess they know better than to shoot law enforcement.'

'Were they wearing gloves?'

'Yup, so we're not getting prints. Honestly, the whole thing was over pretty quickly. I guess they knew that I'd hit the alarm and half the town would come running. You should have seen the crowd here earlier.'

'If you're sure you're okay, I'll go and speak to Connor and Stan.'

'I'm fine. Once the cavalry arrived, I called Chris. He was out on a swim, but he's on his way now. I said I'd stay until you came in.'

'I appreciate that. And Sidnee? I'm glad you're okay.'

'Me too.' She gave me a relieved smile that told me she wasn't as relaxed as she was trying to appear.

I went to see the guys out front. I felt vaguely awkward at seeing Stan; the last time we'd been together, I'd drunkenly slammed the door in his face. Still, this was work. 'Thanks for coming so quickly,' I said.

'We're arranging extra protection here until the drugs have been moved,' Connor said firmly. 'If they've tried once to get their gear back, they'll try again. We'll maintain a visible presence. Juan and I both have daylight charms, and we'll have other vampires cover the night.'

Juan gave me a friendly nod which I returned.

'Doesn't matter for us what time of the day it is,' Stan said, boasting a little. 'We'll provide round the clock cover, too.'

I interrupted before a pissing contest could begin. 'Wonderful! Thank you both. Did any of you see the vehicle they arrived in?'

Connor shook his head. 'We checked the security footage. They left on foot.'

Dammit, that was even more evidence that it was a local outfit. With the barrier, there wasn't much chance they'd be anything other than local but I knew that somehow the Keelut had got in. If there was a fissure, the perpetrators might not have been from town – but if they'd left on foot the chances were they were Portlockian.

'Can one of you secure the front door?' I asked.

'I'll do it,' Stan volunteered hastily.

'Great.' I smiled. 'Gunnar keeps pre-cut pieces of wood in the back. You can just board it up for now.'

'Nah,' Stan said. 'I'll have a new door fitted within the next couple of hours.'

I smiled. 'I really appreciate that.' He puffed out his chest.

Chris's car pulled up and screeched to a stop. 'Is Sidnee okay?' he asked as he got out.

I grimaced. 'She's a little shaken, more than she'll admit. But we've arranged plenty of security around the clock – she'll be safe from now on. Can you take her home? See her safe? It's been an emotional few days for her.'

He nodded. 'Of course I will.'

'In that case, I have some little reprobates I need to question. Excuse me, gentlemen.'

I went round the back and climbed into the SUV, praying to all the gods that were holy that I would remember to drive on the correct side of the road, at least while the guys were watching me.

# Chapter 20

On the way to the Riverdreams' residence, I called April Arctos on the handsfree system to get an update on Russell. Like Gunnar, he'd been admitted to hospital and given a plethora of potions; unlike Gunnar, his organs hadn't been shutting down. Russell had been high and ill but not in danger of death; even so, he was being kept in for observation. Well, that was something.

I spent the rest of the drive focusing on what I needed to know. What was fisheye? How was it taken? Where did Skylark get it from?

I knocked on the front door of the Riverdreams' house, nerves jangling in my stomach. Fluffy stayed at my side; apparently, once a witch hits your boss with a fireball, you become wary about home visits.

Skylark's mum answered with a smile that instantly faded when she saw me. 'Oh, did the Grimes brothers press charges after all?'

I didn't answer that. 'Is Skylark home? I have a few questions for him.'

She frowned but nodded. 'Yes, all right. Hold on.' She retreated into the house, leaving Fluffy and me on the porch. I could hear her arguing with a very angry-sounding son. Soon she was back, teen in tow.

'What do you want now?' Skylark snarled at me. I wondered if he'd show the same disrespect to Gunnar. Evidently Fluffy wasn't impressed by his attitude either because he gave a low, threatening growl. The teen gave him a wary glance but it didn't affect his manners.

'This is about your friend, Russell Arctos,' I said. 'He's in hospital, very sick. Apparently he took something you gave him, and we're here to see what it was.'

For a moment, the boy looked his age – young, shocked, and nervous – then in a beat the bravado was back. 'I didn't give him anything. You're trying to blame me for everything. I don't believe you. Russell's not sick! You're lying to trick me.'

I raised my eyebrow, pulled my phone out and hit re-dial. 'Mrs Arctos, would you mind telling me where you are right now?' I put the phone on speaker.

Skylark looked a little green when he heard April's frightened voice say, 'At the hospital with my son, Russell.' With my supernat hearing, I could hear the beeping of the machines in the background and I wondered if Skylark could too. He'd gone very, very pale and very, very still.

'Thank you. I'll be in contact soon.' I hung up.

'I just gave him a little bit,' Skylark muttered. 'It's not supposed to be dangerous.'

'What's not?'

'Fisheye. It's not dangerous; it just gets you high and messes with your powers a little. It can make you stronger or it can have weird effects, like Russell couldn't control his shift. It was hilarious.'

'Where did you get the drugs from?' He shrugged and didn't answer. I tried again. 'Who did you get the drugs from?'

Skylark stayed silent.

'Tell her what she needs to know,' his mother snapped.

He sneered at her. 'No chance. They'll kill me.' She paled. He looked at me, 'It's harmless. You're wrong.'

It wasn't harmless, and he'd just admitted to possessing and distributing drugs; this kid needed a reality check. Though I was certain the charges wouldn't stick, I was sure that Gunnar would agree with my next course of action. Hopefully it would loosen Skylark's tongue a little.

'Skylark Riverdream, you are under arrest. I will now read you your rights.' I recited the Miranda rights that Gunnar had taught me. 'Since you're a minor, you're entitled to have a parent with you while you're being interviewed.' I cuffed him and looked at his quietly sobbing mother. 'I suggest you get a lawyer.'

Skylark looked sick; he was all out of snark and bravado. As I guided him towards the Nomo vehicle, he looked back and called out plaintively, 'Help me, Mom!'

She looked stricken. 'I'll get a lawyer,' she promised. She stood in the door as we drove away.

# Chapter 21

I put Skylark in a cell far away from the drugs – not that he could get to them. He looked scared, which he should have been. Depending on the amounts he had distributed, and if any money had exchanged hands, he might go down for dealing drugs. If he did, he would more than likely end up in an out-of-town juvenile facility. If so, a trusted member of the magic user group would use a spell to block Skylark's magic during his prison term.

The thought made me shiver. I hadn't been a vampire for long but I was already growing used to my sharpened senses and extra strength. I couldn't imagine them being removed and living like a normal human again; I would feel terrifyingly vulnerable.

I went back outside to look for Connor or Stan and found them both. Lucky me. 'Hey,' I greeted them. 'I could do with a warrant for the Riverdreams' house. Can either of you sort that out for me?'

'Consider it done.' Connor pulled out his phone and walked away a few paces. 'Calliope? I need a sign-off on a warrant.'

Stan had been true to his word; the Nomo's office already had a new and shiny door. 'Thanks for that,' I said awkwardly. 'Sorry about the whole slamming-the-door-closed thing the other night.'

He smiled. 'It's okay. You were trashed. Maybe my animal magnetism made you feel threatened.'

That made me laugh. 'Maybe it did.' I let my smile fade. 'I ... um ... I like you, but maybe not like that. Friends?'

He sighed loudly. 'Friend-zoned. And so soon.' He clutched a hand to his heart. 'You're killing me.'

I elbowed him. 'No, I'm not. Drama queen.'

The huge man let his jokey exterior drop. 'I like you, but I respect that it doesn't seem to be reciprocal. Plus, I'm not the only man with my eye on you, am I?' He flicked his gaze to Connor, who was still talking on his phone.

My skin warmed. 'That's got nothing to do with us. Regardless of any third parties, I just think of you as a friend. Maybe it's because Gunnar and Sigrid treat you like a son.'

'And you like a daughter,' he murmured.

'A little. Sigrid mothers me. It's nice. But ... that makes us kinda siblings.'

Stan rubbed a hand through his hair and flashed me a warm grin. 'From sexy debonair date to brother in one fell swoop.'

I grinned. 'You weren't *that* debonair.'

'You bet your ass I was. You're just not refined enough to realise it.' He stuck his nose in the air and I gave him a light slug on the arm.

'Are we okay?' I asked in all seriousness.

'Course we are. But does this mean I get to let out all the bunny rabbit jokes I've been holding in?'

'I bet you haven't got a single one I haven't heard a million times already.'

'What do you call a bunch of rabbits hopping backwards?'

I shrugged; actually, I hadn't heard that one.

'A receding hare-line!'

I snorted. 'Okay, that wasn't too bad.'

'I have more.'

'Maybe let's ration them, okay?'

'One per social interaction.'

I found I was smiling not because of his stupid jokes but because he was being kind and making this so easy. I'd seen the quick flash of disappointment that he'd tried to hide. It wasn't that I'd broken his heart – he hadn't been *that* invested – but he'd liked me and I was sorry to let him down. But not sorry enough to date someone I wasn't truly into. In the long run, that would be far worse.

I was being kind, too, even if he didn't see it that way right now.

# Chapter 22

'Got the warrant.' Connor waved a document at me.

'Great, thanks.' I went to take it from him and he quickly yanked it back.

'I'll ride with you, since Gunnar can't.'

I thought about arguing but he had the warrant so I didn't. 'Fine. Let's go. I'm leaving Fluffy here. I don't want him to accidentally touch any of this shit.' I turned to my dog. 'Stay here with Stan, okay?'

'Oh, so now I'm guarding your office *and* your dog?' Stan said, but he was smiling.

I winked. 'Fluffy's guarding you. He'll keep you safe, tough guy.' Fluffy barked. 'Do you mind driving?' I asked Connor. 'I'm still not used to the other side of the road.'

'No problem.'

I threw him the keys and we drove to the Riverdreams' house in companionable silence. One of Skylark's siblings answered the door. 'Hi. What's your name?' Connor asked gently.

The girl, who appeared to be about twelve, gave him a wide smile. 'Peregrine.'

'Okay, Peregrine, is one of your parents home?'

'Yeah, just a minute. I'll go get my mom.'

A minute later, Mrs Riverdream came to the door. She looked harried. 'Haven't you done enough?' she snarled at me. It was hard to blame her; first the Grimes' break-in, then the drugs – she'd been through the mill because of her son. And, indirectly, because of me.

'Sorry, ma'am,' I apologised lightly. 'But we have a warrant to search the house. If you and anyone else in the residence would step outside, we'll be as quick as we can.'

She sighed and threw us a dirty look, but dutifully ushered her other two children out of the door. I hoped we wouldn't emerge to find our tires slashed; if we did, we'd know who'd done it.

We didn't find anything until we searched Skylark's room. He had used his limited imagination to find a place to hide his drug stash, and we found five tiny bags of hot-pink crystals under the mattress. I photographed them and then put them in evidence bags.

We searched the rest of the room but didn't find any more fisheye, just marijuana vape juice, the vape and the usual electronics and dirty clothes that live in a teenage boy's bedroom. We took all the drugs and their paraphernalia and let ourselves out. 'You can go back in,' I said to Mrs Riverdream.

She was vibrating with anger. 'My husband will be at the Nomo's office shortly with my son's lawyer.'

'Noted. I'd best get going then.' I gave her a polite smile that she didn't return.

It was a shame she was pissed off, but I was more concerned about finding the people behind the fisheye. It had nearly killed Gunnar and it could have seriously hurt Russell; whatever it was, it needed to be off the streets as did whoever was distributing it.

Connor drove us back to the office and parked out back. 'Do you know what kind of a shifter Skylark is?' I asked him as we walked inside.

He shook his head. 'I don't know what he is exactly, but his family is listed under the Siren group.'

Crap: that meant dealing with Calliope Galanis. I'd interviewed plenty of people but the heads of the supernatural council still made me nervous. I'd only met Calliope twice, and that was only briefly. 'Can you get me a meeting with her?' I asked, hiding my nerves as best as I could.

'Sure. You want me to come with you?' Okay, maybe I hadn't hidden my nerves so well. He pulled out his phone and fired off a text.

Yes, I did. 'No,' I said. 'It's fine. I could do with someone here who can call me when Skylark's dad and lawyer show up. I can't question the boy until then, and I want to do that ASAP.'

'No problem. Will you be okay driving?'

No. 'Yes,' I said firmly.

His phone pinged. 'Okay, Calliope has agreed to talk to you. She's at South Harbour – she owns the fish-processing plant there.'

The fish-processing plant had been at the heart of a lot of local controversy. In one of the council meetings, people had come to blows over the price of fish; it had seemed odd at the time, but now I knew how vital the industry was to the town. If Calliope owned the plant, she held a lot of power. That thought only made me more nervous.

I steeled myself. I could do this. I'd learnt all kinds of skills during the last couple of months; I just needed a good dose of self-belief to go with them. Unfortunately, that seemed the hardest type of belief to come by.

'Do I just go into the plant and ask for her?' I asked.

'She said to go to her office on the second floor. You'll have to leave Fluffy here. No pets allowed since it is a food-processing plant.' That seemed reasonable enough.

'Okay. Can you settle him?'

'Sure.'

I took the car keys back from Connor and motored off to see the queen of the fish. The tingle on the back of my neck told me that the vampire leader was watching me leave.

# Chapter 23

I'd never been inside a fish-processing plant; I'd never particularly *wanted* to go inside one. The first thing I noticed was the strong scent of fish. Go figure.

I entered through a large steel door, passed several huge, blue, fish coolers then went up a staircase. I only got a brief glimpse of the warehouse floor, which was full of equipment and people. A large cargo door headed out to the dock.

A fisherman passed me as he went down the stairs and grunted a greeting. He did a double take when he saw the Nomo officer badge proudly displayed on my shirt.

At the top of the stairs was a grubby office with a stern-looking woman sitting behind a desk. With silvered hair and a stiff bun, she looked like she should be a librarian. A couple of fishermen were in there picking up cheques. 'Bunny Barrington to see Ms Galanis,' I introduced myself.

Her glare did not waver as she gestured to the office behind her. She didn't move to announce my arrival. Okay, then.

I knocked on the doorframe, hesitating to walk in because I could hear raised voices. Then, because I am super nosy, I pushed the door open. There was a tall, blond, athletic-looking man fronting up to another man who was brown-haired, stocky – and vibrating with anger.

Calliope Galanis had warm, tanned skin, ageless light-blue eyes and long blue hair. I wasn't positive, but the blue looked natural. Today, she'd braided it in a thick rope that draped over her shoulder. Her teeth were small and pointed. On land she moved with smooth grace, as if she were in water. I shivered. I'd almost forgotten that the most beautiful things in the sea were often the deadliest.

She was sitting behind her desk, her face carefully blank, but her eyes were raging. Eek. Maybe I should have waited; curiosity killed the cat, and it could kill the new vampire, too.

I froze as all eyes swung to me. 'Sorry,' I said faintly. 'The receptionist said to come in. Connor arranged a meeting for me?'

Calliope looked at the clock. 'So he did,' she said mildly. 'In any event, Mr Mahoon was just leaving.' Her voice was hard.

The brown-haired man bobbed a bow to her but, despite the deferential action, his hands were still clenched with rage. There was trouble at the fish plant all right. He stalked out, slamming the door for good measure. Calliope's eyes narrowed at the blatant disrespect.

The taller man returned to the desk and shuffled some papers together. He put them into a folder and filed it away in a cabinet before turning to face me, his expression bland.

Calliope smiled. 'Do take a seat, Bunny. How is Gunnar doing?'

I had used the drive over here to call the hospital for an update. 'He's doing well,' I reassured her, 'though I didn't get to speak to him. Apparently he's chomping at the bit to get out of there.'

'No doubt. He is not a man to take confinement well. I shall visit him and impress upon him the need to recover fully.'

I nodded. I wouldn't mess about if Calliope told me to do something. There was a depth in her eyes, a heaviness that made me feel uncomfortable; she had seen some shit in her day, and her soul still bore the scars.

She turned to the man. 'How remiss of me, I haven't introduced you. Bunny, this is my second, Soapy Willoughby.'

I'd seen him at the council meetings but never learned his name. Soapy always walked in with Calliope and another woman, all three bearing tridents, but they filed their weapons under their boss's name. He was attractive in a rugged way, and it was clear that Calliope agreed; even as she introduced us, her eyes were roaming up and down his body. With his broad shoulders, narrow waist and muscular arms, he had a classic swimmer's physique. The proprietary way she gazed at him felt like a mark of ownership, and the way he gazed back suggested he had no issue with being her chattel. He obviously served her in all sorts of ways.

'Nice to meet you Soapy,' I said with a tight smile.

'And you,' he replied, though nothing about his body language said he was happy to see me. Maybe I'd interrupted something important with those papers he'd been shuffling. 'Take a seat,' he said. It was just a shade off an order.

I sat. The office was plain and utilitarian, with an old metal desk and metal chairs, straight out of a World War II movie. The only modern item was the laptop on the desk and some contemporary seascapes on the wall. Behind Calliope was a row of filing cabinets – and an incredibly large saltwater tank with dozens of colourful fish darting around inside it.

'So how may I help the Nomo's office today?' she asked, her voice like honeyed silk. Soapy moved around to stand behind her.

For all Calliope's strange beauty, she was dressed in business casual, a crisp white shirt tucked neatly into a pair of black trousers, though I had noticed a set of rubber overalls and those ubiquitous brown rubber boots behind the door. She might be the picture of sophisticated elegance, but she could get dirty.

Somehow that knowledge made me even more aware that I needed to tread carefully. The drugs were being moved via the water, and here I was with the water-shifter leader. There was every chance that someone she commanded was involved – it might even be her. I needed to not fuck this up. No pressure, then.

I sat back in the chair and tried to look relaxed. 'We have an issue we're trying to contain.' That was a royal 'we' since Gunnar was out of action.

She frowned slightly, encouraging me to say more. I didn't want to give too much away, but if she knew about Gunnar being admitted to hospital then surely she already knew something about the drug.

'There is a new street drug called fisheye,' I explained. She didn't react, not so much as a flicker of shock or dismay. Hmm. 'A large shipment was recently recovered.' I liked that: 'recovered' made it sound like there'd been a successful drugs' bust rather than us just finding a tonne of drugs floating in the water.

'As part of the investigation, we've questioned a number of teenagers who've been using the drug. One of them is from your siren group.' I watched for any sign that she already had the information, but she had one helluva poker face.

She shrugged lightly. 'Teens will be teens.'

'Could you tell us what kind of water shifter Skylark Riverdream is? It might or might not be relevant to the case, but we'd like to have as much information as possible.'

'Shouldn't you just ask the boy?' Soapy asked gruffly.

'We can't speak to him without his parents or lawyer present. We're hoping that by getting as much knowledge as we can before we do that, we can move the investigation forward in a timely fashion.' Man, I was good at this police-speak.

Calliope leaned back in her chair. As she studied me with those icy eyes, I wondered if she was going to tell me to take a long walk off a short pier. 'Skylark Riverdream is a bit of a troublemaker,' she said instead. No shit?

'I don't know how this will help,' She tapped her full lips with one tanned finger. 'But you've come all this way and it seems churlish to send you away empty handed.' Soapy made a murmur of protest and she shot him a warning look. 'The family are dolphin shifters.'

'Thank you.'

Her gaze sharpened. 'Will that information help?'

Skylark could have found the stash, but there was also a distinct possibility that he'd got it from a dealer. There was even a remote possibility that *he* was a dealer – though five little baggies did not a dealer make. I smiled blandly. 'It certainly won't hinder the investigation.' I paused. 'You said that Skylark is a troublemaker. In what way?'

'The usual nonsense – truancy, going to places where he shouldn't.' Her voice held a warning, and I wondered if 'places where he shouldn't' included a certain underwater cave. Suddenly she turned back to her paperwork. Without saying a word, she had quite clearly dismissed me.

I stood. 'Thank you for your co-operation.' I paused before leaving. 'What kind of a supernat are you?' The question was gauche at best, rude at worst, but I was new so I was hoping she'd put my lack of manners down to that.

Soapy didn't. His lips drew back in a snarl and revealed partially shifted, very spiky, teeth. In response, my fangs dropped.

The tension rose until, inexplicably, Calliope laughed. She touched Soapy's arm and murmured something I couldn't hear even with my vampire hearing, then she turned to me. 'I'm not shy, little rabbit – though you should be careful who you ask that question of. Ask the wrong person and you won't like the answer.' She smiled but there was nothing friendly about it. 'No doubt in my case, you could simply ask around town. I am a Scylla.'

I blinked. My mother's idea of a fine education had included me learning Latin and I'd read Homer. 'A barking, grisly beast with twelve legs, six long necks and six hideous heads, each with three rows of fangs?' Staring at the woman before me, suddenly, that didn't seem like such an impossibility.

Calliope gave a tinkling laugh. 'That bastard Homer was a little miffed at me when he wrote that. Some men hate being told "no". I'm what you would probably call a water dragon shifter.'

Holy heck. She'd known Homer? That was – what? Seventh or eighth century BC? How old was she? And why the fuck was she running a fish-processing plant in the middle of Alaska?

I realised abruptly that I was staring. I flushed and hastily looked away. Holding her gaze felt a little like I'd inadvertently been challenging her; like holding a wolf's gaze, it was a bad idea.

She looked smug; she'd been fishing for a reaction and she'd got one. 'Don't worry, Bunny. I think I rather like you.'

I wasn't sure if I should be happy about that or terrified. A dragon, a water dragon – an honest-to-goodness mythic beast. And she was looking at me like the cat that was ready to drink the cream. 'Thanks,' I managed. And, because I didn't know how to quit when I was ahead I asked, 'Why on earth would you stay *here*?'

'Because I grow bored easily. So far Portlock has kept me entertained.'

'Do you look similar to the dragon protector in the bay?' I asked nosily.

This time Soapy's growl wasn't hidden and Calliope looked mildly affronted. 'Of course not! He's a dragon, not a *shifter*. It's like comparing a human to a monkey.'

'Sorry. No offence meant.'

'Yet you seem determined to give it,' Soapy rumbled, his eyes narrowed.

'Don't be churlish,' Calliope chided. 'She's new – you're like a babe in the woods, aren't you, little Bunny? Off you hop now. I have things to do.' She turned back to her paperwork.

I told myself I wasn't fleeing from her but making a strategic exit. Yes, I was getting really good at this business talk.

# Chapter 24

I couldn't stop thinking about Calliope Galanis. If she hadn't been bullshitting me, then she truly was ancient – and a water dragon shifter, to boot. She was a sea serpent who'd been written about in ancient literature; she'd had whole legends constructed about her. I was twenty-three and the only thing I'd achieved in my short life was death. To her, I was nothing, a blip on her ancient radar. It was humbling, to say the least.

Back in the car park, I rang the hospital again and asked to speak to Gunnar. I got patched through. 'Bunny! How are you?' He sounded exactly like his usual jovial self; if it hadn't been for the machines beeping in the background, I could have imagined that he was on his lunch break with Sigrid.

I bit my lip; he wasn't on his lunch break, though, he was ill in hospital and I shouldn't be bothering him with work. 'I'm good. How are you?'

'Never better,' he said airily. 'I'm going a bit stir crazy. Update me on the case.' I hesitated. 'Officer Barrington,' he said firmly, 'update me on the case.'

'Yes, sir.' I snapped him a cheeky salute that he couldn't see and gave him the run down on everything I'd been doing.

'You've been busy,' he said approvingly.

I filled him in on my chat with Calliope. 'Did you know that Calliope was in *The Odyssey*?'

'The poem by Homer?'

'Yes.'

Gunnar frowned. 'No. I didn't. I don't know much about her at all – she's very private.' That didn't match with what she'd told me: she's said the whole town would know what she was and that she wasn't shy about it.

'Do you know her supernatural type?' I asked.

'I assumed she was a siren.'

'According to her, she's a Scylla – a water dragon.'

'Water dragon? Like the one in the bay?' He seemed genuinely surprised.

I frowned. 'She said she was different but, even so, she's an ancient water dragon. I can't get my head around it.'

He laughed. 'You're a vampire in a town of supernaturals. It's not that odd.'

'I was blown away by Mrs Wright's age. I can't imagine someone that's three thousand years old.'

'Mrs Wright likes to claim she's the oldest resident of the town but it doesn't surprise me that Calliope is older. There are other ancients in the village, too.'

'Who?' I asked.

'If they want you to know, they'll tell you.' He moved the subject back to Skylark and the case. 'What is the Riverdream kid?'

'Dolphin shifter.'

'So he could definitely have accessed the drugs in the cave. Interesting. You need to question him.'

'I'm on it. His father is coming in later with his lawyer.' It was almost 3am now; the lawyer had called while I was out and made an appointment for 10am, no doubt to fuck with me and put me on the back foot.

'Okay. Make sure Stan and Connor have your back. I'll contact someone to move the drugs to another secure facility, but it'll probably take a few days.' His voice hushed. 'Got to go – Sigrid's coming back from the bathroom. Make sure Sidnee is okay after the scare.'

'I will,' I promised.

'When I'm back,' he said gruffly, 'heads will roll.' He hung up.

I really hoped that was just an expression because I could remember all too well the sound that heads made when they rolled.

After I'd collected Fluffy from the office, we walked home for some food. Normally, I'd have finished for the day about now, but since we were a man down I needed to grab a quick nap before going back to interview Skylark. If his lawyer thought his timing meant that Sidnee would be conducting the interview, he was going to get a surprise.

I gave Fluffy a bowl of dog food for his supper. As I put it on the floor, he gave me a look of utter disdain. 'I'm having a frozen meal,' I protested. 'Your food is better for you than mine is for me!' His eyes narrowed and he gave a grumpy growl before turning his back on both me and the bowl.

'Oh, come on.' I ruffled his ears. 'Don't be like that. I'll chop up a frankfurter to go with it.' He wagged his tail. I opened a jar of the brined sausages and mixed in two with his biscuits and wet food. He gobbled it up.

I drank my cup of warmed blood and took my microwaved meal to the leather sofa so I could curl up and watch some trashy TV. Fluffy jumped up next to me, kicked off all the cushions, turned around three times and sat down, pointing his bum towards me. I wasn't totally forgiven for the dog food.

I ate quickly, surprised by how hungry I was even after the blood. We were watching a soap opera and the wife had just confessed her baby was her husband's twin brother's, when Fluffy's ears pricked. 'Guests?' I murmured. 'Anyone we like?'

Fluffy put his head down again; not someone he disliked, but not someone he liked enough to go and greet.

I went to the door. It was Thomas Patkotak. Huh? What the heck did he want?

# Chapter 25

I couldn't keep the surprise out of my voice. 'Hey, Thomas, what brings you to my door?'

The human hunter smiled grimly at me. 'Heard you have a new drug problem.'

'Not me, personally,' I sassed. 'I was taught to "just say no".'

'Funny. Can I come in?'

Not so long ago, in a moment of drunken revelry, I'd inadvertently put him at the top of Portlock's list of most sexy men so I didn't want to give him any ideas. However, in an oblique way he'd helped me solve my first case so perhaps he could help me with the fisheye situation too.

'Sure.' I stood back and let him enter. Since the guest was actually coming into the house, Fluffy moved languidly off the sofa and came over to say hello. He sniffed Thomas a bit, and Thomas stood patiently while my dog undertook a full examination. Once Fluffy was happy, he gave him a pet. 'Handsome dog,' he commented.

'Thanks. Would you like a cuppa? Or a coffee? You Americans prefer a cup of joe, right?'

He waved away the offer of a drink. 'I'm fine, thanks. I've heard some rumours.' Evidently small talk wasn't Thomas's forte.

'Oh?'

'The drugs are coming in from the sea, not the air.'

I'd already suspected that since we'd found the stash of fisheye floating in the harbour. I was a mistress of deductive reasoning, sharper than a tack. 'Do you know who's moving them?'

'Not yet. I heard you made an arrest.'

So that was why he was here, not to give me information but to dig for it. I looked at him sternly over my teacup. 'You need to let the Nomo's office deal with this.'

He sat down across from me at the kitchen table. 'Bunny, Gunnar is in the hospital and – with respect –

this is above your paygrade. You were made an official Nomo officer about a hot minute ago. We can help each other. I'm not fond of drug dealers, nor their effect on the community. They almost killed Gunnar.' He leaned forward. 'If you want to bring them in, you'll have to be faster than me.'

Holy heck, was he saying he would kill to take them down? I frowned at him. 'You would rather kill them than try to rehabilitate them?'

'It's cheaper in the long run.' He shrugged nonchalantly, like we weren't casually discussing death.

'Do the rest of the council feel this way?'

He shrugged again and didn't answer. A passing comment from Gunnar had led me to think that Thomas had done 'wet work' for the council before. I needed to cool down his jets before this got messy.

'We arrested a minor, a *kid*,' I said. 'I don't have any information for you yet.'

He stared at me a moment, assessing whether I was telling the truth. 'Okay.' He stood. 'Keep me posted.'

'Thomas, I like you – but this is the Nomo's case. Stay out of it.'

He gave me the ghost of a smile. 'Nice to see you growing that backbone.'

'Fuck off,' I said mildly, which made him laugh. I watched him walk out then locked the front door behind him. That was just what I needed, Patkotak sticking his oar in. I hoped he'd heed my order, but something told me he wasn't going to.

Fluffy whined after I'd shut the door and I looked down at him. 'I don't know what to do.' He cocked his head, and I guessed he didn't either.

I was tired and frustrated. Since I was already feeling shitty, I decided that now was the time to contact my parents – I might as well pile on all the shit in one go. I'd been deliberating whether to text my mum or my dad. Mum was difficult and would either scold me or guilt trip me, but Dad had refused point blank to help me get away from his partner, the Vampire King of Europe. That had *hurt*.

I took a deep breath and texted my mother: *I'm doing fine, Mum. I'm in the States. I have a good job.* It would give her a heart attack if she knew I was working in law enforcement, so I omitted that.

I doubted she'd keep me waiting long. It was 1pm her time, so she would be finishing lunch – or luncheon, as she insisted on calling it in a painfully embarrassing attempt to be posh.

I got ready for bed. As I slid under the duvet, I checked my phone. Sure enough, I already had a response. Lucky me.

*It's about time, Elizabeth Octavia! I've been worried sick. No word for months! You could have been dead in a ditch somewhere.*

And there it was: she'd gone with guilt. I grimaced; if I'd believed that her message was genuine I'd have felt bad, but I'd asked for my parents' help to escape so it couldn't have been a big shock when I disappeared.

I replied: *You know that I had to leave. I couldn't face a hundred years in the conclave.*

*We could have worked something out. You should have come to us.*

I had done! My temper was starting to fray. I *had* gone to them and they'd told me life with the Vampire King would be *wonderful*. As if.

I jabbed my reply: *Dad was going to hand me over with a flourish. You know what? This was a mistake. I shouldn't have contacted you. You know I'm okay, that'll have to be enough for now.*

I wanted to throw the phone at the wall, but that wouldn't solve anything. It beeped again and, despite myself, I looked at the message: *Oh, honey. I'm sorry. I miss you. I worry about you, that's all. I love you.*

My eyes burned. She did love me in her own way. It had to be enough, but somehow it never was.

*Love you too, Mum. Got to go.*

Since it was my work phone, I couldn't turn it off, but I silenced the notifications. I wished I could silence my brain in the same way.

Despite my exhaustion, sleep took its sweet time arriving.

# Chapter 26

It was too early and I hadn't had enough sleep; less than five hours rest was never enough for me. To combat the fatigue, I chugged an extra cup of blood. It took the edge off, but the tiredness persisted. Stupid daylight exhaustion.

I showered and got ready in record time; I wanted to be at the office for nine so I had plenty of time to prepare for Skylark and his lawyer. My nerves were clanging and I didn't want to fuck this up. At this point, Skylark was pretty much our only lead.

Fluffy and I stepped out of my house and stopped abruptly when we found Connor on my front step. 'How did you know I'd be up?' I blurted.

He shot me an amused look. 'As if you'd miss the chance to question Skylark yourself. The lawyer flew in from Homer. He just landed. I figured you'd be up soon.'

'And you thought you'd track me down and accost me outside my home?'

'Accost?' He raised an eyebrow and looked amused. 'We need to look at your definitions. You'd know if I was accosting you.' His voice was warm and flirty.

How did the man make everything seem like an innuendo? I huffed a breath. 'I'm grumpy. I had to deal with my mother, thanks to you.'

'You had to deal with your mother because she is your mother,' he responded evenly. 'I just passed along a message.'

I sighed. 'You're right; I'm not being fair. But I *am* grumpy. And tired. Did I mention tired?' I looked around. 'Where's Juan?'

'Guarding the Nomo's office.'

'So who's guarding you?'

'I'm responsible for myself today.' He winked.

'Terrifying.'

He looked amused.

'What gives?' I asked impatiently.

'What gives ... what?'

'Why are you here? Besides a need to fill your soul with my sunny disposition.'

He battled a smile but lost. 'I *do* enjoy your disposition: British, prickly, with a hint of fun.' He sounded like he was describing the bouquet of a glass of wine.

'Funny guy.'

'Looks like we're both a laugh a minute.' Connor's face grew serious. 'I'm here representing the council.'

'And?'

'You have a minor in custody and the council wants some answers. To give you leverage, it has declared that if Skylark answers your questions truthfully and to the best of his knowledge, we will grant him time served and community service. He won't get sent to juvie.' That at least gave me something to work with. Connor continued. 'The council wants a report on this new drug.'

'I can do that. Tonight?'

'Tonight would be good.'

'Okay.' I paused. 'You could have phoned me.'

'I could have,' he agreed. 'But it's much more pleasant to take a stroll with you.'

'Even if I snap at you?'

He studied me, eyes twinkling. 'Well, I guess it would be even more pleasant if you didn't.'

That made me laugh out loud. Suddenly, the remnants of my bad mood were gone.

'Have dinner with me,' he said suddenly.

'Okay.' My mouth agreed before my brain could catch up. Oh shit: I'd just agreed to go on a date with Connor! And worse, I really *did* want to go.

'Is it okay for us to date?' I blurted out. 'You're a councillor and I'm working for the Nomo. And then there's my age and your age? I mean – you're how old?'

He laughed. 'It's rude to ask a gentleman's age. Let's just say I'm well-seasoned.'

'Like a steak?'

'Like whisky. I have depth.'

I smirked. 'Did someone shove you in a barrel for a while, too?'

'I've never been *in* a barrel,' he reflected. 'I've been over one a time or two, though.'

'If you're super-old, how come you're so good at modern stuff? You drive a truck, you dress normally...'

'The best vampires are excellent at moving with the times. Some still cling to old-fashioned ways, but in my view embracing modern fashions and conveniences is necessary camouflage.'

'That's a bit disappointing,' I admitted. 'I half-expected you to wear lace and bemoan the good old days.'

He grinned. 'The good old days weren't that good. Disease was rampant; nobody bathed much or brushed their teeth. And believe me, central heating and air conditioning are hard to beat, not to mention email and cell phones. Do you know how long it used to take to send a message with a damned pigeon? And even then, there was every chance it would get eaten by a hawk.'

'Huh. Hashtag fifteenth-century problems, hey?'

He laughed again. 'I'm not *that* old, Bunny.'

We'd reached the office and I found that I was disappointed that our walk was at an end. 'How old *are* you?' I asked once more, hoping to draw out the conversation.

'You'll have to come on a date with me to find out. I'll call you with a few options once I work out the details. Have a great day, Bunny.' He turned and walked towards Juan, who was loitering by the office, leaving me in the street wondering what had just happened.

I looked down. Fluffy was watching me closely. 'What the heck was that?' I asked. He wagged his tail and barked then his tongue lolled. He was laughing at me. 'Shut up, fur face,' I muttered.

As I walked into the office, Sidnee's face lit up. 'Bunny! I didn't expect you in this morning. You've got to be shattered. I really don't mind handling the interview.'

Even as she said the words, she started fidgeting her hands anxiously. 'It's fine,' I answered. 'I need to feel like I'm doing *something*, you know? No progress on identifying the men that broke into the office?'

'None.' She sighed. 'Chris was really worked up that someone had come in and threatened me. Said I should quit my job or at least take some time off, that it was too dangerous for me.' She snorted. 'I told him to eff off. I've worked for Gunnar ever since... Well, ever since I've worked.'

She looked away, then started to say something else but changed her mind. I'd thought Sidnee was an open book but evidently I'd been wrong. Was nothing in this town the way that it seemed?

Fluffy lay on his bed by my desk as I logged on to my computer. I figured it was too early to have anything back from the lab, since the package would have only arrived yesterday afternoon or this morning, so I was shocked to see an email from them.

*Dear Ms Barrington, Portlock Nomo.*

*I've worked with the Nomo office in Portlock before. I worked through the night to examine the substance you sent. It is extraordinary. I've never seen anything like it. It's not a drug – at least it's not a chemical substance. I don't want to say too much in an email, but I'm sending a registered letter to your office and I'll include my preliminary findings.*

*I'll have to send it on to another expert. More details to follow in the letter.*

*Sincerely, Tony.*

*Anthony Brown*

*Alaska State Crime Lab*

*(907) 269-5740*

*anthony.brown@alaska.gov*

I printed off the email and added it to the file. Anthony Brown had obviously watched too many spy movies and now he was reacting all cloak and dagger, which probably wasn't warranted. Plus, I now had to wait for the damned letter to tell me *how* this substance was extraordinary and I sucked at waiting.

I wanted to call Anthony at the lab and demand some answers, but I didn't know him well enough to dismiss his paranoia. I didn't know who'd care enough to intercept the correspondence in a small town, but I guessed someone could be monitoring supernaturals. Our secret communities were mainly hidden from the wider world, but various government bodies were supposedly fully aware of our existence; an organisation called the MIB – Magical Investigation Bureau – worked for them. I'd been sorely disappointed when Gunnar explained that MIB didn't stand for Men In Black; that was an excellent movie.

Luckily, at that moment the Riverdreams and their lawyer showed up, so I couldn't dwell on the mysterious properties of the drug. I ushered them into the interview room and did the polite girl thing of offering them beverages. The lawyer clearly thought I was the office junior and accepted a coffee. The parents refused a drink, and I excused myself to get Skylark and the coffee.

When I unlocked Skylark's cell, he looked young, small, and scared and my heart twanged. The night in jail had knocked some sense into him and the anger and bravado that he normally carried were subdued. It was a real effort to maintain my poker face but I needed answers from him and I couldn't let my sympathies get in the way of the case.

When I took him into the room he ran to his mother, who gathered him into her arms and started sobbing. I left them to it. Legally, they needed a chance to discuss Skylark's situation and what statement, if any, he was going to give.

I just hoped he knew enough to shine a light on some of this mess because I was sick of stumbling around in the dark.

# Chapter 27

An hour later, there was a knock on the door and the lawyer announced brusquely that they were ready. His eyebrows shot up when Sidnee and I entered the interview room; he'd expected Gunnar.

I said that the session would be recorded, set the device on the table and hit record. After everyone in the room had given their name, I announced the date, time and the charges. Sidnee had offered to take notes in case the recording failed or someone magicked a fault on it. Although the chances of that felt low, I said sure: she needed to feel useful and I was grateful for the backup.

I turned to Skylark. 'Do you understand the charges against you?' He nodded, eyes on the desk in front of him. 'Please answer yes or no,' I said.

'Yes,' he responded dully.

'I'm going to ask you some questions about fisheye. Are you ready to start?'

'Yeah whatever.'

'Who sold you the fisheye?'

'I don't know his name.' He looked down and away; he was lying.

'Please describe him then.'

'He's about my dad's height, blond dude.'

'Weight?'

'I don't know, not fat. Sort of muscular.'

I studied him. He looked uncomfortable, shifting in his seat, looking between Sidnee and me. My gut said Skylark had seen this guy more than once and he knew his name. Whether it was his legal name was another matter altogether. I decided not to press for now; I'd circle back to it. 'Did you buy the fisheye?' I asked.

'No, he gave it to me, told me to give it to my friends.' That part sounded about right. Get the kids hooked, then make them pay.

'Did you take some of it?'

He licked his lips. 'Yeah, I took some.'

'How did it affect you?' Evidently it hadn't made him KO like Gunnar or get sick like Russ.

'It made me shift,' he admitted. 'I knew that it would, so I was by the water when I took it. It made me super-fast and strong.'

'How did you know you were stronger?'

He shrugged. 'I could just feel it, feel that I was powerful.'

I didn't tell him about the placebo effect; he'd expected an effect, so he'd felt one. 'Where were you when the dealer gave you the fisheye?' I pressed.

He gave a one-shouldered shrug. 'By the docks.'

'Which harbour?'

'North.'

Bloody North Harbour. That was where Eric had been murdered and where we had found a tonne of fisheye floating around. It was my least favourite of the harbours. 'Who did you give it to?'

'No one.' Skylark glared at me.

I leaned back and stared at him. He was lying, and he knew that I knew it. 'Should I call Russ in?' I asked quietly.

Skylark studied the surface of the table and said nothing.

The lawyer broke in. 'You don't have to answer anything you don't want to, Skylark.'

'I've been authorized to make a deal with you,' I said finally. 'If Skylark answers all my questions truthfully and to the best of his knowledge, the council will grant him time served, and community service. He won't get sent to juvie. But he knows the dealer's name and I need that information.'

'Let me consult with my clients,' the lawyer said.

'Interview paused,' I said for the recording before turning off the equipment. Sidnee and I left the room for them to discuss my offer. 'Do you think that will work?' I asked anxiously. 'And if they accept the offer, how will we know if Skylark is telling us everything he knows?'

Sidnee grinned and pulled out a set of handcuffs. 'Because Gunnar had Sigrid spell these with a truth spell. If Skylark and his lawyer agree, we pop them on and we get our answers.'

I smiled back at her, relieved we had a plan. 'Nice.' Thank goodness I had Sidnee at my back.

It wasn't long before they called us back in. 'We'll take the deal,' the lawyer said. 'Skylark will answer your questions.'

Sidnee presented the cuffs. 'Since you've agreed, we would like to use these cuffs to guarantee that he is telling the truth.'

The lawyer whispered to the parents and eventually they nodded. Skylark looked panicked; he hadn't been expecting us to enforce anything magically.

'Sky, hold out your hands,' the lawyer said kindly.

The boy hesitated, but then presented his wrists. Sidnee cuffed him.

'I'll resume the recording,' I announced. 'Now, let's start again.' I looked directly at Skylark. 'Who did you give the fisheye to?'

He grimaced. 'My friends, Russ and Jake.'

'Anyone else?'

The boy shrugged.

'Please answer out loud for the recording.'

'No one else.'

'We retrieved several baggies from your house. How many were you given?' I asked.

Skylark looked sullen. 'Twelve.'

'Ah, an even dozen. Minus the two you gave to Russ and Jake, that should have left ten. Where did the others go?'

Skylark obviously wanted to spit nails at me. 'We tried it one other time.'

'When you broke into the Grimes' place?' I asked, though the question was rhetorical. He nodded. Now we were getting somewhere. 'Who gave you the drugs?'

Skylark started to answer then froze. He couldn't lie but he wanted to, and his face was turning bright red with the effort of trying not to tell the truth. He looked desperately at Sidnee because she was playing good cop, then turned to whisper to his lawyer.

The lawyer whispered back and Skylark shook his head firmly. 'Could you give us a moment, please?' the lawyer asked.

Sidnee and I stood up. I picked up the recording device, then we left the room. 'Do you think Skylark will tell us who the dealer is?' Sidnee asked.

'He's a fool if he doesn't, but he's trying his hardest not to.'

'Yeah. Poor kid.' Sidnee sighed.

I was sympathetic but Skylark was making things harder for himself. Arresting him had been a scare tactic, and I'd fully expected to let him go soon afterwards. If the council was baying for blood, I might not be able to do that. Politics were murky, and even though I felt like they had no place in law and order, small towns like Portlock were something else. 'He's not making good choices.'

'He's a teenager – making bad choices is part of the job description,' Sidnee joked.

I wondered what bad choices my best friend had made in her teens. My bad choices had come when I was older; for all I loved the new life I was carving for myself, kissing Franklin in that bar was still top of the list.

I looked at the door to the interview room. The soundproofing was good; I could hear arguing, but it was muffled and indistinct, and it was impossible to tell what they were saying, even with enhanced hearing. This was the longest break in the proceedings so far.

The voices grew louder and angrier, then they stopped. After several beats, the lawyer opened the door. 'Skylark says he will not take the deal. He has nothing more to say.'

My gut churned. Without the deal, he could go to trial and end up in juvie with his magic frozen until he turned eighteen. It seemed extreme. Whoever the dealer was, Skylark was scared shitless of him.

When his parents walked out, Mrs Riverdream's eyes were red from crying and her husband looked furious. 'Can we take him home?' she asked plaintively.

'We'll have bail set up for you by tomorrow. You can get him then,' I explained.

They left the office looking stunned. The lawyer shrugged. 'It was a good deal,' he said before he left.

Sidnee went in and removed the truth cuffs from Skylark. He was shaking as she gently escorted him back to his cell. 'Meatloaf tonight,' she said softly.

'I don't like meatloaf.'

She gave him a flat look. 'Don't get thrown in jail, then you can have choices.' I heard the cell door shut and the lock turn.

She came back to me. 'That poor boy is scared. The only reason I can come up with for why he wouldn't take that deal is that he's more afraid of the dealer than juvie.'

'I reached the same conclusion,' I admitted.

Maybe he'd shared something with his buddies. We could start by pulling them in again – they were all walking a fine line after the stunt they'd pulled at the Grimes' place, and Russell was bound to be more tractable after his hospital stay.

'What do we do now?' Sidnee looked lost. 'Gunnar would have a plan.'

'I have a plan,' I protested. 'We'll bring in the other two boys and see if they know anything about the dealer.'

She brightened. 'Yeah. Kids talk to other kids. And we should probably check in with April Arctos because she was pretty upset. I'm sure she'll give us permission to talk to Russ.'

Skylark was risking going away for a couple of years and ruining his future because of a stupid teenage decision. He was protecting the dealer, not out of loyalty but out of fear.

If he was so scared, who – or what – were we up against?

# Chapter 28

April gave permission for us to talk to Russell and brought him straight over. The boy looked scared; a night in a hospital would do that to anyone, let alone a teenager.

Whilst April was obviously a firm disciplinarian, it was equally obvious that she loved her son deeply, and despite her disappointment in his actions she was here to support him.

'Skylark told us that he gave you the fisheye,' I started after I'd done the spiel about the recording. Russell nodded reluctantly after giving his mum the side eye.

'Were you high when you robbed the Grimes?'

He froze then gave a weak, 'Yes.' He paused. 'I already apologized, and I got a job to pay my share.'

'That's good.' I pretended to look through some papers, like the question was unimportant. 'Did Skylark ever mention who gave him the fisheye?'

This time, the boy looked panicked. He knew something. April obviously thought the same. 'Tell what you know,' she ordered firmly.

'I don't know much. They call the guy the Candy Man. I don't know his real name.' Russell licked his lips. 'Skylark knows it. He said he's in his shifter group.'

There were more than three hundred shifters in the siren group. We'd already suspected one amongst their number must be involved, though it was good to have it confirmed. 'Can you describe him?' I asked.

'I–I've never seen him.'

Frustration roared through me; I'd really hoped we'd get more about the dealer from Russell, but if he didn't know anything there was nothing to get from him. Maybe we could at least learn a little more about the drug? I switched tactics. 'How do you take fisheye? Is it swallowed, injected? What?'

Russell looked at his mom. He evidently recognised that she was already furious, so nothing he could say would make that worse. 'You mix it with some salt water and vape it.'

'You've been doing drugs *and* vaping?' his mother shrieked. Turned out, she *could* get more upset.

Russell hung his head. 'I'm sorry, Mom. I won't do it again. Any of it.'

'Too right, you won't! When we get home you're handing over everything. I mean *everything*.'

I doubted she'd let him out of her sight until he was thirty. I almost felt sorry for him but he'd made bad choices; even worse, he'd got *caught*. I cleared my throat. 'If you could allow us to collect all of Russell's drug paraphernalia, I'd be grateful.'

April nodded briskly. 'Of course you can.'

'It's potentially dangerous,' I warned. 'We'll come by in the next couple of hours to retrieve everything. Please make sure it isn't touched in the meantime.' I turned back to Russell. 'How long does the high last? And how does it affect your powers?'

The boy side-eyed his mom again but she was staring stonily ahead, lips pursed.

'A packet makes a full bottle of vape juice. I only need about three hits. It lasts about an hour.'

Gunnar had touched the raw crystals whereas the boys had diluted it in the vape. Could that be the reason for my boss's reaction to it? Was it more potent in its crystal form? 'Were you warned not to touch the crystals?' I asked.

Russell shook his head. 'Not as far as I know. I'm sure Sky touched them when he mixed them up.'

'You vaped it a couple of times and you were fine, then another time you got really sick?'

'I got stuck and I couldn't shift back into human,' Russell admitted. 'It made me panic.' Was it the multiple exposures that had made him sick, or had he got a bad batch of the stuff?

April's face was red and I was afraid she'd explode. 'How many times did you take that stuff?' she asked through clenched teeth.

'I, umm, used one full vape bottle but only one double hit off the second one,' he said quickly.

'That's why you were so wasted? You took a double hit?' She leaned over him with her hands on her hips. 'You could have died! You don't know anything about this drug.' She whirled on me. 'How dangerous is it? What is it?'

I exchange a helpless glance with Sidnee. Frankly, Russ knew more about fisheye than we did. 'We sent it out to be tested but we don't know much about it,' I confessed. 'It is worth noting that it hospitalised the Nomo when he simply touched it.'

'Gods! It brought down *Gunnar*?' April turned back to her son. 'And you've been sucking it up with goodness knows what else in that vape? That's it! You will never see Skylark or Jacob alone. Never again!'

Russ's eyes flew open. He looked like he was going to say something, but then shut his mouth, sensing that now was not the time to plead with his mum. He probably sensed right.

April's tirade reminded me of Jacob: we needed to get hold of him as well. If he still had some fisheye, he could be in danger. 'Mrs Arctos, what did the hospital say about Russell's condition?' I asked. 'The more information we have now the better, especially if other kids get hold of this stuff.'

'His vitals were fine, but they took blood to check everything over. I don't know the results yet. But the drug affected his shifting.'

'In what way?'

'At first he'd flip in and out of his bear form and he couldn't control his shift. Then he got stuck in bear form and that's when I really began to worry. After that, it wasn't until the drug wore off that he could shift at will again.'

'Interesting. I know I asked this last night, but could we get a copy of Russ's blood work when it comes in?'

'That's fine. I'll send it over.'

'Thank you. We don't have any other questions right now. Thank you both for coming in.' I smiled at Russell but, if anything, he looked even more miserable. He'd ratted on Skylark, his best friend.

April grabbed him by the arm and hauled him out. I had a feeling poor Russ was very sorry he'd ever looked at fisheye.

# Chapter 29

Connor organised a warrant for us in case the Olsens weren't in a co-operative mood. There seemed to be some tension between Stan and Juan, so I left Connor to mediate between them. Cowardly? No. Sensible? Yes.

Rather than call and give the Olsens prior notice, Sidnee and I drove to their home. If Jake had fisheye, it was best to get it from him now, before he took any more of the deadly stuff. We needed to get the word out about this drug, too. There had to be a newspaper in this town.

We knocked on the door and this time Jake answered. He looked confused by our presence. 'I already sent my apology to the Grimes,' he said.

'We aren't here about that. Are your parents at home?'

'Mom is out, and my dad is asleep. He works swing for the borough,' he explained.

'You'd better get him,' I said.

Jake let us in and walked through to the back of the house to get his dad. The three other children were watching a children's movie on TV, and it was clear that Jake was watching over them. Unlike Skylark, he had a responsible head on his shoulders.

A few minutes later, he returned with a tired-looking man in flannel pyjama bottoms and a T-shirt. His hair was mussed and his eyes were tired. I sympathised: I was tired too after only snatching a few hours' kip.

I looked at the small children watching the movie. 'It's probably better if we speak somewhere they can't hear,' I suggested.

'Jake, take the kids up to their rooms.'

'We'll need Jacob back here when he's done,' I said hastily.

Mr Olsen nodded and Jake gathered up the kids. When they were out of earshot, I quietly filled him in on the fisheye and Jake's purported involvement.

The man only looked more tired and defeated, like we'd kicked his favourite dog. I looked down at Fluffy, who'd come in with us, and he whined a little. I guessed he felt bad for Mr Olsen too.

Jake came down the stairs, looking worried. When his dad pointed at a chair, he dutifully sat. 'Do you have fisheye in this house?' Mr Olsen asked.

The boy blanched then looked at me and Sidnee. 'Y-yes,' he stammered.

'How much have you taken?' I asked. 'This is important. Fisheye can be really dangerous.'

'I only took it twice,' he said. 'I have to watch my little sister and brothers so I can't get high too often.' He wrung his hands nervously. That was something; he was responsible enough not to do it around his siblings.

'You still have a full bag?' I asked.

The boy nodded. 'And half a bottle of vape juice.'

'Vape?' His dad said, uncomprehendingly. 'You've been *smoking* it?'

'Vaping,' Jake corrected.

I tried to steer things back on course. 'Who gave you the fisheye?'

Jake squirmed in his seat. 'Sky.'

'Were you high when you robbed the Grimes?'

He straightened a little and looked me in the eyes. 'Yes, ma'am.'

'Who is the Candy Man?'

The boy went a little paler if that were possible. 'I don't know. All I know is that he's in Skylark's Siren group.'

'Have you ever seen him?'

Jake started to shake his head, then froze. 'Actually, I think I did once. He was far away, so I don't know if I can tell you much but he was blond and sort of bulky. Muscular.' That probably described about a quarter of men in Portlock; in a town of supernaturals, everyone was more muscular, the shifters particularly.

I nodded briskly. 'We're going to have to take the fisheye and your vape paraphernalia.'

The boy let out a breath but he nodded. 'I'll get it.'

I shook my head. 'You can show us where it is, but we'll collect it. That stuff is extremely dangerous to the touch.'

Jake looked shocked. 'I've touched it but it didn't do anything until I vaped it.'

That was interesting; it was just like Russell had said. 'What kind of supernatural are you?' I asked bluntly. Manners be damned. Russ was a bear shifter and Skylark was a dolphin shifter; maybe the drug affected each type differently.

'We're wolverine shifters,' Mr Olsen said wearily.

'Did the fisheye affect your shifting?' I asked Jacob.

He shrugged. 'I guess so. I didn't *try* to shift while I was on it, but I did anyway.'

I nodded. 'Okay. Show us where you keep the stuff.'

Jake guided us to his bedroom. He'd been a little more imaginative than Skylark: his stuff was stored in a shoebox at the top of his closet. I flipped open the lid: it contained vape juices, a couple of different vapes, an unopened baggy of fisheye and a half-full vape bottle of bright-pink fluid that I assumed was the fisheye vape juice. Rather than bag up each item individually, we took the box.

Jake looked ashamed and his dad looked hurt. It must be hard to receive blow after blow about how your previously super-responsible teen wasn't what you thought he was. As I left, I made sure to give Jacob one last warning; this mess could be the kick up the ass that he needed to sort out his young life. 'We don't want to be called back here, young man. If we are, you'll be looking at jail time. Do you understand?'

Looking shaken, he nodded.

With a shoebox full of drugs, Sidnee and I made tracks to the Arctos' residence. Time for another pick-up.

# Chapter 30

Sidnee went home whilst I sent the vape juice to the same lab we'd sent the drugs to; we needed to find out if salt water had changed anything in them. I was still waiting for that damned letter from that guy, Anthony.

After preparing the package for the post, I finished some paperwork. I was dead on my feet but there was one more urgent job before I could call it quits and leave: I needed to get word out about fisheye and make sure kids – and adults – knew how dangerous it was.

I rooted around the office until I found an old copy of the local newspaper, *The Supernat Sentinel*, with a phone number at the bottom of the front page.

'*Sentinel*?' a bored-sounding woman answered when I rang it.

'Hi, I'm Officer Barrington with the Nomo's office. I need to speak to someone about an urgent article?'

'Really?' Her voice perked up. 'That's great! I'll come to the Nomo's office. See you in five!' She rang off before I could ask anything pertinent, like her name.

Five minutes later in whirled a woman who was five foot nothing tall, with short, blue-black hair, a shaved patch on one side of her head and a pierced nose. She couldn't have been much older than me. 'Barrington?' she asked as she strode in.

'That's me. You can call me Bunny.'

'As in Bugs?'

'As in Bunny,' I said firmly.

'I'm Lisa.' She held out her hand out and bounced a little on the balls of her feet. 'What's so urgent that you need me now?'

I explained about the fisheye and Gunnar's hospitalisation – I even included the attack on the office to make it clear that these guys meant business. I explained that the drug could make your ability to shift wild and uncontrollable.

Lisa's eyes were wide. 'This is *so* cool.'

'It's a deadly drug,' I pointed out.

'Yes, exactly! Circulation of the paper will go through the roof. Everyone will want to read this article!'

'That's the point,' I said drily. 'We need everyone to watch out for anything suspicious. I'd like you to include a hotline for anonymous tip-offs.'

'You've set up a hotline?' Lisa looked impressed.

'Well, no. We'll just put in one of the Nomo's numbers. It'll work fine.' I gave her one of the office's mobile numbers, which she jotted down. She had me stand by the desk and took a photo of me looking stern. I didn't have to try to pull that off – this *was* serious. People needed to know not to touch this stuff. When Lisa left the office, she vibrated with energy and excitement. I was glad someone was happy.

Connor knocked on the front door before he came into the office. 'Hey,' he greeted me. 'You must be dead on your feet.'

'Undead on them,' I agreed.

He gave a lopsided smile. 'Time to go home.'

I really wanted to take him up on that, but... 'I can't. We still have Skylark in lockup and someone needs to be here for him.'

'I'll stay,' he volunteered. 'You go.'

I hesitated. 'What about our date?'

'Another time.' He smiled again. 'I prefer my dates conscious.'

'You have all these standards,' I mock-complained.

'Yeah, I'm picky like that. Go home. When Gunnar's back and this drug mess is sorted, we'll go out for dinner. Maybe somewhere out of town.'

'Out of town?'

'We'll get on a plane and go somewhere else,' he explained. 'The Garden of Eat'n is good, but there's only so many grilled chickens you can get excited about. If I want to wine and dine you properly – and I do – then I want to do it somewhere far away from hundreds of other nosy supernats.'

I gave him a small smile just before a yawn cracked my face. 'Sounds nice,' I admitted wistfully.

'I can do better than *nice*,' he purred.

'We'll see,' I said but I was still smiling. For some reason, the thought of dating Connor didn't give me heart palpitations like it had with Stan.

I could still remember the feel of Connor's arms around me as he'd raced me through the woods to safety. Okay, so I shouldn't have been proud of needing the rescue but it had been awfully nice – if we ignored the blood, fear and pain.

Fingers crossed that the next time his arms were around me, the only gasps I'd be making would be from something other than pain.

# Chapter 31

The next day, Anthony's registered letter finally arrived. It wasn't the only new arrival in the office: Gunnar was back at his desk with Sigrid sitting huffily in his guest chair.

'Gunnar!' I cried when I walked in. 'I'm so pleased to see you!'

Sigrid looked grumpy. 'The man doesn't know how to rest. He's been told to take it easy for a day or two and yet here he is, sorting out bail and letting Skylark go. He can't sit still for long.'

Gunnar smiled at her indulgently. 'Skylark's had a taste of jail life. Hopefully that is the wakeup call he needed. Besides, his parents were frantic. It was the right thing to do.'

'I don't contest that.' Sigrid folded her arms. 'But did it have to be *you* that did it? Bunny had it handled.'

'I did,' I promised hastily.

'I know you did – I saw you'd already started the process.' He looked at his wife. 'Go home my love and get some rest. You've been driving back and forth to the hospital non-stop. Go relax.'

She threw up her hands in frustration. 'That's what I've been saying to you!'

'I've done nothing *but* rest. Go on, now. Loki will be missing you.'

Her eyes softened. 'I'll go – but I'll be back.' She wagged a finger at him. As she bustled away, she reached over and hugged me. 'You've done the most wonderful job in his absence,' she murmured. 'Well done, Bunny.' She gave me one more squeeze and left.

'She's not wrong,' Gunnar rumbled. 'I'm seriously impressed.'

'Sidnee helped,' I said quickly.

'And this?' He tapped a newspaper on his desk.

I blinked. There I was, splashed across the frontpage under the title: *Unprecedented Danger! Deadly Drug Sweeps Portlock!* Lisa had wasted no time at all getting the article published. I was impressed.

Next to the picture of me was a nametag that said: *Officer Bunny Barrington aka The Fanged Flopsy*.

'The Fanged Flopsy?' I said, startled. 'What the fuck?'

Gunnar grinned. 'I wondered what I'd missed.'

I groaned. 'Looks like Lisa decided to give me a nickname.'

'She also gave you a decent back story.'

'What?'

His amusement grew. 'Just read it.' He handed over the paper.

*Bunny Barrington is a British aristocrat turned vampire who has already killed one rogue werewolf since arriving in Portlock. Now this deadly woman has turned to the side of the law and bears the Nomo's badge of office. Despite her chequered past, she is keen to put her lawless ways behind her and focus on delivering justice. Watch out, Portlock! The Fanged Flopsy is on the case.*

*A confidential informant told me, 'I heard that she got experimented on by the British government. She has all these extra skills!'*

I groaned and buried my head into my hands as Gunnar guffawed at my expense. 'I wasn't lawless when I killed the werewolf, I was the law! She's twisted everything!'

'She's a reporter, it's part of the job,' he said. 'I loved the bit about the government experimenting on you.'

'I was joking with one of the teenagers that works at Pizza Kodiak Kitchen. I didn't realise she'd take it seriously!'

Gunner laughed again. It was nice to see him looking relaxed. I didn't even mind that his amusement was at my expense – though I was seriously contemplating strangling Lisa when I saw her next.

He went back to business, 'I have a letter from the lab.' He passed it to me.

*Dear Portlock Nomo*

*This is fascinating. I'm having a physicist look this over, but from what I can tell this is not a chemical I've encountered before. It appears to be radioactive, though not enough to worry about unless you ingested it or spent a lot of time rolling around in it.*

*I've run some tests on myself, and I haven't had any issues since touching it. I accidentally came in contact with it before I read your warning note, but I had zero reaction – it appears completely inert around me. However, my supernatural lab partner came into contact with the crystals and instantly shifted, so I think it may only affect supernaturals.*

*Have you discovered how it is being taken? We discovered that the bag the drug was in was Kevlar and the box was made of an aero graphene. I can only suppose that was used to block the radiation coming from the substance. Very clever.*

*I'll pass on anything I get back from the physicist. Tony Brown.*

Gunnar and I looked at each other. 'Radioactive?' I squeaked.

He shrugged. 'Yeah. Maybe that's what caused my organs to shut down.'

I frowned. 'It's weird, though. Some of the boys touched it and were absolutely fine.'

'Different batches?' he mused.

'Either that, or different supernaturals react in different ways. Or maybe both.'

'It's possible.' His brows drew together. 'But the radioactivity surely can't be good for humans.'

Sidnee had told me Gunnar was a demigod and I'd never quite been sure if she was messing with me. But demigods were mainly human – was that why he'd been so sick?

We hadn't had any calls about our human residents and fisheye, and hopefully Lisa's article would help get this drug stopped before it got truly started. Only the three boys had taken it that we knew of, though I had no doubt others had tried it. However, they'd probably done it in the privacy of their own homes and not gone on a crime spree afterwards.

Even so, I didn't think fisheye had spread that far. Had we accidentally acquired the full supply, apart from what the dealer had already dispersed to get his clients hooked? Was it addictive? 'Hey, Gunnar. Have you got any urge to break into the jail cell?' I asked.

He blinked, then his eyes cleared as he followed my meaning. 'No. Not yet, anyway.'

'The boys took the drugs the way they were supposed to, by vaping, and then they vaped it again a few more times so it *could* be addictive. There's a reason the dealers gave it away for free.'

He frowned. 'You're right. Let's ring the parents and ask them to keep an eye out for any withdrawal symptom.'

At that moment the office mobile number that I'd given out as our hotline rang. 'Barrington,' I answered gruffly.

'Oh my God! It's The Fanged Flopsy,' a teen voice squealed, clearly as an aside to a mate. Kill me now – and I would take Lisa down with me if that ridiculous nickname stuck.

'How can I help you?' I pressed.

'There's a drug deal going down right now! We saw it happen. Some dude passed some bags of stuff to another dude, and the other guy gave him cash!'

'Where was this?'

'North Harbour.' Always the bloody North Harbour.

'Are the suspects still there?'

'For now. I took some pictures!'

'Great. Stay there and we'll be with you in five minutes.' I hung up. Dammit, I should have taken their names and numbers. Too much haste, less speed! 'Apparently there's a drug deal going down at North Harbour,' I said to Gunnar as I started to leave. Fluffy didn't even raise his head; like me, he was running on empty. I'd leave him here to rest.

'Let's go!' Gunnar rumbled, grabbing the car keys.

'Um, should you come? You know, because of the taking-it-easy thing?'

He glared at me. I guessed that was answer enough.

# Chapter 32

We screeched into the harbour, lights out and sirens silent. Two Goth kids were drinking from cans on a bench. As we jumped out, they pointed to a couple of men; obviously subtlety wasn't in their skillset.

Unfortunately, the movement also caught the men's eyes. They saw us and one of them reacted instantly by turning and diving into the water. Without thinking, I broke into a run and jumped in after him.

The harsh cold took my breath away, but I was determined not to get wet for nothing. I took a deep breath and dived. Opening my eyes in the dark water, I looked around for any sign of the man – and that's when my brain connected with my instincts. If he had dived into the water rather than running back along the pier, he was probably some kind of water shifter.

I was in his territory right now – and I wasn't the best of swimmers.

Seeing nothing in the dark water, I headed for the surface but something grabbed my left ankle and yanked me down. I tried to kick back with my right foot but my movements were sluggish. I kept on trying because otherwise I was about to learn exactly how well vampires coped with deep water. We were undead, right? Even so, we breathed, our chests rose and fell, and my heart gave a thump now and again. I wasn't sure where I fell on a scale of alive to undead.

I kept trying to kick at my assailant but he was completely unaffected by my weak efforts. I was absolutely taking up kickboxing after this. If I survived.

I felt something tighten around my ankle – then his hold on me vanished. I looked down but couldn't make out more than a shape as he swam away. He'd tugged me into deep water, and the moonlight didn't reach this far. I was trapped.

Panic flared, but I tried to stay calm. I fought to reach my ankle, to work out what was tying it down. It was slimy and slippery – some form of seaweed? I tried to untie the knots that he'd tied but I couldn't even find them: it was like the seaweed had somehow *grown* around me. With magic, it might well have done. Ugh.

I yanked at it, but nothing seemed to have any impact on the sturdy plant. Fuck, my chest was burning. I needed to take a breath...

Then impossibly large, bright-yellow eyes latched onto me and, despite my aching lungs, I stilled. Better to drown than be eaten, right? The eyes glowed for a moment, then the gargantuan creature lit up and shone with the blue light of bioluminescence. Eye to eye with me, it looked even bigger and I was paralysed with fear. The thing looked – amused?

It opened its huge jaws and snipped the seaweed cord that was holding me down. As a clicking noise filled my ears, it lowered its gigantic head between my legs and *pushed*, flipping me upwards with such force that my ears popped. I broke the surface of the water with a yell and shot ten feet into the air, desperately gulping in a lungful of oxygen.

What comes up must come down and I hit the water again, but this time I didn't go down far. I broke the surface with some more ungainly gasps. Gunnar was at the dock's edge, and he thrust an arm towards me. I swam to him and gratefully grasped his hand. 'It's a little late for a swim,' he said lightly, but I could see the worry on his face.

'That was so cool!' one of the Goth kids said to the other. 'She totally *hopped* out of the water. That must be one of the things the government experimentation did to her.'

Fuck my life.

# Chapter 33

I was soaked to the skin and shivering uncontrollably. Gunnar had wrapped a blanket around me and suggested I get in the car, but fuck that: I hadn't come through all this to huddle around a heater. Besides, he had only just come out of hospital so no way was I leaving him to do this alone.

Gunnar had secured the other half of the drug deal whilst I was taking my moonlit swim. The buyer was Edgy, our one-armed pilot. The Nomo had cuffed his ankles and put him in the car whilst he came back to help me. 'I know you haven't been here in Portlock long,' he said, 'but you don't go swimming in the drink, not at night. There are all kinds in the depths.'

I glared at him. 'Yeah, I know that *now*. If the water dragon hadn't rescued me, I'd have been a goner!'

'Did it?' He eyed me with interest. 'It seems to have taken a liking to you. And you would have been okay, as long as you didn't get eaten.'

'Eaten?' I said faintly.

'I told you, no swimming in the dark.'

I wasn't sure if he was messing with me; given the vastness of the water dragon, I figured that he probably wasn't. 'Being eaten wasn't the problem, it was the whole lack-of-oxygen thing that was getting to me.'

He smiled. 'Bunny, I hate to break it you but you're a vampire. You don't *need* to breathe.'

I took a breath. 'See? I absolutely do.'

He shook his head. 'It's an affectation, a habit left over from life that the body can't quite forget. But you don't *need* to do it, your brain just thinks you do. That's where stories of zombies come from. You can bury a vampire in the earth and it can claw its way out, though it takes longer than you'd think and they run the risk that it's going to be sunny when they burst out of the ground.'

I gaped at him.

'You weren't really in any danger,' he reassured me.

'It felt like I was,' I said drolly. I felt pretty embarrassed. I'd thought I was going to die from lack of oxygen, but if what Gunnar was saying was true I could have hung out in the water for days as long as nothing ate me. But the burning in my chest had been hard to ignore.

'Come on,' I said, needing to focus on work. 'Let's speak to the kids that called it in.'

Gunnar introduced me to them. Aoife Sullivan was a teenager with vampire-pale skin, and hair so blonde it was almost white. Her eyes were an unnerving shade of light yellow, giving her an almost animalistic feel. I checked her hands: no claws. I had no idea what she was, but she was definitely *something*. She had accentuated her paleness by dressing in Goth clothes: heavy black boots, black jeans, a black lace top and a black jacket.

Her friend, Joanne Gregson, was dressed similarly but her clothes looked significantly less otherworldly next to her brunette hair, blue eyes and warm skin tone. She was bouncing with excitement. 'The way you leapt in after him!' She looked at me with amazement. 'That was so cool! Course, you knew you could do that extra hop thing, right? Wow.'

I stifled a grimace. 'Can you tell us what you saw?'

'Absolutely. Was our tip-off helpful? We're basically crusaders.' Joanne's enthusiasm was cute, even if she was looking at me with far too much hero-worship in her eyes.

'Very helpful. You said you got pictures?' I prompted.

'Yes! Let me show you. I got them both – dealer dude and buyer boy.' She pulled out her phone and found a couple of photos. They showed two men standing together, and another shot with their hands outstretched towards each other, but there was no 'money' shot: no drugs visible, no cash changing hands. Dammit. And the one she'd said was the dealer dude had his back to us.

At the distance it had been taken, and with the dim evening light, I couldn't make out much more than he was tall and broad shouldered. I could now add that he was a strong swimmer. Though he'd stayed in human form whilst I could see him, I was convinced he was some sort of water shifter; his instinct had been to go into the water and that had to count for something.

'The pictures are great, right?' Aoife asked, grinning.

They weren't great; they were helpful but had missed the essential moment. I forced myself to smile. 'Really great, thanks.'

Gunnar took brief statements from them then we cut them loose and joined Edgy in the car. 'Sorry to keep you, Mr Kum'agyak,' my boss said.

'No worries, mate, I could see the drama from here. You fancied a swim, Flopsy?'

I gritted my teeth. 'It's Bunny. And I was chasing a suspect.'

'Right into the drink! That's dedication for ya. Far out, Bunny.'

'Can you tell us what you were doing at the docks?' I asked.

Edgy sighed. 'Well, given that the Nomo here already found a pink baggy on me, there's no point lying. I wanted to have a Captain Cook at this new drug here.'

'Captain Cook?'

'It means have a look, mate.'

I pinched the bridge of my nose. 'Did you not see the papers this morning?'

'Yeah, I did. You looked great. Very tough.'

That was *not* the point. 'The drug is deadly.'

'I heard that, but I also heard it changes your shift, makes you more powerful, into something *else*. With me only having the one arm, I can't fly under my own power anymore. I thought maybe this drug would change that. Worth a try, hey?'

'Not if it killed you!'

'Sure – then I'd be dead.' He shrugged. 'But I wouldn't know any different, would I?'

I tried a different tack. 'How much did you pay for it?'

'Nothing, mate. He insisted on giving it to me for free. Nice bloke.'

'What's his name?'

'I don't know. I'm new in town. Tall guy, and he had a hood on so he didn't let me see his face. It was dark, and all that. To be honest, I couldn't promise to pick him out.'

'How did you find him?' Gunnar asked.

'Well, *he* found *me*. After I'd been to the store this arvo to get some of my marijuana, someone approached me and offered me something harder. Called it fisheye. Said to meet him here at the docks at midnight – and here we are.'

Gunnar removed the cuffs. Edgy hadn't paid for the drugs, and one tiny baggy did not make for a possession charge. Plus – and here was the *real* kicker – we needed a pilot. Without one, this whole town would grind to a halt. The days after Jim's death had been tough; Portlock might be damp, but it ran on liquor.

'You can go,' Gunnar said gruffly. 'But if someone calls you and offers you more drugs, you contact us.' He passed over his card.

'You got it.' Edgy opened the door and slid out.

We watched him leave, and another lead bit the dust.

# Chapter 34

Back at the office, Juan was guarding the building. He grinned when he saw the state of me. 'You wanted a midnight swim?'

'If one more person asks me that, I'm going to punch them,' I muttered. His grin widened. I stepped closer and asked, 'Vamps really don't need to breathe?'

He barked a laugh then held his nose and covered his mouth. After three minutes, I sighed. 'Okay. I get the point. No breathing. So why did it feel like my lungs were burning?'

Juan tapped his head. 'Psychological shit. The brain is a powerful weapon.'

That was one way to look at it. 'Right, thanks.' I walked into the office. Fluffy woke up and gave a low growl at the state of me, then trotted over and sniffed pointedly.

'Yes, I know – I stink.' His growl deepened and he glared at me; he was peeved by being left out. 'You were sleeping!' I protested. He barked. 'Okay, okay. Next time I'll wake you up. Now keep an eye on Gunnar while I get changed. Apparently I smell ripe.' Fluffy's nose recoiled; he agreed. Charming.

I'd dried out a little in the warmth of the car but still I smelled of the water, and my clothes were uncomfortably damp. I used a towel to dry off, then found a change of clothes. Unfortunately, it didn't include underwear; for now, I'd go commando and stay dry.

While I changed, Gunnar had put the little baggy in the jail cell with the rest of the stockpile and flipped on the kettle. The office had a coffee machine but he'd bought a kettle when I'd started work. He knew about a British person's need for tea; he was the best boss.

We sat in his office with our hot drinks. 'Edgy,' I started. 'He only recently came to Portlock, right?'

'Right.'

'And now we have a drug problem.'

'You think he's bringing it in by air?'

'It's a possibility isn't it?'

'Didn't Patkotak say it was coming in by sea?'

'Yeah, but—'

'Occam's razor, Bunny: the most likely explanation is probably the right one,' Gunnar said gruffly. 'We found the drugs in the water, they were wrapped up to survive being stored in the water, ergo they were most likely transported through water.'

I sank back into my chair. He was right. 'The girls saw some stuff exchanging hands and Edgy had a roll of cash on him, but we didn't see any other evidence that he was the buyer rather than the dealer.'

'That was to pay for the drug, but the dealer let him have it for free.'

'That was his explanation,' I agreed. 'But what if the roll of cash was money he'd been paid, and that solitary bag was all he had left after the deal had gone down?'

'It's possible,' Gunnar said finally, 'but not probable. That's not how it struck the girls, and they were there to see it.'

'They're teenagers,' I snorted, like I hadn't been one of their number only a handful of years earlier. His amused expression told me the same thought had occurred to him.

As he was absently checking his emails, he stilled abruptly and his eyebrows shot up. 'Well now,' he murmured. 'That's interesting.'

'What is?' I asked.

'Another email from our friend, Anthony Brown.'

'The lab guy?'

'The lab guy. The physicist – whom he wouldn't name – told him off the record that he'd seen this effect before.' Gunnar paused dramatically. 'In a government project he can't talk about.'

I was stunned. Maybe all my jokes about government experiments weren't totally off base. 'The government knows about supernats?'

'Oh yes,' he said grimly. 'A few people in power – not everyone, but the president and some of his advisors – know. There's a whole government branch dedicated to keeping us all nicely hidden.' His voice was grim.

'The MIB? But isn't that what we want, too?'

'Whether we want it or not, it's the reality. Anyone tries to out themselves, and the MIB will be knocking on their door.' The Magical Investigation Bureau sounded scary. Gunnar had told me that they had all sorts of dangerous powers and they ran black sites for supernat containment.

'You reckon someone stole this drug from the government? So maybe this really is a limited stash. We get rid of it and the problem goes away.'

'Maybe,' said Gunnar. 'But the dealer is out there and still peddling. He still has something to give away.'

'He gave the kids a dozen bags but he only gave Edgy one. He must be running low.'

'We can hope,' he agreed.

'I'm not up on witchy things, but couldn't we ask someone to scry for the drug dealer?'

'Good thinking – but there's a snag. Technically we can scry for our guy, but we'd need a personal item of his, which we don't have. The drug bags aren't personal enough because they wouldn't contain enough focused emotion for the spell to work. And witch-wise, Sig can't do it for us. By community standards she's not very strong. She's more of a hearth witch, good with homey things.'

I didn't know much about different types of witchcraft. I was the only supernatural in my family and I'd come to this world late, but even so I was picking up knowledge. Shirley had thrown fire at us, the Grimes could do illusions, and Sig was a hearth witch – whatever that was.

'Is there an encyclopaedia of magical beings?' I asked Gunnar. 'Sometimes I could do with a cheat sheet.'

'No. Each species guards its secrets well. None of us want a book of our strengths and weaknesses lying around for the MIB to find.'

'Good point.'

'I'll teach you as we go,' he promised. 'You'll pick things up in no time with that memory of yours.'

'So – hearth witch?'

'Oh! It means she's magical at domestic things. In Sigrid's case, it's cooking. That's one of the reasons she prepares the meals for any prisoners here – she laces calming magic through their dinners. It's reduced the frequency of incidents,' Gunnar explained.

'Cool. So who would be strong enough to scry for us?'

'I know of one witch in Portlock that can do it. There may be more but, as I said, we play our cards close to our chest. Even so, we'd still need to find something personal belonging to the dealer.'

'If we knew who it was, that would be a whole lot easier,' I said drily.

'It really would.' Gunnar grinned.

'Okay, I'll stop suggesting unhelpful ideas.' I often felt like I was working blind. For example, would it have killed Connor or my vampire liaison Hester to mention the breathing thing? I'd taken a computer course and nothing about that had been mentioned. Gunnar was right: no one liked being up front about their strengths or weaknesses, even to their own kind.

Gunnar was watching me. 'Hey, now. Your suggestions are great and one of them is going to work out. If we don't keep thinking outside the box, we'll never get anywhere. You've done great work on this case so far. I'm really proud of you.'

I nodded because suddenly I couldn't speak; a rock had taken up residence in my throat. He was *proud* of me.

The door dinged and Sidnee came in. She squealed when she saw Gunnar through the glass, ran in and hugged him. 'Gunnar! You're out and about already! How much trouble are you in with Sig for being here?'

He laughed. 'She's posturing, but only a little. She knows I need it.'

'She knows you well,' Sidnee agreed. 'How's the case going?' We filled her in on the hotline tip, the drug deal and my impromptu swim. She stared at me in horror. 'You *followed* him into the bay? What were you thinking? And in the dark, too!'

'You swam in there at night,' I pointed out mulishly.

She rolled her eyes. '*I'm* a mermaid. If something tries to bite me, I bite back!'

I smiled sheepishly. 'Trust me, I won't be doing it again. Anyway, I was thinking about the case. Our only remaining lead is Skylark. He knows who the dealer is and I think we should take a run at him again. Now his parents have had time to make him reconsider his position, maybe he'll tell us more.'

'Can't hurt,' Gunnar agreed.

'Later,' Sidnee said firmly. 'Now go on home, the pair of you. I've got the office. Get some food and rest, in that order.'

I stood. 'You don't need to tell me twice,' I admitted.

'You've been burning both ends.'

'Well, I'm back now so no need,' Gunnar said firmly.

Sidnee and I exchanged looks. Until he was back to full power, we would both be pulling extra hours. No way we were leaving Gunnar by himself – what if he relapsed? What if the drug *was* addictive and he broke into the jail? It was unlikely, but I wasn't risking him for a minute.

'Bunny, come on home with me,' he said. 'Sig made dinner and you're invited. Fluffy too. We've missed you both since you got your own place.'

I smiled. 'Thanks, Gunnar. I'd love to.' Sofa-surfing had been grim, but it had been nice to have some company that wasn't furry.

'I just have to call Chris,' Sidnee said. 'He's anxious about me since the whole break-in thing. I'll let him know I'm here safe and I have the guards outside. I won't be long.'

'You chat with your beau on your mobile as long as you like. If the Nomo's phone line isn't tied up, I don't mind. Anyhow, you've got the quiet shift.'

We left Sidnee on the phone to Chris and drove to Gunnar's house, a charming dark-red place with green trim and hand-painted flowers. It looked charmingly old world for this wild place, but it suited Sigrid.

Fluffy ran to the door to greet Sigrid as soon as she opened it. She smiled warmly at him and me, but her eyes were really only for Gunnar, and she checked him over anxiously, looking for any sign that he wasn't okay. Finding none, her shoulders eased. She gave Fluffy a thorough pat, and let him in.

He raced to join Loki. Loki could get quite exuberant around him, and my dog was quick to put him in his place, but they seemed to enjoy playing together. Sig let them into the back garden to enjoy the dawn air. Fluffy rarely got a free run since he was with me all day in the office or cooped up in the house. Our tiny garden was barely large enough for him to take care of business. Once I had enough cash saved, I was going to have a doggy door installed so he could go in and out when he wanted.

Sigrid was putting some finishing touches to supper, so I set the table and tossed the salad. It was nice to work alongside someone I cared about without needing to talk or having to impress. My stress melted away and I let my mind rest.

After a time, she broke our companionable silence. 'So, I hear you're going out on a date with Connor?'

'How did you hear that?'

'Sidnee,' she smiled. 'She's excited for you.'

I was uncomfortable at the thought that people were gossiping about me and Connor, especially since we hadn't even been on a date yet. No wonder he wanted to take me out of Portlock. 'Actually, he's asked if we could go out of town. If we do, could you look after Fluffy? I'm not quite sure when.'

'Of course. Anytime, sweetie. We love Fluffy. He reminds Gunnar so much of his old dog, Killer. I think Fluffy has really helped heal that empty place in his heart.'

'That's lovely – I'm so pleased. And thank you.'

She smiled at me and pulled a large casserole dish out of the oven. 'That smells divine,' I licked my lips and my stomach cramped. Dammit. Blood! I hadn't brought any with me.

'It's just food, nothing special.'

She didn't understand that Fluffy and I ate frozen dinners or takeout almost all the time, not anything home made with love. Mum had a chef and rarely cooked; that was probably why I could burn water. 'It's special to me,' I said softly. 'Um, I'm sorry, Sig, but I've screwed up. I don't have any blood with me.'

'Not a problem. We always have some in the freezer in case of vampire guests! We'll get you sorted in a jiffy.' She rooted around in a chest freezer, pulled out a small bag and placed it in a bowl of just-boiled water. In a couple of minutes, it was warm and ready to drink. She poured it into a mug for me and I downed it in one. The cramps eased instantly.

'Thanks so much.'

'Not a problem, now go and wash up. Dinner is ready.'

'Yes, ma'am,' I only half-joked.

She placed the dish on the table with the warm crusty rolls and salad while I went to the bathroom. When I came back, the dogs were already helping themselves to the food Sigrid had served them. Lucky pups.

After the meal, Gunnar drove Fluffy and me home and idled at the kerb until we were safely inside, only driving off when I'd locked down the metal shutters. As I went to bed, I tried to analyse what I was feeling. It was an old sensation, one I hadn't had since Nana had died.

With a jolt, I realised I felt cared for; more than that, I felt loved.

# Chapter 35

When the jangle of my phone jarred me from the vice-like grip of sleep, I assumed it was Gunnar or Sidnee calling me about something important. 'Hello?' I answered, my voice croaking.

'Bunny! You've got to help me! Skylark is missing.' I recognised Cordelia Riverdream's voice straight away. Just like that, the last vestiges of sleep fell away.

I sat up. 'When did you notice he was gone?'

'About an hour ago, but his bed is empty and it hasn't been slept in. I called his phone, but it's here. He would never leave his phone!'

Skylark had been let out on bail. It hadn't even been that expensive: he was a minor without the means to leave the area without help from his parents who were established members of the community. He hadn't been considered a flight risk, but maybe we'd got it wrong. 'Have you checked with his friends?' I asked.

'Of course I have, it was the first thing I did! No one has seen him.' Her voice caught. 'I called the hospital but no one matching his description has come in.'

'I'll run down some other options and call back as soon as we know something. In the meantime, phone me if he walks in.'

'I will! Thank you.'

'I'll be in touch,' I reiterated, then hung up.

After I'd called Gunnar to fill him in, I went into the shower; I needed the pounding of the hot water to convince myself that I'd slept enough. But then, if I was undead did I really need sleep? Maybe my exhaustion was in my head, like the burning lungs thing. I cracked a yawn and dismissed that idea: I was *exhausted*.

I stood under the spray and considered our options. Option 1 – and the most likely: Skylark was up to no good with his friends; Option 2 – he'd shifted into dolphin form and jumped bail; Option 3 – and my least favourite – the dealer knew he was a weak link and had taken care of him before we had an opportunity to come knocking again. This was a small town so everyone would know about Skylark's arrest.

I drank my blood, grabbed a piece of toast and a travel mug of strong tea – I needed a pick-me-up this early – and Fluffy and I headed in. I might need Fluffy's nose later if Skylark really was missing.

When we arrived, Gunnar was just stumbling in; he looked tired, too.

'I'll ring Russ and Jake, then I'll get a list of his other friends from Cordelia,' I said.

'I'll call Calliope and see if we can get some help from the water shifters in case Skylark is just out having a swim,' Gunnar said. We both knew he meant the kid was jumping bail, but neither of us wanted to call it that. If he had jumped bail, when we found him he'd be remanded in custody until his trial and neither of us wanted that. If we found him in the bay, we'd call it a swim and make sure his parents kept a better eye on him.

We went to our desks to make calls. Russ and Jake said that Skylark wasn't with them, so Cordelia gave me some other names and numbers to try. Maybe she hoped they'd tell the Nomo's office something that they hadn't told her.

An hour later, I'd struck out completely. There was still no sign of Skylark. 'I'll go to the Riverdreams' place and conduct a search,' I suggested.

Gunnar looked worn out. 'I'll come,' he said as he pushed away from his desk.

'Maybe you should rest—' I started.

'Maybe you should can it,' he replied sharply. A beat later he rubbed his forehead. 'I'm sorry. I *am* tired, but there's a missing boy out there and it's my duty to find him.'

'It's my duty too.' *My* voice was a little sharp now.

'I know. But on missing kid cases, time is of the essence. We find him quickly or we don't find him at all – not alive, anyway.'

I swallowed hard. 'Then let's go.'

The three of us loaded up and headed out. Understandably Mrs Riverdream was a mess: her hair was dishevelled and her eyes were red from crying. As we pulled on nitrile gloves, she showed us to Skylark's room.

'Have you noticed anything missing?' I asked her as I photographed the scene.

She shook her head. 'Just the clothes he was wearing when he went to bed last night – a pair of athletic shorts.'

There was an old pair of ratty, well-loved trainers at the base of the bed. 'What about shoes?'

She blinked. 'I didn't think to look.' She scanned the room and pointed to the pair I'd spotted. 'Those are the ones he had on.'

'Are there any others missing?' I hoped there were, because a kid wouldn't leave his room without shoes if he were planning a lark with friends. A wolverine shifter, perhaps; one of those might shift in his room and climb down the tree next to his window. But Sky was a *dolphin* shifter, so he'd have to walk or climb out. If he'd left voluntarily, he'd have needed shoes; my gut telling me that his disappearance was anything *but* voluntary.

Cordelia dived frantically into the closet and tore apart his shoe rack. 'They're all here!' she cried and the sobs started again. 'Oh my god.' She started to hyperventilate. 'Someone took my boy!' she wailed.

I wanted to reassure her, but I feared exactly the same thing.

# Chapter 36

Fluffy was snuffling around the room. Head low by the window, he let out his 'I've found something' alert so I went straight over. I took out an evidence bag and frowned at the item: it was a girl's hairpin with a sparkly butterfly at the end.

'Is this one of yours or your daughters?' I asked, holding it out.

Cordelia shook her head. 'No, I don't think so. Kestrel has a tonne of pins so I can't be positive, but I don't think so.'

'Did Skylark have a girlfriend?' I asked.

'Not that I know of – and he definitely hasn't brought anyone over here.'

I showed it to Gunnar. 'It could be nothing,' he said. 'He might have picked it up off the ground or taken it from a girl he liked. But we're going to see if there is anything to find from it.' Fluffy gave a sharp bark as if he agreed.

I noticed a scuff on the windowsill and looked down to see how hard it would be to sneak out – or steal a teenage boy. Since he was a shifter, I was sure Skylark could jump the distance without much effort and land safely; I was pretty sure even I could. But the tree close by would make everything a hundred times easier.

I took a picture of the scuff mark, then opened the window and leaned out so I could look at the torn bark on the tree. It was clear someone had climbed either in or out of the window. Bare feet made it easier to hold onto the bark, but twin marks on the trunk made it look as if a ladder had been leaning against it. 'Mrs Riverdream, do you have a ladder?' I asked.

'Yes, in the garage.'

'Mind if I use it?'

'No. Why?'

'I want to get a better look at that tree.'

'It's been a while since we used it.'

'Let's go find it.' I was thinking that the ladder had been used as recently as last night. Sure enough, when Mrs Riverdream opened her garage door, the ladder lay right alongside it.

Either Skylark had set up the ladder in advance and waited until his parents were asleep to go play in the water, or someone else had gone up the tree and convinced him to shimmy down of his own accord – or someone had climbed in, rendered Skylark unconscious and dragged him out. With his shoes by the bed, I was leaning towards the third possibility.

I leaned the ladder against the tree to see if it lined up with the marks; it did. I climbed up and used a small flashlight to see if there was anything else that could count as a clue, and my breath caught as I saw a few strands of hair caught on a piece of bark. I took some photos of them in situ, then went back down to get some tweezers and another evidence bag. I scuttled back up and harvested the hair. It was dirty blond and about two inches long. Skylark had brown hair. Bingo.

We might be able to scry the dealer after all.

# Chapter 37

I showed Gunnar the hair and he gave me a fist bump. 'I'll contact Sally, our local scrying witch,' he said.

We now had two items to scry with: the butterfly hairpin and the strands of hair. Surely we'd get a hit off at least one of them. I had also asked Skylark's mother for something important to him and she'd given me a small childhood teddy.

Back at the office, I processed the evidence and wrote up the reports. By lunchtime Gunnar still hadn't reached the witch that we needed. He was getting frustrated and I was getting worried.

Fluffy and I ran home for lunch and I had a quick cup of blood to see me through. I didn't want to take too long because I was keen to see the witch work her magic. So far I'd seen a necromancer, a mermaid shifter, a couple of werewolves and vamps, but the only active magic I'd seen had been from the witch that threw fireballs at Gunnar.

When I got back, Gunnar's hair was wilder than usual because he'd been yanking on it so much. 'I called a few other high-powered witches I know. I have four messages out there, but I'm waiting for call backs,' he said. 'I might have to call Liv – and you know how much I like to talk to her.'

Liv was the magic leader and the necromancer I'd seen in action, although she didn't end up raising the dead – there'd been no point when his soul had already fled. But she had a thing for Gunnar and she wasn't shy about letting anyone know about it. It made Gunnar hugely uncomfortable because he loved his wife and other women didn't exist for him.

'I'll give it one hour then I'll call Liv. Again.' He sighed. 'I asked her to come by earlier and ward the cache of drugs more securely. Since they were bold enough to come in here when Sidnee was manning the desk, I wanted a little sting in the tail if they try it again. My friend is arranging to pick up and dispose of the shipment, but getting that amount secure is taking more time than I want.'

I bit my lip. 'I can call Liv for you, if you want?' I offered, although Liv frightened me, too. A couple of times she'd sent me a vision of herself in ancient times wearing a crown and covered in gold. When I'd examined the memory, the shadow behind her right shoulder looked like a pyramid. If it was, we were most likely looking at Egypt, Sudan or Iraq, all of which I knew very little about.

Wherever she was from, Liv had some serious magic – and that magic dealt with the dead. As I was one of the undead, that made me a little nervous. Besides, I also had no idea what her agenda was.

Gunnar shook his head. 'I'm a big boy. I'll call her if we need to.' He paused. 'Though I appreciate the offer.' His phone rang and when he looked at the screen, he gave a fist pump – not Liv, then. He hit the speaker. 'Gunnar here,' he said.

'Gunnar, it's Sally Marsh. You need some scrying?'

'Yes. It's pretty urgent – a missing child. Are you available to assist?'

'I can do it, but I'll need to invoice you. Scrying is hard magical work and I won't be able to undertake any other magic for a few days afterwards. It'll be expensive.'

'Fine,' Gunnar snapped, but I could see he was annoyed she wasn't doing it out of the goodness of her heart.

'Great. I need to prepare. Say an hour from now?' she said briskly.

'That would be fine.' He smiled at me in triumph and I smiled back. 'Where would you like to do it?' he asked.

'I'll come to you, but I'll need a level table.'

'We'll have it ready.'

'Okay. See you shortly.' She rang off.

'Thank God!' Gunnar breathed. 'We can use the table in the interview room.'

'I'll go clean it,' I offered. I scrubbed it until it shone just in case cleanliness was important in witchcraft, then quickly took Fluffy outside to do his business.

Sally Marsh showed up promptly, precisely one hour from when she'd said she would. She appeared to be in her sixties; her brown hair was streaked liberally with grey, her skin was lined, but her eyes were warm. She was carrying a large bag. 'Mrs Marsh?' I offered her my hand. 'Please come this way.'

I showed her to the interview room and she nodded that it would do. She set her bag on the floor and started pulling out supplies. First there was a black cloth, with which she covered the table, then a large copper bowl, candles, crystals, and some items in various jars. Finally, she pulled out two maps, one of Portlock, one of the world. I guess she was prepared for two extremes: Skylark was either in town, or waaaaay out of town.

I watched closely but didn't disturb her with the litany of questions I had. Something about the process lit a fire in me, and the crystals fascinated me.

'Could you get me a pitcher full of water?' Sally asked, pulling me from my reverie.

'Of course.' I found one in the break room, filled it and took it to her. 'Is there anything else I can do to help?'

'Yes, I need the items that are linked to the person I'm scrying for.'

I went to get them. She looked at the hair, still in its evidence bag, and frowned. 'Do you know how this works?' I shook my head. 'When I use the items they'll disintegrate, so we won't have any evidence left. Are you sure you want me to use the hair?'

I frowned. 'Can you, like, use half of it?'

She examined the few strands of hair. 'I'm afraid not – it's already a very small sample. It might not work even if I use it all.' She shook her head. 'I've never scried with so little,' she admitted.

'What about the toy or the hairpin?'

She hefted the pin in her hand. 'This might survive the scrying because it's metal, but the toy probably won't. Do you want me to start with this?'

'I'll ask Gunnar. Hold on.' I knocked on his door. 'Sally is ready to start the scrying, but we've got a problem.'

He gave a barely audible sigh. 'Of course we have. Hit me.' I explained that scrying would destroy the hair and he frowned. 'That's not good. If we find the dealer, we won't have any hard evidence to link him to the kidnapping.'

'She can start with the hairpin, then the teddy, then we can decide about the hair,' I suggested.

'Yeah. Let's leave the hair as a last resort.'

I let Sally know our decision and asked if I could watch her work. She didn't mind, so I stood out of the way in the corner and Gunnar loitered in the doorway. Fluffy stayed glued to my side – he wanted to see as well. He was trembling slightly and I rubbed his head. I guessed he was sensitive to witch magic; maybe he thought he was protecting me. He was the best pup.

Sally filled the bowl and added the contents of three small jars. I didn't know what they were, but my vampire nose found them pungent. Fluffy's nose must have, too, because he sneezed violently three times.

Next she lit the candles and we turned off the overhead lights. She placed the crystals around the bowl, waved her hands over it and chanted, then dropped the pin into it. She spoke a few more words in a language I didn't recognise. The air tingled like it does before a lightning storm, and the smell of ozone filled the air. The hairs on my arms rose.

'Look!' the witch commanded me, her voice unnaturally low.

I looked.

# Chapter 38

The bowl showed the inside of a kitchen, a home I recognised. It was Skylark's home, dammit. His younger sister, Kestrel was having a teddy bears picnic. The hairpin was nothing to do with the case at all. We were chasing our tail.

'Dammit,' Gunnar muttered. 'A dead end.'

We should have started with the teddy – that was Skylark's toy. That would show us *him*. Live and learn. 'Let's try the teddy now,' I said urgently.

The witch blew out the candles and wiped her brow. 'I'll need a few minutes. I'll have to cleanse everything.'

'Can I help?' I offered solicitously, partly to help but mostly to get a move on. I was itching to get some results.

I reached towards the crystals but she handed me the copper bowl instead. 'Thank you. Take the bowl, empty it, and wash it.' She gave me a container of salt. 'Make sure you scrub it with salt and then rinse it thoroughly. And I'll need fresh water.'

When I returned, she started the process again. At the appropriate moment, she added the small cuddly teddy bear and said the words. We gazed into the bowl.

My heart lurched because it revealed a cavernous space in which Skylark was tied to a chair, his mouth duct-taped shut. He looked wet, muddy, and seven shades of scared. At least he hadn't jumped bail, but I kind of wished that he had because he looked young and terrified. He was wearing his bedtime athletic shorts and he was shivering. Leaning over him was a man with dirty-blond hair and a muscular build, dressed in loose black combats and a black hoodie: the dealer who'd dived into the water.

The man appeared to be observing or talking to the boy; it was hard to tell because his back was turned to us. We couldn't see his face, nor hear what he was saying, but the way Skylark flinched told us it wasn't all sunshine and rainbows. He was clearly terrified.

'Can you tell us where he is?' Gunnar whispered, as if his words might travel through the bowl.

Sally was sweating now and her hands were trembling, but she nodded. She pulled her necklace over her head and held the crystal pendant over the map of Portlock, then whispered a few more unrecognisable words. The pendant moved and stuck to the map.

A few seconds later, her knees gave way. Gunnar caught her before she slid to the ground and placed her gently on a chair. She was already coming around as we scoured the map. 'The industrial part of town,' he muttered. 'That's AML's warehouse, I think. I'm ninety percent sure.'

'Who?' I asked.

'AML – Alaska Marine Lines.'

'Let's go then!' I said.

'We need to take care of Sally first,' Gunnar murmured reproachfully.

I was chomping at the bit but I nodded. I hastily packed up her stuff whilst Gunnar gave her a glass of water. Sally came back to herself pretty quickly, and though she was tired she insisted she was fine to drive. We helped her into her car then ran out to the back of the office, dived into the Nomo's SUV and squealed out of the car park.

As we headed to the water, we kept the lights and sirens off. This part of town was industrial and it looked the part. We parked a few warehouses away from our target; from our spot we could see where Alaska Marine Lines loaded and offloaded the barges. There were stacks of shipping containers piled up, and a crane that was used to load and unload the boats. There was also a small warehouse for storing goods – and that was where Skylark was being held.

'Who owns this place?' I asked Gunnar. 'I know AML is operating out of it, but do they rent it from someone?' Maybe a name on a deed would crack this whole case wide open.

'AML owns it,' he grunted. 'We'll get a list of employees that have access. First, let's find Skylark.'

We left the vehicle as quietly as we could. Fluffy was wearing his vest and he vibrated with a low growl next to me as we edged nearer to the warehouse. There was a roll-up loading door and a regular entry door next to it. Gunnar tried the knob but it was locked. He did his thing, and the knob turned.

The building was silent and my stomach clenched. We'd taken too long to settle Sally. If we'd missed our opportunity to save Skylark, it would kill me.

Gunnar put his finger to his lips as he slipped inside the door. I followed closely behind, mouth suddenly dry. He unclipped the gun at his hip, drew it out smoothly and held it down next to his leg.

The warehouse wasn't totally dark; light leaked around the doors, and I could see just fine with my vampire eyes. I heard a splash nearby and wondered what had fallen...

That was when I spotted Skylark; he had duct tape over his mouth, he was tied to a chair and his eyes were bulging with fear. He shot a look to his left and nodded his head, and I looked in the direction that he was desperately indicating. Was the kidnapper hiding? It was certainly possible because there were boxes everywhere.

Gunnar holstered his weapon and ran forward to untie the boy. His eyes wide and frantic with fear, Skylark tried to say something but the duct tape was muffling his voice.

I finally realised what he was trying to tell us. To his left, hidden behind some boxes, a gun was pointing directly at him. If we bumped him or tripped the line, that gun would blow the boy's head off.

'Stop!' I shouted to Gunnar. 'He's been booby trapped!' Gunnar froze and I pointed at the gun. I didn't feel confident enough around weapons to untangle the trap myself, but I trusted my boss could do it without setting it off.

Gunnar studied the trap then backed up and walked behind the boxes. I moved in front of Skylark in case the gun went off by accident. It was aimed at Skylark's head so, shifter or not, it would kill him. Now the gun was pointing at my torso and I was a vampire; I'd survive being shot.

'It's okay,' I said. 'We've spotted the trap and we're undoing it. You're going to be okay.'

Skylark sagged against the chair and started to cry.

I waited tensely for Gunnar to disarm the trap. I would survive a shooting, but the memory of being shot was all too fresh in my mind and it had *hurt*. I didn't particularly want a repeat experience, though that would be better than witnessing Skylark's brains being splattered on all those boxes and knowing I could have saved him.

Finally, Gunnar put the gun on the ground. 'All clear!' he called. The trap had been a rush job; the kidnapper must have seen us arriving. That splash I'd heard was no doubt him or her jumping into the water.

I knew that we had to push harder on Calliope; this was being carried out by one of hers, and she couldn't be the gatekeeper anymore. And maybe after this, Skylark would start talking.

I turned on the lights. The old fluorescent strips were audible as they flickered slowly to life. Once we had full light, I moved closer to Skylark and double-checked for more traps. Seeing none, I carefully untied him.

He jumped into my arms and I patted him awkwardly as he sobbed into my shoulder. He'd just had the scariest experience of his life; he was shaking and he smelled faintly of wee. I didn't blame him because I'd have pissed myself too in those circumstances.

I led him away from the scene of all that trauma and wrapped him in a blanket. 'Let's get you into the warm,' I said as I coaxed him into the car.

Gunnar frowned. 'We need to look around but Skylark needs medical attention first to check he's not hurt. He's certainly in shock, so there's no point trying to question him now. I'm going to run him to the ER and call his mom. Can you stay and secure the scene?'

I nodded confidently and started collecting the equipment I needed: scene of crime tape, camera, notepad and forensics kit. I slid on nitrile gloves. 'I'm pretty confident the kidnapper jumped in the water,' I said. 'I heard a splash as we entered the building.'

'Okay. Keep Fluffy with you. Once I get the all clear from Skylark's medical team, I'll see if he's willing to talk to me. Are you sure you'll be okay alone?' Gunnar looked distinctly uneasy about leaving me.

'I'm a vampire,' I said airily. 'And Fluffy is pretty fierce. We'll be fine.'

'Well, ring me if there is even a hint of trouble. I'll call Stan and Connor while I drive to the ER and ask them to send back up.'

'No problem.'

Gunnar drove off with the newly rescued kid. We'd finally done something right. I hoped the kidnapper had done something wrong, like dropped his driving licence at the scene. A girl could dream.

# Chapter 39

I taped off the area and started my search. First, I returned to the chair where Skylark had been tied up. It was a metal folding chair and he'd been tied to it firmly. The rope lay where I'd left it when I'd released him. I photographed the scene and laid out cones near anything of interest, then I put the rope and the duct tape into evidence bags.

Fluffy helped, too, snuffling along the floor and letting out a whine when he found anything. I followed him as he followed the path the drug dealer had taken to the back dock. Naturally, the trail ended at the water where he'd jumped in. A floating sock was all that was visible.

I checked the area thoroughly for any other discarded clothes but I couldn't see anything; he'd probably ripped off his shoes so he could swim more easily, though there was no sign of any footwear. I took a quick shot of the sock then found an oar leaning against the building and used it to drag it in. As I bagged it, I wondered if Sally could scry from a sock. It was worth a try. Of course, it was possible that the sock didn't belong to the kidnapper, but it was all I had. I scoured the area but didn't find anything else.

I stifled a scream as a man dropped down beside me. My fangs shot out and without thinking, I punched him in the face.

'Ow,' Connor muttered. 'You throw a good punch.'

'Oh my god! I'm so sorry! You startled me.'

'Evidently,' he muttered, rubbing his jaw. 'I came to watch your back but now I'm not sure I'm needed.' The shock of the punch had worn off and he looked amused.

'Well, any backup is appreciated,' I admitted. 'I was a little jumpy by myself.' Fluffy growled and I laughed. 'Yes, I know you're here too, but this warehouse is huge and there are so many boxes. I was worried someone was slinking around watching me. I can't shake the feeling I'm being observed. Overdramatic, I know.'

Connor frowned. 'Let's work together to clear the warehouse.'

There was a small office, little more than a lean-to, which held a computer and a filing cabinet. The door was locked. Dammit, where was Gunnar when I needed him? Connor studied me for a moment before reaching into his back pocket and pulling out a slim leather pouch. He opened it and slid out two tools: lockpicks.

He raised an eyebrow at me and I nodded; okay, so maybe we were skirting around the edges of the law a teensy bit, but Gunnar clearly had no issue with opening locked doors. And what difference did it make if it was by magic or lockpicks? Absolutely none that I could see.

After a minute, there was a snick and the door opened. 'Nice. Can you teach me how to do that?' I asked.

Connor grinned. 'If you like.' He held open the door for me and we went inside.

The computer was password protected – no surprise there – and the filing cabinets were full of printouts for orders and deliveries. I was about to give up on finding anything helpful when I spotted something on the printer. It was a list of authorised visitors and one name struck me: Soapy Willoughby, Calliope's second in command. No wonder she was being difficult about helping the investigation; her second looked like he might be hip deep in the whole mess.

By the time I'd finished combing the warehouse, Gunnar was back. He seemed relieved to find Fluffy and me as he'd left us, and he gave Connor one of those man hugs. 'Thanks,' he murmured. 'Appreciate the assist.'

'Anytime,' Connor said simply.

'How's Skylark?' I asked.

'Overwrought. Physically he's okay, but mentally...' He trailed off. 'He's being kept in overnight. I've got Stan on his door.'

I nodded with relief. Stan was a huge deterrent – he'd joked once that *he* was a weapon; I'd seen him shut down a huge bear shifter without getting a hair out of place. He was formidable.

I was running through the evidence I'd collected with Gunnar and showing him the logbook when Connor's phone rang. He listened for a moment, and his eyes widened in shock. 'Call an ambulance, send it to the Nomo's office. I'll ring you as soon as I know more!'

He hung up and dialled. 'Get more men down to the Nomo's office, NOW!' he roared. He turned to Gunnar and me. 'That was Juan's wife. Their bond just snapped.'

Gunnar swore. 'What does that mean?' I asked.

'It means,' he said grimly, 'that someone just killed Juan.'

# Chapter 40

'Juan was guarding your office,' Connor said darkly. 'Someone has used Skylark's kidnapping as a smokescreen, a diversion to pull us away from the drug cache. I've sent more men, but we may already be too late.'

Gunnar shook his head. 'I already had Liv put some extra wards around the cache. If they tried to get in, they're in for a shock.'

'They didn't save Juan.' Connor's tone was grim. 'Let's move!'

We ran out to the Nomo's SUV and leapt in. 'Where's your truck?' I asked Connor.

He shifted a little in his seat. 'I ran,' he admitted.

'What?'

'I ran to the warehouse.'

'From where?'

'Your office,' his jaw worked. 'If I hadn't left Juan...'

I turned to face him. 'You can't think like that.' Because if he blamed himself for leaving his post, then I'd have to blame myself for having him act as backup for me.

Connor shook his head and fell silent then reached out to Fluffy and patted him on the head.

It couldn't have been more than ten minutes before we finally pulled into the Nomo's office but it felt like a century. A small crowd had gathered out front. 'My men,' Connor noted.

My shoulders eased. If the drug dealers *had* been trying to get their stash, it looked like they were long gone. I was disappointed we couldn't apprehend them, but also a little relieved that I wasn't heading straight into a gun battle.

We piled out of the vehicle. Connor went straight to his men whilst Gunnar went inside to check on the drug's cache. After hesitating for a moment, I followed Gunnar to the jail cell.

He stopped abruptly. The cell door had been cut open and a body was lying face-down on the floor.

From the dead man's stocky build, I could tell straight away that it wasn't Juan.

The Nomo knelt down and checked the body for signs of life, then shook his head wordlessly. We had two bodies to deal with: Juan's and this dude's. Liv's ward had more than a little sting.

We pulled on nitrile gloves and started documenting the scene. When everything was photographed, we checked the man's pockets. Nothing: no ID, nada. Gunnar carefully rolled over the body and I gasped. I recognised him. 'Mr Mahoon,' I said.

Gunnar's eyebrows shot up. 'And how do you know Mahoon?'

'I saw him arguing with Soapy and Calliope in her office.' I hesitated. 'You don't think Calliope's involved in all this?'

He shook his head automatically then stopped as he considered the idea further. 'I don't know,' he said finally. 'I don't know that she would involve herself in drugs. She has a good thing going here – she earns a tonne, and Merric doesn't bother her.'

'Merric?'

'Another water-shifter leader, one she's had issues with in the past. She came here for –sanctuary, I suppose, like plenty of others have done.'

That made me swallow. Whatever – whoever – Merric was, I didn't want to meet him. Calliope was scary enough; to imagine there was something out there that scared *her* was enough to make me want to pee my pants like poor Skylark had done.

Gunnar continued, 'I can't see her risking all that she's achieved. You'll have noticed,' he said drily, 'Portlock is a bit of a mishmash. We take in the strays from other supernat towns. Portlock is your last call and if you can't survive here, then you're out into the world on your own with the MIB and the hunters watching your every move. One misstep and it's curtains. Calliope wouldn't risk that.'

'And Mahoon?'

'Well, he evidently *did* risk it.' Gunnar looked disappointed. 'He'd had trouble settling in other communities – he was ex-military and he struggled to adjust to civilian life. He was booted out of the supernat town of Bay Ocean for brawling too much. Maybe I should have dug more deeply into his background, but there was nothing to suggest there was a problem with either drug use or drug dealing.'

There was no incriminating evidence left in the cell; whatever the dealers had used to cut through the metal doors they had taken with them. All they had left behind was what Mahoon had been carrying with him. Either they'd been disturbed or they couldn't be bothered to remove his body. Liv's deadly ward had been enough to stop them from reaching the cache; the price of that had been Mahoon's life.

'I'll call for another ambulance to transport the body.' Gunnar sighed. 'And I'll notify Calliope.'

'I'll check on the situation with Juan,' I volunteered. I went to the group of men gathered together outside. 'Excuse me,' I said politely. 'Where is Juan?'

One of them squared up to me. 'This is a vampire matter. We don't need the Nomo's office.'

For once, my fangs did what they should do: flashed down. I gave a toothy smile. 'Luckily, I'm a vampire too. Move.'

The man met my eyes and I held them; I felt him *push* at me somehow, but I pushed right back and his eyes widened.

'Kole,' Connor barked. 'Let her through.'

'Yes, boss.' He stepped aside, as did the others, and I moved to where Connor was sitting next to Juan.

Juan was propped against the wall of the Nomo's building where he'd died; were it not for the blood trickling down his nose and his fixed gaze, it would have looked as if he and Connor were having a chat. But they weren't.

I remembered Juan's gentle teasing only a day ago, and my heart gave a distinct twang. I hadn't known him for long, but for what it was worth I had liked him.

Connor's expression was blank but his eyes were not; they were filled with rage. 'They touched the fisheye to his skin and it killed him,' he snarled. He pointed his toe at some crystals in the ground. 'They must have tossed it to him and he caught it reflexively.'

A chill ran through me. Fisheye was deadly to vampires, and it would also have been to Gunnar if we hadn't got him medical attention so quickly; this shit wasn't a recreational drug, it was a weapon. 'I need to photograph the scene,' I said softly.

'Yeah, all right.' Connor sighed. 'Do your job, Officer Barrington.'

It stung a little, hearing my title from him. He was distancing himself from me. Did he think, like Kole, that this should be a vampire matter? Because it wasn't, it was a *Portlock* matter.

Anger pulsed through me at whoever was doing this to us. Heat fired through my body and I felt the flicker of flames lick my insides. Fuck. Not now!

I let my eyes close and took a few deep breaths. For some reason, I pictured the bay and the water dragon, pictured him lighting up with his blue magic. I remembered the feel of the water around me, and slowly the heat inside me cooled.

When I opened my eyes, Connor was kneeling next to me. I hadn't realised I'd dropped to the ground. The rage in his eyes had been replaced with concern. 'Bunny?'

'I'm fine,' I managed and pushed him away. 'I just had a moment,' I said firmly.

I busied myself getting out the camera and ignored his inquisitive eyes. I photographed the scene, including the scattered fisheye crystals, then carefully picked them up in gloved fingers and slid them into an evidence bag.

I checked Juan's pockets but found nothing of note. He carried a few knives, so he'd been armed and potentially dangerous, but it hadn't stopped him from dropping where he'd stood.

'You need to tell your vamps to be careful,' I said. 'Until we've got this shit nailed down, they need to wear gloves and keep their skin covered.'

Connor nodded. 'Fine. I'll call a meeting for tomorrow night at the warehouse at Kamluck. Vamps only. I want you there.' Kamluck Logging was

Connor's business and it made him a powerful man in town. Something to remember.

It wasn't a request, but I nodded as if it were. 'Okay. I'll see you then.'

Connor looked at the sky. 'The sun is coming. We need to go, and we'll take Juan with us. His wife deserves to see his body as it is now, not have it burnt and blistered.'

'I'll check with Gunnar, but that should be fine. We don't need an autopsy – we know cause of death. Start loading him up.'

As I walk away, he said, 'I'll be back after I've spoken to his widow. I won't leave the office unguarded. Those fuckers don't get their hands on this shit.'

'Thanks.' I touched him lightly on the shoulder and he leaned into me. I gave him one last squeeze then I walked back into the office. 'Juan Torres is dead,' I confirmed to Gunnar. 'Looks like he touched some fisheye and KO'd there and then. Connor is raging.'

'Understandably,' Gunnar rumbled. 'First Kivuk, and now Juan. I thought only a stake through the heart, a beheading, or complete exsanguination would kill a vamp, but it seems that fisheye will do the trick as well.'

'We can't let this shit be distributed,' I said.

He grimaced. 'My friend is stepping up his extraction plans. He'll get it out of town tomorrow and destroy it in a specialist facility.'

'Connor's furious,' I warned him again. 'He has it locked down tight for now, but when we find out who's doing this…' I trailed off.

He threw me a sidelong glance. 'Connor's a good man but he comes with some baggage.' His comment felt pointed. Was he giving me a warning?

I shifted uneasily. 'Are you saying I should stay away from him romantically?'

'I'm not your father, Bunny. You're an adult. Just … be careful, okay?'

I didn't know how I felt about Gunnar's words. Of course Connor had baggage; he was old – although I didn't know how old – and he was the vampire leader. I assumed that his vampires would always come first. If anything, the warning made me want to know him better. My mum wasn't wrong when she called me contrary.

# Chapter 41

The atmosphere in the office was sombre. Gunnar contacted Calliope and put the call on speakerphone. 'I'm sorry to disturb you again so soon,' he said.

'And yet you are doing so,' she said sharply. 'I am trying to attend to Mahoon's body.'

'I appreciate that, but he isn't the only one dead. I need a note of any of the siren group that were known associates of Mr Mahoon.'

'I am far too busy to attend to your every request. You are an investigator, I suggest you compile a list yourself,' she snarled.

When he replied, Gunnar's tone was deliberately mild. 'Fine. In that case, I will haul in, and question every single siren I know. The drugs are coming in from the water, Calliope, and they were found in the water. The dealer jumped into the bay to get away from us. It's someone in your camp, and I am going to be hauling you all in and looking at your lives under a microscope. Or,' his voice hardened, 'you can give me that damned list.'

There was a beat of angry silence. 'Fine,' she spat.

'Wonderful.' His voice was genial once more. 'You and Soapy can bring it in person tomorrow.' She hung up without responding.

'You're in danger of burning bridges,' I murmured.

He shrugged. 'I'm the Nomo. I am a part of the council, yet I am also outside of the council. If they have an issue with me, they're supposed to call in the MIB – and only a fool would do that. Calliope is no fool.'

'Maybe not, but I imagine she can hold a grudge.'

'No doubt,' he agreed wryly. 'But I'll worry about that on another day when my residents aren't dropping like flies.'

'Whilst we're waiting for the list, I assume you've got files on the residents, their applications to move into the town?'

'Not all of them. Some of them came before my time. The last Nomo wasn't big on paperwork.'

I grimaced. 'That's a shame. I was thinking that we need to look into people with military backgrounds.'

'Why's that?'

'This drug. The physicist said they'd seen it before on a government job. And Mahoon was ex-military – maybe Uncle Sam tapped him again.'

He looked at me, shocked. 'You think this has come from the *government*?'

'Maybe. They see us supernats as a threat, right? They keep us contained in our little towns – but what if we get out, and the MIB and the hunters can't contain us? What government wouldn't have some sort of emergency plan? They need a weapon that can bring down supernats.'

'But it didn't kill the shifters.'

'No, but it fucked with their shift. When they were smoking fisheye, they shifted involuntarily. What could be worse to a shifter than losing the ability to control their shift? Russell got stuck in his bear form. Fisheye killed Juan and laid you low… The CIA were responsible for bringing LSD into the States. Maybe this could be something similar.'

Gunnar looked troubled. 'The siren group has a lot of ex-militaries. Soapy used to be a Navy Seal, but I can't see him working against us supernats like that.'

'People will do crazy things for money.'

'Maybe you're right – but I hope to hell you're wrong.'

'Me too.' I moved away from the volatile subject. 'Besides the sirens, we have Skylark to question and we have the sock. Could Sally scry it?'

Gunnar shook his head. 'She was wiped out – I don't think she could scry her own breakfast at this stage. I'll have to ask Liv who else could help us.' He grimaced at the thought.

'While you do that, I'll contact Cordelia Riverdream and ask if we can see Skylark.' I stepped out of Gunnar's room and went back to my desk. I gave Fluffy a pat and picked up the phone to ring Skylark's mum.

'He's shaken,' she admitted when I asked how her son was. 'He's a shell of his former self. The hospital let us go because there was nothing physically wrong with him, but mentally... I'm so grateful you found him when you did. He told us about the gun.' She let out a sob. 'I can't think about it.'

'He's really been through the mill, but we do need to talk to him. When would be a good time?'

I heard her say something but it was muffled, like she'd put her hand over the phone rather than just hit mute. Then she said, 'Sorry, he's just gone out for a swim with his dad.'

'He isn't supposed to leave town.' There was a faint note of warning in my voice.

'I know, but they're only swimming in the channel. Going for a swim is the best way to relax dolphin shifters, and Skylark isn't doing well. He needs the water.'

'I'm sure, but this is important. Can you call me when they get home?'

'All right,' she murmured. 'But can you question him here?'

'That's not a problem,' I reassured her. 'We'll come to you.' I tried to keep the impatience and worry out of my voice because there was no point worrying his mum, but Skylark held the key to all of this. Now he was in the water with his dad, where no doubt other sirens were swimming too. I prayed that he'd come back.

# Chapter 42

Gunnar was on the phone when I went into his office. He held up a finger, then said firmly, 'We're on our way.' I waited until he'd hung up and raised a questioning eyebrow. 'We've got two missing hunters,' he said grimly.

'Hunters like Patkotak?'

'No. Sorry, I just meant men that go on hunting trips.'

With Juan's death fresh in my mind, I asked, 'Did they take drugs?'

He gave me an approving look. 'No, neither of them did, according to their wives. But they haven't been seen for more than twenty-four hours and they haven't checked in.'

'Where were they hunting?'

'Outside the barrier,' he confirmed.

A chill ran down my spine. After the incident with the rogue werewolf and the beast beyond the barrier, this couldn't be good. 'Why on earth would they go outside of the barrier?' I asked incredulously.

'It's maybe hard for you to believe after all you've seen since you arrived, but for years there was no need to worry about going through the barrier. These guys grew up hunting there – subsistence hunting is a way of life.'

'But the beast…?'

'It's been dormant or hibernating. We haven't had a peep out of it for at least a couple of decades. It's one of the reasons why some people have started complaining to the witches about the barrier tax. It takes away money you could use to feed your family, and people were saying there was nothing to worry about.'

'Surely that's been silenced since Kivuk was found! And that cairn!'

He shook his head. 'Plenty of people think that was vamp business. It was a stake through the heart – he pissed off the wrong person.'

'And the rogue werewolf with red eyes?' I asked incredulously.

'An attempt to turn someone into a werewolf gone wrong.' Gunnar shrugged. 'You'll find conspiracy theorists in every part of the world, and Portlock is no exception. I've even heard rumours that the witches killed the werewolf and Kivuk to justify keeping paying them for the barrier.'

'That's insane.'

'Unfortunately, we're in an age where people are happy to like and share misinformation without checking its veracity. False news spreads as fast as true news. It's dangerous.'

'These hunters? They were in the camp that didn't believe?'

'I'd guess so if they went beyond the barrier. Come on, we're gonna interview the families and see if we need to call in search and rescue. Grab Fluffy, his vest, and your jacket and boots. More likely than not we'll be going outside.'

Outside as in beyond the barrier? Call me crazy, but that was not a place I wanted to go. Stifling a groan,

I slipped on my boots and picked up my jacket, then went in the back room to get Fluffy's vest and put it on him. We were as ready as we could be, which was to say that I felt wholly unready.

'Grab your weapon and day pack,' Gunnar added. He had buckled on his gun belt and both guns were in their holsters. If he hadn't been so big and looked so much like I imagined Thor did, I'd have said he was the spitting image of a Wild West gunslinger.

I picked up my gun case with a little more confidence this time; I'd been practising. In the Nomo SUV, Gunnar handed me a package. 'It's for you.' I opened it and saw that it was a shoulder holster. 'I ordered it to fit your gun. As the only other police officer in town, you should have one so you can get to it fast.' His voice was gruff but warm.

'Thank you so much.' My own holster! I really was an American now. Next thing, I'd be drinking coffee.

He shrugged. 'No big thing,' he muttered.

I untangled the holster and put it on. As well as the gun, I kept a knife Connor had given me in my boot. I grinned to myself; I was a regular Alaskan now, wearing at least one gun and one knife.

I checked that my revolver was loaded and put it in the shoulder holster. I was slightly more comfortable now that I knew how hard it was to accidentally fire it, and I felt slightly safer having a weapon. Surely even the beast couldn't survive modern weapons.

'Our hunters are Akiak and Lukas Savik, brothers, both in their late forties. Akiak is the older of the two. They both have a wife and kids. It was Akiak's wife, Talia, that called us in,' Gunnar explained as we pulled up to a white house with a black metal roof.

He went first and asked Fluffy and me to hang back. I grimaced, but we fell back to our go-to position since the fireball incident. When Gunnar knocked, a woman answered and invited us in.

Talia was red eyed and clutching a tissue. The other woman in the room introduced herself as Olena, Lukas's wife. The TV was blaring in the lounge and there was a whole bundle of kids in front of it, ranging from primary-school age up to older teens.

Olena closed the door. 'We're trying not to worry them,' she said with a pointed look at Talia.

Talia sniffed. 'I can't help it,' she said. 'Akiak *always* checks in. *Always*.' Fluffy gave a sad whine and rested his head gently on her knee. She stroked his head and tears fell again.

Olena's eyes softened. 'I know. That's why the Nomo is here.' She led us into a cosy kitchen with a heavy wooden table with bench seating on one side and chairs on the other.

We sat and Olena poured us each a cup of coffee. Since she didn't offer tea, I accepted it gratefully; any hot drink was better than no hot drink.

'When did they go out?' Gunnar asked, pulling out his notepad.

'They've been out hunting since last night – they were due back this afternoon. As darkness crept in again... We're worried,' admitted Olena.

Talia gave another sniff. 'They *always* check in.'

'Even if it was just one night away?'

'They check in when they make camp and again when they're heading home to let us know when to expect them,' Talia said.

'So, we can make their dinner,' Olena huffed. She was trying to be humorous but it fell flat; the worry in her eyes undid the effect.

'Where did they go?' Gunnar asked.

'I have the coordinates of their camp – Lukas sent them from his satellite phone.' Olena passed Gunnar a piece of paper and he put the details into a map app. He showed me the location; it was three miles outside the barrier.

We talked with the women for a few more minutes, asking about the men's hunting habits and what guns they used. They described the brothers' truck and where they had most likely parked to get through the barrier. We tried ringing the satellite phone but it didn't do a damned thing; it was broken or out of battery, or both.

It wasn't looking good for either of the Saviks. My mind flashed back to Kivuk, impaled on top of a rock cairn just outside the barrier where a creepy doll had been laid only a few weeks before; a sinister warning. A warning they had disregarded.

# Chapter 43

As we climbed into the SUV, something else pulled at my memory. Years before, the first time the creature had attacked the town, it had apparently left the mangled bodies in the river. 'Do you think we should check the river first?' I asked Gunnar. 'If it's the same creature, the bodies might be there.'

Gunnar scrubbed his fingers through his hair. 'You're right. We'll start there before we hike outside the barrier.'

Oh crap: I so didn't want to go beyond the barrier. It was there for a reason. I looked down at my toes and my gaze caught on my badge on my chest. Dammit – for good or ill, I was *Officer* Bunny. I was no longer a trust-fund kid or a dirt-poor waitress; I was an officer of the Nomo. That meant I had to do things like find missing kids and missing hunters.

Only days ago, I'd been hoping for a fun case to sink my fangs into. Now I had two, I wished I was back at my desk twiddling my thumbs and feeling bored.

Gunnar nodded decisively. 'May as well check the river first. It's going to be tricky getting help outside the barrier. We could call in the search and rescue from Homer and get them to bring in their helicopter, but they aren't supernaturals and they don't know about the beast. We could be condemning them to death.'

I blew out a breath: *we* didn't know about the beast, either. We hadn't seen it, and all we had were rumours, superstition and supposition. But that was more than search and rescue had – and we *were* supernaturals to boot.

A slightly hysterical laugh escaped me. 'Share the joke with the class,' Gunnar murmured. 'I could use a laugh right about now.'

'I was just thinking that all you've got is me, a naïve city girl from London, and you think I'll be useful in the wilderness?' I snickered. I had no bushcraft and almost no shooting skills. I was as much use as a broomstick with no bristles.

'That's what you get for having a name like Bunny,' he quipped.

'Ha-ha.'

Gunnar was the only person who could tease me about my name without me wanting to punch him in the throat, mostly because he did it with real affection.

The car jolted as we went over a huge pothole; the road was getting rougher the closer we got to the river. 'Do witches really use broomsticks?' I asked curiously.

The Nomo slid me an amused look. 'I would love to know how your mind works. To answer your question – yes and no. They don't fly on them, but they do use them to cleanse a house of bad vibrations and negative energy. Sig's great at it.'

'Is that one of the reasons why your home always feels so positive?' I asked nosily.

'Partly, but also because Sigrid and I are positive people. I'd rather see my glass as half full than half empty. Life is better when you look at it with positive eyes – you see opportunities others might miss. After all, you only live once.' He flashed me a grin. 'Though in your case, it's going to be real long ride.'

We pulled up near the river and parked on the side of the road. As we climbed out, I felt a mix of dread and excitement: dread because I really didn't want the men to be dead, excitement because if they weren't there Gunnar and I would be going where no man had gone before – well, not recently. Beyond the barrier.

Though the thought terrified me, this was the *new* Bunny and she was going to kick ass no matter where she was.

Gunnar looked at me. 'You ready?'

I nodded. We walked quietly down the trail to the water. I prayed no bodies awaited us there.

---

My eyes were sharper than Gunnar's; even so, I scanned the dark depths of the water, the banks, the rocks, and I saw nothing sinister. We walked up and down the riverbank for over an hour, but there was no sign of anything amiss: no stray shoes floating down the river or an abandoned rucksack or a severed head.

'Nothing,' I muttered aloud.

Gunnar grunted as he swung his flashlight back and forth over the water. 'All right, let's call it. Hopefully this means they're still alive.'

I didn't share his optimism. 'They might still be alive, but if they are they're in real trouble. We don't know how long they've got before the beast finds them.'

We walked back to the vehicle silently, both contemplating the Saviks' fate. 'Are you ready for this?' Gunnar said finally. 'I can leave you guarding the office.'

I glared. 'Absolutely not. I'm coming.' There was no way I'd leave Gunnar to face this alone when only days earlier he'd been at death's door! Besides, even if I was as useless as a witch who'd just scried, Fluffy wasn't. He had a sharp nose and keen instincts, and he'd be an asset beyond the barrier.

I bit my lip. 'Are we calling in search and rescue?'

'No, it would be a death sentence and I can't do it in good conscience. I'm calling Patkotak. He's the only one I can trust with this.'

I was surprised. Out of all the supernatural creatures at his disposal, it was a human he wanted by his side?

Gunnar pulled out his phone and spoke briefly to Thomas then cut the call. 'He'll meet us at the edge of the barrier by the Grimes' house. That's the closest spot to the trail where the hunters went.'

I nodded, my mouth suddenly drier than a woman's lady parts as she watched her boyfriend clip his toenails.

We drove over the rough, unpaved roads to the Grimes' brothers shed and parked next to an old truck. It was dirt encrusted and beaten up, but the tires were new: it belonged to the hunters. I followed Gunnar to the back of our vehicle where he handed me my rucksack.

I checked Fluffy's vest, then put his small saddlebags onto his back; they held his portable dishes, food and water. I checked my daypack and made sure I had water and my insulated lunch bag with enough blood for a day trip. There was also a first-aid kit. I adjusted my new holster, checked my weapons again, and put on my rain jacket and the pack. I was good to go, even if I didn't want to.

I heard a vehicle straining up the last steep part of the road to the Grimes'. Thomas parked beside us and climbed out. He armed himself with enough weapons to take down an army, and then we were ready. Once more unto the breach, dear friends...

Here's hoping we came back.

# Chapter 44

Gunnar shared the hunters' GPS coordinates with Thomas in case we got separated, then we started to hike. It wasn't far from the trucks to the barrier; Gunnar had told me that those who belonged to the town could pass from inside the barrier to the outside without a problem, but going the other way was another story.

The boats and planes that regularly went back and forth had a charm embedded into their hulls so the barrier would accept them. If you were supernatural, you could pass with a few carefully uttered words because of a spell the witches had set up, but pedestrian humans would never even know that the barrier was there. The uninitiated saw barren wilderness with the ruins of the original Portlock from the 1930s. Those that ventured in thought they were exploring the whole area, but in truth the spell confined them and they were walking in circles.

When we stopped at the barrier, I felt a slight, dissonant hum at the edge of my senses. It was all in my head, of course; Gunnar had told me there was no way to identify the barrier unless you were a magic user, and I definitely wasn't one of those even though I could occasionally summon fire. Nope: nothing magical about that.

Even so, I felt a slight resistance like pushing on gelatine. When I tested it by pushing my hand into it, it moved slightly more slowly than it should have done. It was weird.

Gunnar frowned. 'Something is wrong. The barrier feels ... off.'

'Did Liv repair the rip that let the Keelut in?' I asked.

Thomas's eyebrows shot up. 'A Keelut got in?'

'According to Gertrude,' Gunnar grunted. 'Liv hasn't found it, but she did find a rip. She had the witches repair it.'

Thomas looked worried. 'We should bring this to the council.'

'We will – as soon as we've found the Savik brothers.' Gunnar reached out and felt along the barrier, then froze when his hand suddenly slid through it. He swore darkly. 'There's another rip right here.'

A chill ran down my spine. Another one? What did that mean? Was the barrier failing somehow? What was making the rips? What if the beast could get inside?

'How large?' Thomas asked.

Gunnar's hand traced the tear. 'Feels about two feet long and maybe a foot wide.'

I was relieved; if the beast was large, there was no way it could get through a hole that size. I guessed Thomas was thinking the same because he put away his knife. 'What does it mean?' I asked.

Gunnar said grimly, 'One rip is an anomaly, but two? I'd say someone is trying to open the barrier. We'll need to get the witches out here pronto to repair it.' He pulled out his phone. 'Hold on a sec while I contact Liv.'

The coward started texting! He sent the message then glowered as he read an incoming text. 'Goddammit. My friend is here to move the cache under cover of night. It couldn't be worse timing.' His jaw worked. 'I'll call Connor.'

When Connor answered, he said, 'A friend of mine is here to take away the cache of drugs. I need you and your men to facilitate that. Keep it as quiet as you can – we don't want the dealers learning we've moved it yet. If they think it's still in the jail, we have leverage.'

There was a pause as Connor replied. 'His name is Henderson,' Gunnar confirmed. 'And Connor – he's MIB.' He winced a little as Connor replied. 'I trust him,' Gunnar insisted. 'He said he'll destroy it and I believe him. Just keep everyone calm while I'm out.'

Connor must have asked where Gunnar was going because a moment later he said, 'Beyond the barrier.' A beat. 'Yes, she's with me. I'll take care of her, son, you have my word on that. You take care of Henderson.' He rang off. 'Shitty timing,' he muttered, rubbing his face.

After sending a message, presumably to Henderson, he put away his phone. 'Let's go. We won't use this spot in case our passing through makes the tear larger.'

We moved a fair distance down, then took turns to go through the barrier: Patkotak went first, then me and Fluffy, with Gunnar bringing up the rear.

Walking through the barrier felt weird, like I was moving in a pool, but I could still breathe easily. I wasn't worried for myself – after all, I was a vamp – but I was worried for Fluffy. I needn't have been because after a few steps we popped back out the other side and everything started to move freely again.

Patkotak, Fluffy and I waited silently for Gunnar. When he joined us on the other side of the barrier, Thomas took point once more and I brought up the rear with Fluffy. My boy was hyper-vigilant, trotting at my side with his ears pricked and his head swinging as he watched for danger.

The road continued for about a kilometre before it faded into a narrow trail. I kept my eyes open and my ears pricked for any sound I didn't recognise, but there was a tonne of them. I'd not had much chance to work on my bushcraft since I'd moved here, and for a city girl the woods were as spooky as fuck. I didn't recognise most of the sounds or smells; I could read about bushcraft and memorise what to do in different situations, but most of what I was seeing now hadn't been in the books – and I wouldn't know what to do until I did it. Book smarts only got you so far.

For such a big man, Gunnar moved silently through the forest whereas I felt like a bull in a china shop as I crunched and crashed my way through. Thomas watched me with amusement, sometimes demonstrating a foot placement or pointing out a quieter route along the trail. He was gliding silently, like he was on a marble floor in stockinged feet.

Another branch whacked me in the face and I grunted. 'Fuck's sake,' I muttered. Fluffy yipped in commiseration and Thomas snickered at me.

'Let's see you navigate the London Underground,' I retorted.

We were on a narrow animal trail that appeared to be well travelled, and it didn't take us long to reach the coordinates the women had given us. The remnants of the camp were still visible – a cold fire pit and small pile of wood – but there was no sign of the men. Fluffy sniffed around but he didn't indicate anything out of the ordinary.

'You're up, Patkotak,' Gunnar said.

Thomas searched the area surrounding the campsite. After a few moments, he said, 'They went this way.'

We followed him.

# Chapter 45

An eerie howl filled the darkness. Fluffy's ears lay back and a low growl erupted from his throat. Thomas paused and said, 'Wolves.'

'Wolves?' I asked. Real wolves or shifters? I'd seen and heard both since I'd come to Portlock.

'Yup. Listen. The pack will join in.' Sure enough, moments later more howls filled the night. Just regular wolves. I shivered: there was nothing *just* about them – they were freaking wolves!

Fluffy leaned against my legs and I felt his unease. Other than the werewolf pack, the only other wolves I'd been close to were the skanky ones in the city that required a solid knee to the bollocks. Those wolves were vile, but they wouldn't rip your throat out.

We started climbing up a steep slope; we were still on a trail, but it was getting rougher. The brush was trying to peel off our skin and some sections were almost impassable because of thick branches.

'It's easier if you try to step over the alders,' Thomas said.

I could see why; it was impossible to walk through them. Even Fluffy was struggling, and he was smaller than us.

A little further on, Thomas paused and pointed a plant out to me. 'Devil's club. Don't touch it.' He turned over a broad leaf with his gloved hand. 'It's covered with prickles that break off into your skin. It's extremely unpleasant.'

I memorised the plant. I had never felt further away from the glitz and glam of London. Thomas took out a machete and started whacking the devil's club away from the path. I was never going to complain about his arsenal of weapons again.

An hour into our hike, he stopped abruptly, squatted down and scanned the ground with his flashlight. 'They left the trail here, but it looks like they split up.'

Fluffy sniffed the two trails and pointed his nose at the one that continued up the hill.

Another eerie howl split the night; this time Thomas jumped up and started looking around. 'Not a wolf,' he confirmed, his voice tight.

Fuck. If it wasn't a wolf, what was it? It had sounded the same to me so how could he tell the difference? I listened; what followed sounded like high-pitched, angry words, although not in any language I'd ever heard. The skin on the back of my neck prickled. Okay, not a wolf.

Thomas and Gunnar froze. Fluffy growled deeply, lowered his head and laid back his ears. 'Nantinaq,' Thomas whispered. 'It's watching us.'

'Is it the beast?' I asked fearfully.

He shook his head. 'No way of knowing. Could be a friendly brother or it could be a monster.' Please God, let it be a long-lost brother.

A crash came to the right as if a large tree had fallen. I peered into the darkness, but even with my sharp eyesight I could see nothing.

'It wants us to leave,' Thomas said sombrely. 'We'd better respect our big brother's wishes and hurry before it gets annoyed. Move!' He chose the path Fluffy had indicated. Rather than split up, we decided to stick together and follow the hunter who'd gone uphill first.

Thomas had to check the path often since we were off the trail now. There wasn't room for us to travel abreast, and Fluffy stayed with him. When Thomas paused for too long, my dog showed us the way one of the Saviks had gone. I *knew* he would be an asset to the team.

'I think one of them went low to drive the game up to his brother,' Thomas mused. He stopped; pointing to some crushed vegetation, he leaned down and picked up a shell casing. 'He lay down here to shoot, then he took off this way.' He pointed and Fluffy started moving in that direction, nose to the ground, agreeing with his assessment.

Thomas started back down the hill in a different direction and we followed. A hollow sounding 'thwack' sounded close behind us and I glanced back but saw nothing. 'We need to hurry,' Thomas barked. No shit!

I upped my pace to a fraction below a run. Gunnar was behind me, probably thinking he was protecting me; since I was a vampire and not a magic user, I was content to let him. My only supernatural weapon was my fangs – and if I got close enough to use them, I was probably a goner.

I suddenly remembered that I also had fire. I had no idea *why* I had fire, or how to use it, but I could definitely do damage. The problem was that I was as likely to barbecue Gunnar and Thomas as our enemies.

There was another crash to our left, but this one was caused by a huge rock. I knew that because I saw the boulder land in the brush. If that had hit one of us...

Thomas was jogging now and I started to run flat out. A scent reached my nose. 'Blood,' I said. 'Up ahead.'

Thomas turned his flashlight back on. 'Here.' He stopped abruptly and pointed the light at a large pool of blood and the body of a mountain goat.

The carcase was torn to pieces and sections of it were scattered around. The shoulder section had a neat hole in it; the brothers had shot the goat but not managed to retrieve their kill. This was *not* good; the chances of finding either brother alive were diminishing by the moment.

Fluffy stared intently into the brush and I wondered what he could see that we could not.

Gunnar and Thomas lit up the goat's remains and I photographed them, then Thomas and Fluffy located the hunter's tracks and we raced off again. This time the sounds that pursued us were growling and screeching. My floppy heart gave a few extra frightened beats.

'We've angered them,' Thomas warned.

'Them?' I asked.

'I mark at least three.'

Great. Fucking fantastic. How many of them lived out here? Apparently there were at least three of these knobheads, one for each of us except for Fluffy, the lucky bastard.

Gunnar scanned the forest and I stayed on Thomas's heels. Running down the hill I could feel the burn in my thighs, but Thomas was like a machine: he wasn't even breathing hard. He avoided branches and brush like he was made of oil, and occasionally he took a swing with the machete and cleared our path. The foliage pulled at my hair and scraped my clothing but I didn't care; I just wanted to be away from these things that were hounding our heels.

Suddenly, Thomas froze and I almost ran into him. 'What is it?'

He pointed to a small ravine in front of him, only about three feet wide. Wedged in it was a body.

Fuck.

# Chapter 46

We stared down at the slash in the earth until Gunnar knelt and pulled some rope from his pack. 'Help me get this around the body and we'll pull him out.'

I had the smallest hands and, since there wasn't a lot of room around the stiff body, I was the one who threaded the rope around him. He was too newly dead to have much smell, but the edge of rot teased my supernatural sniffer.

Once the rope was tied, Gunnar effortlessly hauled the body out of the ravine and laid it on the ground. I immediately recognised the man from his photo: it was Akiak. Poor Talia. He didn't appear to have been brutalised; there were no sign of any wounds and I didn't smell any blood. 'His neck's broken,' Gunnar noted.

Thomas nodded. 'He could have tripped in the dark and broken it when he fell into the ravine.'

'Entirely possible,' Gunnar agreed. He had a body bag in his pack that he wrapped around Akiak, then he effortlessly slung the corpse over his shoulder.

Fluffy, who had been watching the brush around us, started to whine. That was all the impetus we needed: we hauled ass. Thomas led us to where he thought we would cross Lukas's trail. Even with the extra burden of Akiak, Gunnar's movements were still silent. I fell behind to watch *his* back; he couldn't look around much with the body on his shoulder.

As we continued downhill, the screeching and growling grew fainter until it faded away, but Thomas said they were still watching. I knew he was right; I could feel the weight of six eyes pressing into my back. That was enough to make me keep moving quickly.

Finally, Fluffy stopped, sniffed the ground and looked pointedly at us. Thomas knelt next to him and studied the earth. 'We've found Lukas's tracks,' he announced.

I wondered if we'd find Lukas's body because finding him alive seemed like a pipe dream. The whole forest had an eerie vibe, and I knew it wasn't just because of the screeching nantinaq that we'd disturbed. I couldn't shake the feeling that the beast itself was watching us and deciding our fate. Maybe the beast was completely different to what people thought was haunting Portlock. Frankly, the nantinaq were bad enough.

I caught a movement in my peripheral vision and whipped my head to the right – then immediately wished I hadn't because red eyes were glowing in the brush and the trees. I blinked and they were gone.

Fuck this. I swallowed hard and sped up until I was almost on Gunnar's back. 'I saw something,' I whispered, although there was no reason to keep quiet. The creature clearly knew where we were.

'What?' Gunnar asked.

'Red eyes in the trees.' I half-expected him to laugh at me, but he didn't. After that, he kept his eyes on the trees too.

Something besides the three nantinaq had us in its sights. My impression of what I'd seen was something dark, huge and filled with malevolence, although the latter might just have been the red-eye thing. Maybe it was an albino creature that was naturally red eyed but was kind and friendly and always up for a jape. Maybe it was a lovely, red-eyed unicorn. But it didn't feel like it; it had seemed full of rage and hatred.

I didn't say anything – we were scared enough already – but I loosened the snap on my holster and made sure I could draw my gun quickly. Thomas had a large gun in his hand now; he must have either seen something or heard my whisper to Gunnar. Gunnar had unfastened both his holsters, although he'd have to drop the body to draw the one on his right side.

Fluffy speeded up and we stayed close together. This time the scream that rent the air made us freeze in our tracks. My blood ran cold. Once my mind was my own again, I whispered, 'What was that?'

'Our signal to get back through the barrier,' Thomas said grimly. 'We'll loop back round.'

As we started to jog, we practically stumbled over Lukas – or what was left of him. He was in the middle of the trail, and it was immediately obvious that his death hadn't been an accident. Only his head remained, his face frozen in a rictus of horror, and I instantly had a flashback of the rogue werewolf I'd beheaded.

Whilst I dealt with my own little trauma, Gunnar was already working like the consummate professional that he was. He carefully lowered Akiak's body, zipped open the body bag and shoved Lukas's head into it, then slung the remains of both brothers back over his shoulder.

A branch soared through the air, struck Fluffy and he yipped in pain. I rushed over to him and looked up to where it had come from. 'Fuck off!' I yelled at whoever – *what*ever – had flung it. It might be an evil demonic beast, but *no one* hurt my dog.

Red eyes glinted in the dark, and I pulled my gun and shot three times at them as I ran my other hand over Fluffy. Nothing felt broken; though he was panting and upset, he seemed to be okay.

'Let's make tracks!' Thomas barked.

Immediately there was a roar from the trees. Something extremely pissed was behind us, breaking trees and flinging branches and rocks. We dodged and dived – and thankfully got lucky.

I had vampire speed and sight, but I had a hard time keeping up with Thomas since he was better at avoiding the obstacles in our path. I wondered inanely if he was being helped by a spell; it was better to focus on anything other than the red-eyed beast that was dogging our steps, whom I had just told to fuck off. That hadn't been my wisest move, but the heat of the moment was a real thing.

Finally, we burst through the brush onto the trail that led to the road and safety. I was panting from fear rather than exhaustion. We were so close now – but just as I thought we were going to make it, something screamed to our left.

Without stopping, Thomas shot five times towards the spot. There was a nasty screech and a crash as something fell. Was it too much to ask that Thomas had just killed the beast and ended its reign of terror?

'Hurry! It's just wounded! It will only buy us a few seconds,' he urged.

On the straight, Fluffy and I quickly pulled ahead of the men. I'd been on the university running team and now vampirism was giving me blinding speed, so I reached the barrier first – but I couldn't get through it without Gunnar's spell. That was something to remedy if we ever came this way again.

I took up a shooter's stance like Gunnar had showed me, drew my gun and aimed it beyond the men, looking for any sign of nightmarish red eyes.

I could hear Thomas and Gunnar's pounding feet, and the creature tearing up trees and hurling them to the ground to our right; it was definitely not dead then. Fear made heat rise in my gut and I struggled to keep it within me because I didn't want to harm Gunnar or Thomas like I had Virginia and Jim. The fire was my own beast, and I battled to contain it.

Gunshots rang out as the men were on the final approach, Gunner still carrying the body bag with its grisly contents. The fire was burning me up, but I pushed it aside and focused. 'I've got your backs,' I shouted. 'Just run!' Behind them, the red eyes were coming closer.

Thomas reached me first, placed his hand on the barrier and mumbled the spell, though I couldn't make it out over the screeching and crashing. Then he swore: nothing was happening. He looked up, dismay on his face. 'Gunnar, it's not letting us through!'

Gunnar dropped the body bag, placed both hands on the barrier and delivered the spell. Nothing. 'It's not working,' he said grimly. 'The rip – it must be affecting this area of the barrier.'

We couldn't go right because the beast was there; it was only a matter of time before it stopped its temper tantrum and came after us with all its might. I'd seen Lukas's body and I knew the extent of its rage and strength.

Thomas ran about thirty feet down the barrier to the left and tried again. 'Nothing,' he yelled.

'The rip is near here, right?' I asked. 'We might be able to squeeze through it!'

'It's here!' Gunnar said, feeling the boundary. His hand sank through it. 'You go first, Bunny. You're smaller – if you can't make it through then none of us can.'

I wanted to argue but there was no time – and he was right: I was the logical choice. I felt around at shoulder height where Gunnar had identified the rip, thrust my arm through and then literally dived. Unlike when we'd come the other way, the barrier now felt solid and about a foot thick, but I kicked my way through and finally slithered through it.

'It worked! Come through!' I screamed. 'Chuck me Fluffy!'

Thomas lifted Fluffy and slipped him through the barrier, then Gunnar lifted the body bag. As it slid towards me, I grabbed it, yanked, and it emerged like a gruesome birth. I dragged it away from the barrier.

Next up was Thomas. He was taller and broader than me, so he jumped and thrust his arms through rather than diving. As he struggled to get his shoulders through the gap. I reached up, grabbed his hands and pulled with all my might. He slid out.

A tree fell only a couple of feet away and landed on the road. A mewing sound came from it and

I saw a fuzzy little creature clinging to the trunk. The beast was coming and anything in its way was going to die. Gunnar also saw it and being a total softie, he grabbed the cat and thrust it through the barrier where it landed at my feet. Then, his expression strained, Gunnar bent and thrust forward both his arms.

No way would his shoulders fit – the rip had barely let Thomas through. My stomach clenched. 'Pull,' Gunnar yelled at us.

Thomas and I each grabbed an arm and pulled, but the huge man was wedged tight. His face turned red as the barrier squeezed his shoulders and chest, and his breath was shallow and fast as he started to panic.

Then I saw something I never wanted to see again, something that would haunt my nightmares and my waking moments forever. I saw the eyes ... and they were coming for Gunnar.

# Chapter 47

The beast was not a nantinaq; I didn't know what it was because it was nothing more than a dark smudge against the night with blazing red eyes, but it was *huge*. For the first time ever, I saw Gunnar looking afraid.

Thomas and I pulled with all of our might, so hard that I heard Gunnar's shoulders pop. The black demonic smudge raced towards him but, just as it reached for his legs, he finally slipped through. We all tumbled to the ground in a heap.

Black smoke poured through the gap and panic raced through me. We couldn't let that thing come through – that was why the barrier was there!

I let my fear unfurl in a wall of heat, and fire exploded from me. A hot fireball ripped from my chest and flung itself towards the gap in the barrier. The beast of shadows screamed as my flames broiled its inky tentacles and it withdrew, no doubt to lick its wounds, though it gave another scream of rage before it went. The threat was clear: it was going, but it would be back.

Gunnar muttered something that sounded Scandinavian, and white light blasted out, temporarily sealing the rift. But the spell had taken something from him and he slumped to his knees, his arms hanging uselessly by his sides. His face was twisted with pain; we'd dislocated both of his shoulders to save his life.

He gave me a small smile. 'I *knew* it wasn't a gas explosion,' he said, referring to the cause of the fire at my last house.

Mouth suddenly dry, I admitted, 'I don't know what it is. It's only happened that one time – well, twice now.' I sighed. 'It isn't normal for a vampire, is it?' I asked unhappily.

'No, not for a vamp,' Thomas confirmed. 'It looks like you've got some elemental witch magic.'

Gunnar nodded. 'Like Shirley.'

Great: I had the same sort of magic as that poisonous bitch. What the fuck had Franklin done to me? Thinking of him made me think of John's message to Conner. It couldn't be a co-incidence that a witch had paid Franklin to turn me and now I had witchy powers...

'Do you mind if we keep this to ourselves until I get a handle on it?' I asked the two men.

Thomas mimed zipping his lips and Gunnar winked. 'Keep what to ourselves? Now, I'll need some help with these arms.'

'I'll put them back in,' Thomas offered. 'But it's gonna hurt like a motherfucker.'

Gunnar blew out a breath and nodded. 'I know. Do it.'

Thomas took Gunnar's right arm and pulled it out straight to his side, then lifted the arm, put it behind Gunnar's head and pushed. There was an audible pop as it slid back into its socket. Gunnar bellowed and I winced in sympathy.

Finally, Gunnar nodded for Thomas to do the other arm. My boss was panting by the end, clinging to consciousness by sheer stubbornness. It looked horrendous; I reminded myself never to dislocate my shoulders.

We waited patiently until Gunnar caught his breath. Fluffy licked his face and eventually the Nomo lifted one of his arms carefully and patted my boy on the head. 'I'm okay. They'll heal fast now they're reset. I'm bushed, though.'

He studied the ground, clearly wondering how he was going to get to his feet. Offering him an arm wasn't the best idea with his shoulders newly put in place, so I carefully reached around Gunnar's middle and helped to pull him up. He swayed; whatever that white flash had been, it had taken it out of him, and he'd already been operating at less than full power thanks to the bloody fisheye poisoning.

Fluffy whined softly and glanced at the small animal Gunnar had saved. I recognised the breed from my first job as the Nomo's assistant: it was a lynx. Unlike Timmy, it was smoky coloured, and its little spots were hard to see under its dark-grey fur. The poor thing was cringing behind a rotten tree stump. Fluffy looked at me and I sighed. 'Go on, then. Why not?'

His tongue lolled and he gave me a giant lick before trotting to the cat. It gave a small hiss as he approached, but he ignored it and nuzzled it with his nose. After a moment, the cat seemed to relax. Oh so gently, Fluffy picked it up in his mouth and trotted to the SUV. I opened the door and he hopped in and set the kitten on the back seat.

'Looks like you're collecting strays,' Thomas said, amused.

'Yeah,' I sighed. 'Well, how much work can one lynx be?'

'Oh, they're super-easy to look after.' I didn't need his snicker to know he was being sarcastic. 'Well, this has been fun. Let's get the body parts secured and get out of here.'

Before I could offer to help, Thomas shouldered the bag and put it in the back of the Nomo's SUV.

Gunnar was still pale and swaying. 'You're gonna have to drive back,' he said to me.

I nodded. 'No problem, boss-man.'

Thomas and I helped Gunnar into the truck. I was trying to keep my worries under control, but when the Nomo closed his eyes and rested his head against the headrest panic wormed its way in. It was too soon after the whole fisheye episode to see him looking this sick again.

'Get him to Sig,' Thomas murmured. 'She'll fix him up. I'll lead the way back to town.'

I appreciated the thought, even though I knew the way back. We chugged into town, dodging potholes as we went. I kept sliding Gunnar worried glances and he caught one of them. 'I'm all right,' he murmured. 'Just beat.'

Beat like a tenderised steak, I thought, though I didn't say it. You shouldn't kick a man when he was down and Gunnar was definitely down.

Once in Portlock, Thomas flashed his lights at me and headed off to do God knows what. I drove us to the hospital and dropped off our gruesome cargo at the morgue so they could perform an autopsy on the Savik brothers' remains. When I climbed back into the car, Gunnar grunted, 'Notification.'

I nodded. The sky was lightening, but the women would want to know, no matter what time it was. My heart aching for the families, I drove to Talia's house and pulled into the driveway.

Gunnar sat up, tried to open the door and let out a low groan. I touched his arm. 'I've got this.'

It was testament to how awful he felt that he nodded and sat back. The lynx crawled forward onto his lap and curled up, purring. Gunnar lifted a hand to stroke it a little. I met Fluffy's eyes and jerked my head at our boss. Fluffy sat up and fixed his eyes on the exhausted man; he would watch over him whilst I did the worst thing I'd probably ever done.

I looked like I'd rolled down a mountain. I tried to straighten my clothes, though it didn't really matter what I looked like. I was there to ruin their lives; even if I'd been dressed fit to meet a king, my words would destroy them.

I knocked three times and waited. It took a minute or so for Talia to answer. The hope in her eyes died as she saw my face. 'Can I come in?' I asked. She held the door open then sagged to the floor.

Olena ran down the stairs, 'Who was—?' She trailed off as she caught sight of me. 'No,' she whispered.

I shut the front door and faced them. 'I'm sorry,' I said uselessly. 'I'm so sorry. Akiak and Lukas are both dead.' I was probably doing it all wrong. I was supposed to say something else, wasn't I? 'I regret to inform you' or something like that? This was awful.

Talia wailed and Olena hastily finished descending the stairs to go to her. 'Hush now,' she said, her voice sharp. 'You'll wake the kids. They've only just gone down. Hush now, Talia,' she repeated. 'They need their sleep.' She pulled the other woman into her arms and rocked her back and forth. Then she looked at me over her friend's shoulder; she'd known on some level that Lukas wasn't coming back to her.

'Let's get you to bed,' she said to Talia. 'Come on, love, it's already been such a long day. You're exhausted.'

'Akiak,' she sobbed. 'My Akiak. How will I raise my children alone?'

'You won't be alone,' Olena said fiercely. 'You have me, and I have you. Neither of us will be alone.'

She half-carried, half-dragged Talia up the stairs, then paused on the landing. 'I'll be back in a moment,' she said to me.

I waited patiently and about ten minutes later she came back down, her eyes red and her cheeks tear stained. 'Sorry to keep you,' she murmured.

'Not at all.'

'How?' she asked.

I didn't know what to say, what details to give. 'Akiak broke his neck. It looked like a simple accident.'

'And Lukas?' Olena's voice wavered.

'He was attacked by something. We couldn't recover all of his body. I'm sorry.'

Her lips trembled. 'Attacked by what?'

'We can't be certain at this time,' I said, hoping that vague answer would satisfy her.

Her eyes sharpened. 'What aren't you saying? Tell me!'

'It appears,' I said carefully, 'that the beast beyond the barrier may have killed him. We'll know more after the autopsy.'

'The beast?' Olena shook her head. 'Lukas said that was a tale made up by the witches.'

'No,' I said bleakly. 'I saw it. It's real, very real. Do you know other men in the hunting community?' Olena nodded. 'Please urge them not to go beyond the barrier. It's important.'

She suddenly looked weary. 'I will. I don't want this to happen to anyone else. I can hardly believe it's real. I keep expecting Lukas to walk back in and—' She cut off with a sob.

I reached out and patted her shoulder. 'Do you want me to call anyone?' I asked.

'No. Everyone I love is already here. Thank you for letting us know. When can we see them?'

I grimaced. 'I'm not sure that is advisable. But the morgue will be in touch once the autopsies have been completed.'

'Okay, thank you.' She was a shadow of the formidable woman I'd met only hours ago.

'I'll go,' I murmured. 'If there's anything I can do, please call me.' She nodded, but we both knew she wouldn't. She showed me to the door and I left her to her grief.

Outside, I breathed in the cool air. That had been horrendous. The Savik families had been torn apart – and for what? Because the men had encroached on the beast's land? As far as I was concerned, the barrier tax was worth every penny. The thought of the death and destruction that beast could wreak on Portlock was terrifying. How did you kill something made of shadows and evil?

# Chapter 48

Gunnar was snoring lightly when I climbed back into the car. I drove him home and gave Sigrid a sanitised version of what had happened. Despite the frustration she clearly felt while I was telling her the story, her expression was gentle when she woke her husband. She helped him from the car and waved me off.

Just this once, I decided to park the car at my house instead of the office. The adrenaline crash was hitting me and I needed to get home as soon as possible; I wanted to lock my doors and windows, close the metal shutters and never look outside again. I was supposed to be a big, tough vampire, practically immortal, but I'd just seen something scarier than my worst nightmare. And I wasn't sure I would *ever* get over it.

Even Fluffy seemed a little cowed as he kept an eye on the lynx kitten.

I was surprised to see Connor sitting on my front step. 'Hey,' I greeted him warily. 'Are you okay?' With the events of the last few hours, I'd forgotten about the mysterious MIB friend of Gunnar's moving the drugs out of the Nomo's jail.

'I'm fine.' He studied me. 'You're not.'

'I've been better,' I admitted.

He didn't press, didn't ask what I'd seen. 'Can I come in?' he said instead. 'I'll check under your bed for monsters.'

'Sold,' I agreed instantly. The shadows would scare me tonight.

I unlocked the front door and flicked on every light I could find, then I activated the metal shutters and locked up. It made me feel marginally safer, although I had the distinct feeling that the creature we'd seen would have zero problem gaining entrance if it wanted to.

I hoped Liv already had people repairing the rip in the barrier. I needed to check. 'Do you have Liv's number?' I asked Connor.

He pulled up a contact on his phone and passed it to me. I hit ring. 'Not now, MacKenzie,' Liv snarled as she answered.

'It's not MacKenzie, it's Bunny.' The handy thing about having a unique name is no one ever said 'Bunny who?'.

'I'm busy, Bunny,' she said, but her voice had a little less bite.

'Are you at the barrier? Gunnar did something temporary to patch the rip, but you need to do something permanent *now*.' My voice wavered.

'Did you see it?' she whispered.

'Yes,' I admitted. 'It can't be let in, Liv.'

'We're repairing it,' she confirmed.

There was a shrill scream. The hairs on the back of my neck stood up and I gripped the phone tightly. 'What was that?' I demanded.

'A sacrifice,' she said wearily. 'The barrier doesn't run on wishes and dreams.'

I went cold. Oh my God.

'A goat,' she relented. 'Just a goat. I have to go.' She hung up.

I passed the phone back to Connor and blew out a breath. Well, fuck. What had I thought a necromancer would do? Liv's power came from death – in this case, a goat's death. I didn't especially like it, but I liked the idea of the beast coming into town even less.

Connor was watching me with stormy blue eyes, but he still didn't press me. He went into the kitchen and flicked on the kettle.

The lynx kitten looked small and helpless on my sofa. Was it old enough to be away from its mother? What did a lynx kitten eat? I should call the vet in the morning but until then I guessed I needed to find it some meat. I had a pack of burgers; they would do.

I started to feed the little cat pieces of the meat and it ate them greedily. When its belly was round and solid, it curled up and fell asleep.

Connor passed me a mug of blood and a cup of tea. I pinched my nose and chugged the blood, then sat on the sofa and pulled a blanket onto my lap. As

I sipped my glorious tea, the whole story gradually came tumbling out of me. 'It's evil,' I finished. 'I don't care if Liv has to kill a whole herd of goats to keep it out. If it gets into town, it'll kill us all.'

'It won't get into town,' he promised.

I hoped not. I was tired, but since I was covered in most of the forest, I mumbled, 'I need to take a shower.'

'If you want, I'll stay until you're ready for bed.'

I felt ridiculous but I *did* want that. If he was there, no shadow monster would sneak into my room to kill me while I was sleeping. 'That'd be great,' I admitted.

I showered quickly, dressed in my pyjamas and dried my hair. Connor was waiting in the hallway and his eyes softened when he saw me. 'You're dead on your feet,' he murmured. 'Come on, Sleeping Beauty.' He took my hand, tugged me into bed and tucked the duvet around me.

'My, Grandma, what big teeth you have,' I mumbled.

'Wrong story,' he smiled.

'I don't believe in Prince Charming,' I countered with a yawn. 'And if he does exist, he should know that kissing unconscious girls is a no-no.'

He looked rueful. 'What about sleepy ones?'

'That's fine!' I said hastily, suddenly feeling a whole lot more alert. He leaned down and tension hummed between us. He flicked his eyes to my lips and then ... he kissed me on the forehead.

I was still blinking in confusion when he slipped out of the room. 'Tease!' I shouted after him. His laughter drifted back.

I sank back into the pillows and a smile pulled at my face. Despite all I'd been through, I suddenly felt steadier. I felt Fluffy jump up next to me and place the kitten on the pillow.

I drifted off with a warm, furry lump purring in my ear.

# Chapter 49

When I woke up, I told myself I had to focus on something else; the monster and the barrier were above my pay grade and thinking about them left a hollow, scared pit in my stomach. Drugs, though: I could deal with those. The cache of fisheye had been moved, but the drug dealer was still at large.

I put together a temporary litter box, left the kitten locked in the bathroom with some hamburger and water, then Fluffy and I marched to the office feeling determined. Calliope still hadn't provided us with the list of water shifters; she was protecting someone and my money was on Soapy. We could push the issue but meanwhile perhaps Sally would recover enough to do some more scrying for us. I wasn't sure if she needed an object that had an emotional or physical link to the scryee, but I had the sock. Most people didn't get starry-eyed over their socks, but if all she needed was something that had been worn we might be in luck.

When I rang her, she said she was still out of action. I went into Gunnar's office to complain about it. He was sitting at his desk looking much better. 'How are you?' I asked, eyeing him cautiously. He looked okay but there was still something missing and I couldn't quite put my finger on it.

'Fully healed, thanks to some witchy potions, though the arms have some residual aches.'

'Glad to hear it.' I paused. 'Listen, I've been thinking about the drugs and I think we need to call Liv. Sally can't scry for us, but we have the kidnapper's sock. Surely Liv will know someone else we can use.'

Rather than looking grumpy about calling Liv, Gunnar just looked resigned. He sighed and picked up his phone, then put it back on the desk with the speaker activated.

'Why hello, Gunnar,' Liv purred.

Gunnar actually shuddered; he really didn't like her come-ons. 'Liv, we need the help of the magic leader.'

That was a subtle plea for professionalism if ever I'd heard one.

She obliged, and her voice was brisk when she next spoke. 'Another rip? We just sealed the last one.'

'No, we need a scryer. We were using Sally Marsh, but she's still out of action. Do you have any suggestions who else we could use?'

'Are you scrying for an object or a person?' she asked. The purr was back.

'Person.'

'What kind of object do you have?'

'A sock.'

'Hmmm.' Even her pause was sexy. I rolled my eyes. 'Well, you're in luck. *I* can scry for you, Gunnar.' Somehow it sounded like she was going to do more than scry.

'Uh.' Gunnar was flummoxed; he hadn't thought that was a possibility. 'I thought it required a witch?' he said lamely.

'People are covered in dead skin cells and they shed them constantly. A sock is like a beacon for a necromancer.'

Gunnar cleared his throat. 'It was soaked in saltwater.'

Silence. 'For how long?' she asked.

'Unknown. Probably a few minutes.'

'Might be fine. Skin cells would still be inside – I doubt they washed away, although salt can make things difficult. We'll see. I'll still come by and give it a whirl.'

'When?' I had a feeling Gunnar was going to make himself scarce.

'Well, I just got out of the shower and I'm standing here naked, so unless you want me in this state...' She paused for a long time. When he said nothing, she finished the call with, 'I'll be there in an hour.' The last bit was clipped and filled with annoyance. She hung up.

Gunnar made sure the line had disconnected, then looked at me pleadingly. 'Yeah,' I grinned. 'I'll handle it. You can disappear. I'll text once she's gone.'

He beamed. 'Thanks.'

'Sure thing, boss.'

'I'm going home. My arms still ache. Call me if we get a result on the scry.' He gathered up his things and went out of the back door. I watched him run away; I would have run away too if Liv had me in her sights.

I sat at my desk and Fluffy heaved himself out of his cushioned dog bed to lean against my leg. 'You're lucky Liv isn't as fond of dogs as she is of Gunnar,' I remarked and scratched behind his ears.

I caught up on some admin while I was waiting for Liv, but thankfully she didn't leave me hanging for long. She pushed open the front door and sashayed in. She had a large bag over her shoulder and was wearing a flowing ivory dress, low cut, belted with a thin strip of gold that set off the burnished bronze of her skin. Her hair was down and the white streak was vibrant among her shiny dark curls. She looked like an Egyptian goddess, a look I knew she cultivated. She was going to be disappointed that her prey had escaped.

'Liv,' I said brightly. 'That was fast. If you come around here, I'll open the room for you and retrieve the sock.'

She looked around – for Gunnar, I assumed. 'Hmm, yes.'

I let her into the interrogation room and she plonked her huge bag down on the steel table and started removing its contents. I went to the evidence room and collected the sock in its plastic bag. When I returned, she asked baldly, 'Is Gunnar here?'

'No, he went home. Dinner was ready.' It didn't hurt to remind her that Gunnar was happily married.

'Shame.' She looked me up and down like I was a viable replacement for Gunnar. 'Too skinny,' she muttered. Charming.

I ignored the slight; she wasn't my type, either. 'Will it affect your scrying to have me around?'

She waved her hand dismissively. 'No, I'm not doing anything for the general dead – or undead, in your case. It will only affect the sock.'

'Will it burn up?' I asked, remembering Sally Marsh's warning.

She looked at me in surprise, then considered it. 'The sock won't, but the dead skin cells will be gone. It'll be worthless for DNA evidence once I'm done.'

That would suck if we needed DNA, but right now we had nothing. 'Go ahead. The risk is worth it,' I said.

Liv put the sock on the table. Her scrying items included a large glass bowl, candles and herbs, all things I'd seen her use when she'd tried to raise Eric Walker for us. Her style was slightly different from Sally's, presumably because she was a necromancer rather than a witch. She didn't fill the bowl with water; instead, she put various items into it and added something from a bottle that held an amber-coloured liquid. At first I thought it was some kind of alcohol, but it didn't smell alcoholic. I didn't ask her about it either: with my luck, it was dead-body fluids boiled down to some sort of broth. I shivered and felt vaguely sick.

She lit her candles, lifted her arms to the ceiling and chanted. The candles flared brighter and I felt that same nauseating tug I'd felt the last time from her magic, like an oily slime was sliding around my guts then yanking me towards her. A chill ran down my spine and I took a step back.

She opened the evidence bag and let the sock slither into the bowl. Once it struck the liquid, the tugging feeling inside me stopped abruptly and the candles flared even higher. She chanted more gibberish and stared into the bowl. 'Look!' she demanded, her voice lower than usual.

I crept closer, peered into the bowl and gave a little fist pump as Soapy Willoughby came into view. He was in what looked like the hardware shop, talking calmly to Sidnee's boyfriend, Chris, over chai lattes. Both men had bags; they'd clearly been shopping and bumped into each other. This was what I needed.

Calliope would *have* to let us interview Soapy now because it looked like he was anything but squeaky clean.

# Chapter 50

Liv let her arms fall, the candles died, and the image disappeared. 'Did you get what you wanted?' she asked, not unkindly.

I nodded. 'Oh yeah.'

As she gathered up her things, I poured the liquid from her bowl into the sink, rinsed it and dried it with some paper towels. I wrung out the sock and put it back in its evidence bag, 'Thanks for doing this,' I said. 'We appreciate the help.'

She shrugged. 'Sometimes we must sacrifice for the good of the community,' she said sanctimoniously, then ruined the effect by adding, 'I'll send you the bill.' She winked and walked back out, not wasting any of her exaggerated hip action on me.

I paused before I rang Gunnar. Okay, so the evidence was helpful, but we had no proof that the sock belonged to the kidnapper. And even though it seemed like it was Soapy's, there was nothing to prove that he was *definitely* the kidnapper. He could just have gone for a swim in the bay and left a sock floating around.

I sat bolt upright. We had a piece of hair! Just a tiny piece, caught on the tree as the kidnapper had stolen Skylark away, but even so we could do a DNA match on that. I rubbed my hands together. Things were cooking.

I picked up my phone to call Gunnar and grimaced when I saw a veritable tonne of messages from my mum. There were twenty texts at least; she did *not* know the meaning of playing it cool. Wincing, I scrolled through them and my breath hitched and my sluggish heart sped up slightly. The gist of her gazillion messages? She and Dad were coming to visit me. In Alaska. Fuck's sake.

I looked at the phone for a long five minutes, then simply texted back: *When?*

The response was instant: *Next month, I'll send you my itinerary. Dad will come a week later.*

A week later? How long was she staying? She'd *detest* Alaska. Maybe I could encourage her to leave after a few days. Or better still, not come at all.

*How long are you planning to stay for?* I asked instead.

*A month.*

I put my head in my hands, then texted: *There isn't a whole lot to do here.*

*I'm sure I'll figure it out. We'll have you interacting with the best the town has to offer in no time.*

I groaned aloud. What did she think was going on here? Balls? Charity events? Galas? So far the biggest social event had been my 'Welcome to Portlock' party, which had ended with me singing my lungs out and passing out, and Connor looking after me. Mum would *not* approve of such behaviour.

The other thing to worry about was the fact that she was human. Even though she knew about vampires, she was as ped as they came. This had disaster written all over it.

I tried again. *Mum, there is no high society here. This is Alaska; I think they might be anti-high society.*

*Nonsense.*

Bugger. This wasn't working and I didn't have the time or patience for her right now. *I've got to go back to work,* I wrote. I had a month to come up with a plan to deal with her. It would be fine.

*Love you, darling.*

A small smile curved up at that. *Love you, mum.*

Fluffy looked at me; I was sure he could feel my anxiety ramping up. 'It was my mum,' I explained. 'She's coming to visit us. Here.'

He shot up, barked once, then growled and bared his teeth.

'It'll be fine. How bad can it be?'

His expression said pretty fucking bad.

Yeah.

# Chapter 51

I called Gunnar and told him about the sock scry. He said to leave it with him for now and he would speak to Calliope. Grudgingly I agreed, though I felt like I had my hands tied. Personally, I would have stormed down to the fish plant and demanded a meeting with Calliope and Soapy. But Gunnar knew the politics of the situation and he knew Calliope better than I did, so his call was probably the better one. Even so, impatience chafed me for the rest of my shift.

Gunnar had given me permission to leave early so that I could go to the vampire meeting that Connor had called to discuss fisheye. When the door beeped to signal Sidnee's arrival, I sent her a grateful smile. 'Hey! Sorry to drag you in early.'

She waved my thanks away as a yawn cracked her face. 'No worries. I mostly intend to nap by the office phone,' she confessed. 'Chris kept me up all night. He's *very* athletic. That man has *stamina.*' She fanned herself a little, and a happy smile danced on her lips.

I smiled back, trying not to show the small shard of jealousy that was burrowing inside me. I wanted to be athletic with a certain man, but all he'd done was kiss my forehead. If he was interested in me, he was moving at a glacial pace. Still, I hadn't exactly shown interest – maybe I needed to flirt a little harder.

I bit my lip. Connor just lost Juan; now wasn't really the time to be putting moves on him. Besides, I had no moves; normally I just made eye contact with a guy in a bar, gave him a smile and if he was interested he'd be over like a shot to buy me a drink. Being in a damp town in Alaska was crippling my style.

I called the taxi company to collect me from my house, said goodbye to Sidnee and went home. After I'd fed Fluffy, I checked on the kitten and let him out of the bathroom. 'I'm sorry,' I said to my dog, 'but I'm leaving you here. I'm not risking any vamps deciding to juice-box you. Plus, that one is yours.' I pointed to the kitten.

He whined but then padded after the kitten, which was lapping up more hamburger. I turned on the TV for them and Fluffy jumped onto the couch to watch a TV show about bikers.

When the taxi arrived, I didn't recognise the driver. He confirmed my destination and set off, not engaging in chit-chat for which I was grateful. My thoughts were chaotic and I didn't have the strength to pull out my mother's social graces.

I got out at Kamluck Logging and headed for Connor's office. Before I could go inside, Connor came out. He gave me a small smile in greeting but I saw grief play across his face. I blinked and it was gone. His calm poker face was back in play.

Another male vampire was shadowing him. Connor said, 'Lee Margrave, my ... second.'

Margrave nodded. Broad shouldered and dark haired, he had a wicked looking scar down his face that had almost certainly been acquired *before* he'd been turned. He was a bruiser; if I'd met him in a dark alley, I would have run the opposite way.

'Nice to meet you,' I said.

Connor came down the steps and offered me his arm. I must have looked a little surprised, because he said, 'It's quite a walk to the meeting area.'

'Oh,' I said and took his arm. It was at times like these that I suddenly recalled he was older than me, born in another era when a gentleman offered a lady an arm. I could walk by myself, but there was something charming about having my arm through his.

We went down the path behind the building. Margrave stayed a few steps back, just as Juan had done. It made my heart twang and I rubbed my hand up and down Connor's bicep in sympathy. His arms were deliciously muscled. 'You have nice arms,' I blurted. I gave a mental head thunk; if this was my way of flirting, I really needed more practice.

Connor smiled, his eyes suddenly dancing with humour. 'Thank you. You've mentioned your appreciation of them before.'

I blinked. 'I have?'

'While you were drunk after your party.'

My skin warmed. 'Oh. What did I say?'

He paused and turned to face me. His gaze flickered to Margrave, who discreetly stepped back. 'You said that my arms are very muscly and you happened to love muscly arms.' His warm breath teased my ear, making me shudder in the most delicious way.

'Oh?' It came out breathless. 'Anything else I need to know?'

A smile teased his lips. 'In the privacy of your own home, you dance like no one is watching.' His eyes darkened. 'Even when I was watching.'

Oh boy. Heat pooled in my belly. I wished to heck that I could remember that night. Why had I drunk so much? Surely being a vampire should have protected me from drunken memory blackouts, but no.

'I'd love to repeat the experience,' Connor murmured, 'but with you sober. That way, I'd know every swing of those hips was really meant for me.'

His hand went from being laced through my arm in a gentlemanly way to sliding around the small of my back. He used the tiniest bit of pressure to move me towards him. I could have resisted if I'd wanted to – but I didn't want to.

We were in the middle of a spruce forest, and the scent of the trees was mingling with the earth and drifting on the air. Then there was the scent of Connor: he smelled like sandalwood, bergamot, and vanilla. He smelled *divine*.

The cold air of Alaska licked around me but I was suddenly very warm. Giving me plenty of time to move away, Connor reduced the distance between us to a finger length. His blue eyes looked at my mouth and he licked his lips. I followed the path of his tongue and wished it was on my skin.

He leaned down slowly and my eyes slid closed as his lips pressed against mine. My hand slid around his neck, pulling him more firmly to me, and I moaned as his tongue invaded my mouth. Hot, dizzying desire roared through me and my mind went blank as I melted into his arms.

And then that *zing* that I always felt with Connor crackled along my skin with so much strength that I pulled back. 'What *is* that?' I panted.

Connor's chest was heaving and he looked a little disconcerted. 'I'm sorry.' He ran his hand through his dark curls. 'I shouldn't have…'

'You absolutely should have!' I interrupted firmly. 'And we're going to do it again. Lots. But that spark? Connor?'

He pressed his forehead against mine. 'Not now,' he murmured. 'We have to get to the meeting. I'll explain on our date – when we finally manage to have it.'

'But … it's a thing?'

He nodded slowly. 'It's a thing.'

Damn. I didn't want to have a thing; I wanted to have something normal for once.

Connor offered me his arm again and led me along the woodland path. I recognised parts of it: it was on the way to the cabin where he'd hidden me after I'd been shot. Soon we reached a much larger building that looked like a warehouse. That made sense since a logging business presumably needed somewhere to store the cured wood out of the rain.

Connor paused outside the entrance and let his gentlemanly arm drop. I felt the loss of that comfort more sharply than I was prepared for, but I did my best to emulate his poker face.

We walked in. The door went directly into the storeroom, where lumber was stacked ceiling high, and the immense space was redolent with the rich scent of freshly cut wood. We passed all manner of logs and boards, then went into a showroom in one corner of the building where a range of flooring and wooden items were displayed. Everything had been pushed against one wall so that chairs could be laid out, and the room was filled with people, my people: the vampires of Portlock, Alaska.

Nerves sprang to life in my stomach and my stupid fangs dropped. Wankers. As I put my hand over my mouth, Connor caught the movement and smiled sympathetically. 'Don't worry about it. Everyone here has been through it.'

Thankfully the crowd had yet to notice our entrance, so I let my hand fall. 'It's embarrassing.'

'It's normal,' he insisted. 'Think happy thoughts and they'll retreat.'

'Just like Peter Pan?' I joked.

'Where do you think J M Barrie got it from?'

I gaped for a moment, which made him grin, then closed my mouth with a clack. 'It's tough to think happy thoughts the first time I'm in a room full of vampires I don't know,' I admitted.

He winked. 'They're just as scared of you as you are of them.'

I held in a laugh with effort; my nana used to say that about spiders. The humour of the moment made my teeth retract: happy thoughts, indeed. No doubt that had been Connor's intention. 'Thanks.'

'Ready?' He seemed to be asking about more than just this meeting.

Was I ready? I wasn't sure, but I nodded confidently. Mum had been preparing me for moments like for this my whole life. Fake it till you make it.

'Liar,' he murmured, his eyes warm. Then he straightened and the humour vanished. 'Come on, Bunny Barrington. Come and meet the vampires of Portlock.'

# Chapter 52

Although the warehouse was cavernous, someone had tried to make it seem a little cosier. There was a table of snacks and treats in one corner, together with bottled water, tea and coffee. No blood in sight. Despite the chairs, the vampires were standing in small groups talking and socializing. For them, this was a regular meeting; for me, it was something else – and I wasn't sure what.

Connor waited until I was ready then jerked his head to the podium, indicating that I should follow him. As he stalked through the crowd, it parted like the Red Sea. All eyes were on him and on me, and I felt the weight of their collective curiosity as I followed him a step ahead of Margrave.

A mic had been set up. Margrave stood behind Connor to his left, watching me appraisingly and with a hint of challenge, so I moved behind Connor's right.

'If you will all sit, we'll begin.' There was immense power in Connor's voice. For a moment my knees wanted to buckle, but I had no chair on the podium so – with an effort – I remained standing, as did Margrave.

Some vampires made it to the chairs, others simply dropped to the concrete floor where they had been standing. Silence fell and Connor let it hang like a heavy cloak. As the tension of the moment built, my scalp prickled. And still the silence held.

Finally Connor spoke. 'By now you'll have heard of Juan Torres' death, our second in command.' He spoke with an almost royal plurality. 'It is a hard loss for us all, especially so soon after losing Kivuk.' He gazed at the assembled vampires but there was nothing soft about his expression, no grief; instead, he looked angry. 'We will find those who took Juan from us and they will be held accountable.' He drew out the last word, each syllable heavy with threat.

'Juan was killed in a way that no vampire has been killed before. I have notified the council, but you also need to be aware of the method of his death. I have invited Officer Barrington of the Nomo's office to talk to you. Listen to her respectfully.' His tone said play nicely, or else.

He stepped back and discreetly placed a reassuring hand on the small of my back as I moved to the mic. I gazed at the assembled crowd of vampires and felt faintly sick. Then I cleared my throat.

'Thank you, Connor. For those of you who don't know me, I'm Bunny Barrington. I've recently moved to Portlock from London, England, and as Connor said, I work at the Nomo's office.' My mouth was dry and I paused, wishing I had a cup of tea. 'We've recently had some issues with a new street drug called fisheye.'

The stony silence held but all eyes were looking at me with eerily rapt attention. 'Juan Torres died, not because he used this drug but because he simply touched it.'

Noise exploded in sharp contrast to the silence a moment before. I looked uncertainly at Connor and he covered the mic. 'Give them a minute to process it,' he murmured. After the promised minute, he uncovered the mic and his voice cracked like a whip. 'Settle down. Listen to Officer Barrington, then we'll answer questions.'

The crowd became mute and stared at me once more.

'The drug looks like bright pink crystals,' I said. 'It can be mixed with salt water and vaped. Do not touch anything of that description and do not vape anything you have not prepared yourselves. The drug is mildly radioactive. It doesn't appear to affect humans, but it affects both land and sea shifters and gives a sustained high when it is vaped. However, it appears to be fatal to vampires. If you know of anyone who has come into contact with it, is contemplating using it or has already purchased it on the streets, please let the Nomo's office or Connor know immediately. Touching it with your bare skin is fatal.'

Connor said, 'Until further notice, you are all to wear gloves when in town. Ensure as little skin is exposed as possible. The drug was tossed to Juan and he caught it – that was all it took to kill him. Take sensible precautions and let me, Margrave or Barrington know immediately if you come across any drugs. Questions?'

'What is the Nomo doing about this drug problem?' one woman called. She was ginger, curvy, and wearing a tight red dress that was out of place in the warehouse. Her red hair made her look a little like Jessica Rabbit: I had a bunny rival.

'Everything we can,' I said confidently. 'We're raising awareness – you'll have seen the article in the *Supernat Sentinel* – and we are working hard to identify who is distributing the fisheye. We have already found and secured a large cache of the drugs, and it's possible we have already confiscated most of the supply. Even so, it's important that you warn everyone you know to stay away from it. If you see it being sold or used, please tell us immediately.'

'Who are your suspects?' Hester called out coolly.

'I can't confirm that at this time, but we *do* have suspects. The Nomo's office is working tirelessly to identify and apprehend the perpetrators.' Thank goodness I loved crime dramas; they had taught me a great deal about how the police presented themselves at press conferences.

The questions continued in that vein, but they were basically variations on those same two questions: what are you doing, and who is doing it? After about fifteen minutes I was exhausted.

'Enough,' Connor called finally. 'You have been warned. I do not want another death because of this drug. Wear gloves, be mindful, be proactive. I want everyone travelling in pairs through town until I say otherwise. Meeting adjourned.'

The vampires filed out, leaving Connor, Margrave and I in the room. Fielding the questions had been surprisingly hard and I felt like I'd been through the wringer, but I hoped I'd done the Nomo's office proud with my professionalism. The badge on my chest felt suddenly heavy.

Connor gave me a warm smile. 'You did really well.'

'Thanks.'

'I'll give you a lift home.' He turned to Margrave. 'Ask Hester to tidy this up, and make sure that gloves are available and handed out to everyone that needs them. I don't want any more mistakes.' Margrave nodded and marched off.

Connor led me back into the woods towards the office and his truck. 'Doesn't everyone in Alaska already have gloves?' I joked.

He shrugged. 'The undead don't feel the cold so much. That's usually an advantage, but not so much now.'

'You're really worried,' I realised.

'If this drug gets out, if people realise how deadly it is to vampires, it could change the power dynamics across the supernatural world. We can't let word of it spread.'

I licked my lips. 'Maybe not every vampire will react the same way as Juan.'

'Maybe,' he conceded. 'But I don't want to experiment to find out. My concern is that other vampire leaders won't be as scrupulous as I am, so we need to shut this down. Hard.'

Connor held the passenger door open and I hopped in. He slid in beside me and let the motor roar. 'Have you named your truck?' I asked suddenly.

'No. Who names their vehicle?' he asked, his tone mocking.

'Stan does. His truck is called Bessie.'

Connor snorted. 'A vehicle is just so much metal. It helps me get from A to B but I'm under no illusions that it's sentient. There's enough weird shit in this world without adding to it.'

I imagined the beast with its shadowy figure and its blazing eyes. 'Yeah,' I murmured. 'You're right.'

It was late – or very early – by the time that Connor dropped me off. 'Good night,' I said as I climbed out.

'Good night, Bunny,' he replied. He made no move to close the distance between us, so I guessed a goodnight kiss was out of the equation. I tried not to feel disappointed – but we had this *thing* between us and I needed to know more about it before we had a repeat performance of the kiss in the woods. Holy moly, though, it had been good and I wanted *more.*

Pulling out my keys, I started towards the house. Connor rolled down his window. 'Bunny,' he called and I turned back to him. 'Dream of me.' His eyes suddenly looked a whole lot more fiery.

My heart pounded. 'Yes,' I managed and then fled into the house.

Where I dreamed exclusively of a certain dark-haired vampire.

# Chapter 53

The next afternoon, Fluffy and I left early to get in a run before work. It was still daylight, but I felt rested for once, and since I'd not been running consistently I figured the exercise was needed. Afterwards, I was energised and rejuvenated. I had a shower, dressed and decided to head to the office early.

When I arrived, it was in total disarray. Gunnar and Sidnee were pulling on rain gear and boots. 'What's going on?' I asked.

'Perfect timing!' Gunnar grunted at me. 'We're going out on the boat, so grab your gear.'

I slung on wet-weather clothes. 'Should we take Fluffy?' I asked Gunnar, but he shook his head.

'We should get out there fast and I don't want to risk him going overboard. He can man the office. We need a mermaid more than a dog for this one.'

I settled a disgruntled Fluffy in his bed in the office and we hightailed it out of there, locking the office doors behind us. It didn't take us long to reach the dock where the Nomo's boat was kept. On the way, I briefly gave them the rundown of my meeting with the vampires. I omitted the kiss; that wasn't Nomo business.

We parked and hurried to the boat. I felt like a third wheel while Sidnee and Gunnar moved around preparing it, so I watched and learned, committing their actions to memory. Next time I would be an asset rather than an *ass*.

'Where are we going?' Sidnee asked, once we were underway.

'You remember that sea cave where you found the fisheye?' Gunnar asked. 'Well, we've had an anonymous call saying there's another one.'

'Another cave full of fisheye?' I asked.

'Supposedly. We'll know for sure when we get there. Sidnee, are you up for a swim?'

'Yup.' She gave two thumbs up and a wide grin; she was bouncing with excitement.

'The sea cave is under Elizabeth Island, so we have a five-mile ride. The sea is a little wild today, so you might want to find a comfortable spot.'

The furthest boat ride I'd taken was a short distance into Port Chatham Bay. We were going out into the ocean, and the ride would be *rough*.

'Ooh, this will be fun,' Sidnee said happily. 'I haven't swum in open water for a long time! Not since my parents...' She trailed off. 'Anyway, I love seeing new things! This will be great!'

It was the first time she'd ever mentioned her parents; there was a story there, but now wasn't the time for prying. I made a mental note to raise it another time.

'I wonder if they had the drugs out here the whole time, or if they moved them once we found that huge cache? Is Elizabeth Island inhabited?' I asked.

'No,' Gunnar grunted. 'Just a few dry cabins, rarely used.' The sea was choppy and he was focusing on keeping the boat moving in the right direction.

'That might make it a great place to manufacture the drug,' I pointed out.

He shook his head. 'There are zero facilities, no services whatsoever. If it's a manufactured substance, or something from the military like the lab guy seemed to think, I don't know if they could put anything together out there.'

A small stone on the bow of the ship lit up and we juddered through the barrier. As we passed through, the light winked out. Travelling through the barrier felt wildly different at sea; it felt stronger, more solid, and I didn't know whether that was a good or bad thing. Either way, a frisson of fear trembled down my spine. The beast wasn't the only thing that the barrier kept out. What kind of monsters were lurking in the water below us?

Fuck. Now I'd gone and scared myself.

# Chapter 54

The boat was really bumping along now. I moved around in my seat but it was still uncomfortable; there wasn't a pad thick enough to compensate for the jostling, and my bony bum was already starting to hurt.

Gunnar's chair appeared to be on hydraulics and he barely moved as it absorbed the bouncing. Sidnee was looking forward over the bow, perfectly at ease, moving in time to the boat's rocking. I decided that vampires were definitely *land* supernaturals, and I wondered how long I'd survive in the freezing Alaskan waters. I had no urge to find out – I'd leave experimenting to another vampire.

We hit an even bigger wave and I shot off my seat as we plummeted down the other side of it. My teeth dropped down and I felt queasy. I pushed it aside;

now was not the time to barf. Then a particularly hard bounce had me letting loose a string of swear words that would have absolutely mortified my mother.

'Not much further. Sorry about the rough ride. Just a small storm brewing,' Gunnar reassured me.

I didn't want him or Sid to see my stupid fangs, so I gave a thumbs up and kept my mouth closed. *Think happy thoughts. Think happy thoughts.* The first thought that came to mind was Connor, his arms around me, his lips against mine. I used my sharp memory to revel in the moment. When I opened my eyes again, the fangs were gone.

Thankfully the sea smoothed out as we approached the island and the wind died to nothing. The coastline was rocky, probably a good place for a sea cave to form, but it quickly changed to grass and then to steeply forested slopes. Like Gunnar had said, there were no signs of inhabitants, buildings or boats: there was nothing. Gunnar checked his GPS coordinates and moved us along the shore until he was sure of our location.

As I saw it, there were three options: whoever had called our hotline had sent us on a wild goose chase, was setting a trap, or had discovered the cache of drugs and wanted nothing to do with them.

'You said the call was anonymous, but we haven't seen anyone out here. Any siren group member could swim out here – it's only five miles,' I noted.

'That wasn't all the caller said,' Gunnar explained. 'He said he'd passed Soapy's boat out here – he was trying to steal Soapy's hot fishing spot. The caller was a siren shifter, so after Soapy left he decided to check out the underwater scene and see if it was fished out. He dove down, found something in the cave and was pretty sure it was a fisheye cache. I didn't get any more out of him, so it's up to us to see what we see. Or, more accurately, what Sidnee sees.' He grinned at her.

She grinned back. 'I brought the camera this time.'

'Perfect. I'm gonna take Bunny to the island. We'll have a mosey round to see if there's a secret manufacturing plant here. You take the water and we'll reconvene on the boat.'

Sidnee flipped him a cheeky salute and started to strip off her clothes. Gunnar dropped anchor and she dived into the ice-cold water. Once she'd disappeared, he used a small hoist to lower the small skiff off the cabin roof and into the water. It was tiny, like a toy boat. I looked at Gunnar's huge size and back at the skiff. No way was I getting into that dinghy.

He untied the skiff from the hoist, then beckoned for me to climb aboard. 'For fuck's sake,' I muttered as I flung my leg over the rail and jumped into the small boat. I landed with a sigh of relief.

Gunnar guffawed. 'Bunnies don't like swimming?' he teased.

'This one doesn't, not in freezing cold salt water,' I grumbled. We bounced merrily in the waves and my stomach lurched. I grasped the sides of the skiff – I could reach both of them at the same time without stretching. It felt like a small wave would capsize us, but Gunnar didn't seem too worried so I clung to his calm. We'd be fine.

When he started the engine, it let out a whine and we moved away from the relative safety of the Nomo's boat. The rocky shoreline was deceptive and some of the stones were huge and dangerous, but the skiff wove through them without issue.

We landed on a pebble beach and, since I was in the bow, I jumped out. I grabbed the rope and heaved, then Gunnar hopped out and dragged the boat out of the water. He left the end of the rope under a heavy stone before surveying our landing area. 'Looks pretty empty.'

No kidding: this was the barest piece of land I'd ever seen. The idea that there was only Gunnar and me on the whole island was strangely fascinating. I'd never been this alone in my entire life; even in our huge house, there'd been my parents, my nana, my nanny, and usually a cook or housekeeper.

'Where do we start?' I asked. 'And what are we looking for?'

'Let's walk the beach and see if we can spot any trails or boat docks, anything that would point to ... well, anything.'

'Okay, I'll follow your lead.'

Gunnar chose a direction and started walking. I kept my eyes peeled but I saw nothing but raw wilderness. Once I thought I spotted a flash of brown fur, but Gunnar shrugged it off as a moose or a deer. Nothing to get excited over. Eventually we ran out of beach; rather than move into the interior, we went in the opposite direction but soon we ran out of beach that way, too. We hadn't seen so much as an animal trail.

'Should we sail around the island?' I suggested.

'Sidnee's probably had time to investigate the cave. Let's go back to the boat and see where we're at, then we can decide what to do next.'

We headed back in the skiff. Sure enough, Sidnee was on the Nomo's boat. She waved but her face was sombre. 'She's found something,' I murmured.

'If she did, that's the nail in Soapy's coffin,' Gunnar said grimly.

The skiff pulled alongside the boat and I climbed aboard. Gunnar and Sidnee hoisted the skiff back up on the roof. 'What did you find?' he asked Sidnee when they'd finished.

'Let me show you the photos and videos. A picture's worth a thousand words, after all.'

We went inside and looked at the video on a tablet so it was on a larger screen than the one on the underwater video camera. We watched as Sidnee approached the cave, a large dark hole in the dark water. 'It's about two hundred feet down,' she said. 'That puts it well out of the reach of humans. Only water shifters would store stuff that deep.'

'What about a submarine?' I suggested.

She shrugged. 'It's possible but not likely – especially when you're talking about something going on right next to a supernatural town.' She was right; this was Occam's razor again. 'Wait until you see the rest of the footage.'

Sidnee entered the cave and various sea creatures swam by her, lit briefly by the bright beam of the camera light. I was entranced by the hidden world under the island. Finally, she came to a familiar sight: mesh bags full of plastic-wrapped bundles. 'That looks like a stash of fisheye,' I said. 'What's the confusion?'

'This,' she said grimly. 'Keep watching.'

On the video, Sidnee swam around the mesh bags; there seemed to be a lot more than we'd confiscated, maybe thirty bags as opposed to the five we'd already seized. 'Zoom in,' Gunnar said, frowning. She froze the video and increased the focus. Gunnar pointed. 'There.'

We looked. Holy hell – it was booby-trapped. The whole thing was rigged to blow.

# Chapter 55

'I see the problem,' Gunnar said drily.

'Yeah, me too.' I folded my arms. 'I doubt that's even fisheye in those bags, just something to draw us in and blow us up.'

Gunnar shook his head. 'We don't know that. It could be fisheye, and they just don't want it stolen like the first batch.'

At least we had a lead now – and things weren't looking good for Soapy.

'Do you want me to go back down and see if I can figure out how to disarm it? Or I could get a sample?' Sidnee asked.

Gunnar shook his head sharply. 'Absolutely not. Too dangerous. I'm not risking you. We have the video and it matches up with what we had in the lock-up. It'll have to be enough evidence for now. We'll call in a specialist to disarm the booby trap, though it will take me a while to find someone qualified for that kind of dive. I'll have to bring Calliope into the mix to find a siren shifter skilled enough.' He grimaced. 'That isn't going to be a fun conversation.'

'You're positive she isn't involved?' I asked. It was her shifter group and her second in command that were involved up to their eyeballs.

He shook his head. 'I doubt it. She has no need to push drugs – she's already incredibly wealthy, and she's never displayed any behaviour that would put our community at risk.'

'What about the fish price thing?' I threw out.

'That didn't put our community at risk. That was business.'

I took a deep breath then let it out slowly. 'I guess we go see her after we get back.'

'Yup. We're done here. Good work, Sidnee.' Gunnar looked at me. 'Let's take that cruise around the island and head home.'

He pulled up the anchor and we motored around the island. A lot of it wasn't possible to approach easily with a boat, and the places that looked like someone could get close enough to land showed no signs of anyone having been there. By the time we'd completed our loop, we were all sure that the drug wasn't being manufactured or packaged there.

We cruised along nicely back towards town; thankfully the sea was calmer and we were all much more relaxed on the journey back. Then *WHAM*! Something rammed into us so hard that we all went flying against the side of the hull. I landed first, then Gunnar's massive bulk slammed into me. I grunted at the impact and my ribs creaked.

Gunnar hastily scrambled off me. 'You okay?' he asked.

'I'm okay.'

'Sidnee?' Gunnar called.

'I'm fine,' she called, pulling herself up.

We were all a little disoriented, and the boat was rocking wildly. We looked out of the windows, but nothing was visible on the surface. 'Did we hit a rock?' I asked.

Gunnar looked over his instruments. 'No, no way – we're in deep water.'

'Something rammed us,' Sidnee said grimly.

I shivered and the hair stood up on the back of my neck. We were on the other side of the barrier... What kind of monster was attacking us? A shark? Please let it be a shark. I could cope with a shark because at least it wasn't a supernatural monster. How my standards had changed. 'What could hit us that hard?' I asked, my mind immediately going to *Jaws*. 'A shark, right?'

'More likely to be a whale,' Gunnar suggested.

In my head I was screaming, *You're gonna need a bigger boat*. Instead I said, 'This is a little boat. Let's get back home. Fast.'

Gunnar pushed the throttle and the boat jumped ahead, its two big engines churning. *WHAM*! This time the boat rocked so hard that we almost flipped over.

'I'm going out there,' Sidnee said, and started to strip off her clothes again.

'It isn't safe! We don't know what's attacking us!' Gunnar barked.

'Not many things can threaten me.' Sidnee smiled, showing her shark's teeth. 'Besides, I'm faster than almost everything.'

'Sidnee!' Gunnar shouted, but she ignored him and went over the side. He blistered the air with swear words, some of which I'd never heard before. I was pretty sure a few of them weren't even anatomically possible.

He slowed the boat to a stop, pulled out a rifle from under the bow and checked it over, then went to the side and watched for something to show up. We had stopped moving; we had to wait for Sidnee and we weren't sure if the boat was compromised. It seemed to be lower on one side, like the ramming had bent it somehow.

Suddenly, Gunnar shot at something in the water. 'What is it?' I asked urgently.

He shook his head. 'A shadow is all I saw.'

'Be careful you don't shoot Sidnee!'

He dropped the muzzle of the gun. 'I couldn't hit her if I tried,' he confessed. 'She wasn't wrong when she said she was fast.' There was pride in his voice.

The boat rocked again, but it wasn't a solid hit. I checked that my flotation device was done up correctly. Again. 'What kind of shifter is Soapy Willoughby? I know he's in the siren group – could this be him?'

'I think he's a salmon shark, so yes, it definitely could. They can be ten feet long and weigh five hundred pounds.' My *Jaws* fears were coming true.

At that moment Sidnee leapt onto the deck. 'Can't find anything,' she said crossly. 'I think the prick swam off. I didn't see a thing – but the boat has a big dent.'

'See any holes?' Gunnar asked.

'No, but you know the deal.'

'Yeah. It'll have to be pulled out of the water.'

We all hurried inside the cabin and Gunnar punched the engines then we raced back to town – this time without incident.

# Chapter 56

I was very grateful when my land-loving vampire feet hit the dock. To say I'd seen my life pass before my eyes was an understatement – and it hadn't been that exciting. My life could be summed up by soirées and serving shots, which was a bit depressing really.

We were all quiet as we walked back to the SUV. We were pretty sure we knew who the drug dealer was, but now we had to confront Calliope. Even Gunnar didn't speak; the boat being rammed had shaken him as well. We would have to inspect it for damage because those hits had been hefty.

Things were stacking up against Soapy. I could understand why Skylark hadn't wanted to point fingers at the second in command of the siren group, and no wonder he'd willingly climbed down the tree when Soapy had come knocking. If we could get

Skylark to corroborate our suspicions, the case would be ironclad.

I climbed in next to Gunnar and Sidnee hopped in the back. 'Should we call in Skylark?' I asked. 'Now we can ask him if it was Soapy that kidnapped him we might get a response, or at least something we can use.'

Gunnar started the engine. 'Yes, we'll talk to him first, then we'll get Calliope involved and hopefully make an arrest.'

I used the drive back to the office to set up a time with Skylark's parents to bring him in for another interview. I was worried that they'd be difficult, but the kidnapping had scared them, and they agreed to an appointment the following evening. The delay chafed, but we had little choice; besides, we were all shattered. Sidnee had put in a ridiculously long shift and was ready to collapse into Chris's arms. He'd already rung a few times to see where she was.

We pulled up to the office and my heart stopped. The door had been rammed open. 'Fluffy!' I shouted.

I rolled out of the car whilst it was still moving, ran into the office and immediately saw him. He had a collar on and he'd been chained to the leg of the desk, but he was okay.

I melted onto the floor next to him. 'Oh my god.' I wrapped my arms around him, letting his solid presence reassure me. 'Thank goodness you're okay.' He gave a soft whine and licked my face, then nuzzled my neck whilst I clung to him in sheer relief. When I'd seen that door busted in…

Gunnar came in. 'You okay, boy?' he asked. Fluffy gave a solid bark. 'Good lad.' Gunnar made short work of freeing him from the chain then went to look in the jail cells. 'Well, looks like Soapy and his crew used the diversion to come in here and try to get the cache.' He smiled grimly. 'The trick was on them because it was already gone.'

'Yeah,' I agreed. 'Small mercies. Shall we do some fingerprinting?'

Gunnar shook his head. 'No point. It's like Grand Central Station in here with people coming and going. Besides, Soapy's not stupid. They will have been wearing gloves.'

Sidnee patted Fluffy and he gave a low whine. 'Glad you're okay, puppers,' she said to him. 'I'm heading off. I'm so tired, I need to crash.' Fluffy lunged forward and grabbed her top with his teeth, tugging her back to him. She laughed. 'I love you too, but I really have to go.' She kissed him. 'I promise I'll go straight home to bed.'

Reluctantly, Fluffy let go of her. An alarm bell rang distantly in my head but I squashed it down because it was ridiculous.

I wrote a few emails while I waited until Gunnar had secured the front door; now I understood why he always had his plywood ready. Once he'd finished, Fluffy and I headed home to check on our little lynx.

The kitten let out a pitiful meow when we arrived, then wound in and out of my legs, purring loudly. I leaned down to pet him. 'Did you miss us, bud?' I asked gently. The cat's purr deepened to a rumble before giving Fluffy the same treatment, winding in and out of his paws.

'We can't call you "Bud", can we?' I murmured. 'What about Shadow?' The name seemed to fit the smoky-coloured kitten. He added a trilling 'mermp' of approval to his thunderous purr. 'Shadow it is.' I smiled. 'Let's get you both fed.'

I made up generous bowls for both of them and a brew for myself. It had been a long shift. My body was aching, but I couldn't be sure whether it was from my earlier run or the horrifically bouncy boat ride. Either way, blood would fix it.

I warmed a small cup in the microwave and managed to drink it without holding my nose. As the rich drink flooded through me, it washed away my aches. As much as the idea of drinking blood revolted me, the effects were totally worth it.

Bed was calling my name; the daytime exhaustion was starting to roll in, crushing me with its weight. But at least we had made progress today. Soapy's days were numbered.

# Chapter 57

I awoke to pounding on my door and blearily checked the time. I'd only been asleep a few hours, and it took a real effort to wrench myself out of bed. I threw on some clothes and willed myself to wake the fuck up.

I opened the front door and blinked when I saw Russell Arctos. How the heck did he know where I lived? 'Russ? What are you doing here?'

'Skylark's in trouble – real trouble. I tried to talk him out of it, but he went to the fish plant. He hasn't come back. I rang the Nomo's office but no one answered. You're closest, so I came to you.' I looked beyond him and spotted his bike.

My brain felt like it was full of wool but I tried my best to focus. 'Okay, come on in. I need to grab my boots. Tell me what's going on.'

'I don't know for sure. When Skylark called me, he was freaking out that his parents had agreed to another interview with you guys. He's scared about ratting. He went to the fish plant to speak to Calliope. He was supposed to call me when he was done, but I haven't heard anything and it's nearly 10am!' The boy was frantic and I couldn't blame him. What the heck was Skylark thinking, walking into the lion's den like that? God save me from stupid kids.

I pulled on my boots and turned to Fluffy. His close brush with the drug dealers at the office was fresh in my mind. 'You stay here,' I told him. 'Look after Shadow. I won't be long.' He whined and paced, but he finally lay down with his head on crossed paws and his big brown eyes pleading.

'You have to stay here. I can't have anything happen to you.' I kissed him, then hightailed out of my house. 'We'll go to the office first,' I said to Russell. 'We'll grab the Nomo SUV to drive to the plant.'

Russell hopped on his bike and pedalled slowly whilst I jogged to the office. He was right; the Nomo's office was empty. I went around the back to where the car was parked. As always, Gunnar had left the keys on the top of the driver's side wheel – not the most secure hiding place for a cop to choose, but handy today.

I pulled out my phone and rang Gunnar. No answer. I left a voicemail, then did the same for Sidnee. It nagged at me that neither of them had answered and dread started coiling in my gut. That alarm in my head I'd dismissed earlier rang again, louder this time.

I hesitated, then texted Connor and Stan. It was broad daylight and, as far as I knew, only Connor and I had daylight charms so the vampires would be of limited help. Stan, though, should have some shifters awake who could help if I needed them.

I didn't wait for either man to respond after I'd sent out my SOS. Concern for Skylark was consuming me. 'Okay,' I said to Russell. 'I've got it from here.' He opened his mouth to protest but I cut him off. 'Go home, Russ. I'll get Skylark out of this.' I hoped.

With a grimace, he hopped on his bike. I checked he was heading for his home then drove fast to Sidnee's house. I needed to reassure myself that she was fine.

But when I arrived at her house, her truck wasn't parked outside and the tendril of worry flared into a flame. The drug dealers had tried to break into the office yesterday and get the cache of drugs but found them gone. Sidnee and Gunnar weren't answering their phones. Had the dealers come knocking at their houses instead?

I tried to calm down. Sidnee's house looked fine, if empty; there was no sign of forced entry or damage. She'd probably gone to Chris's house. Then worry turned to panic because one thing had been nagging at me. If the call to get us out to Elizabeth Island had been nothing more than a diversion so they could break into the empty office, why had they thrown Soapy under the bus? The caller had said they'd followed Soapy's boat, which had cast more doubt on him. If Soapy *was* involved in all of this, why would he do that? And if Soapy *wasn't* involved in all of this ... then the other person who'd been scried by the sock was Chris.

Chris Jubatus, a selkie who could easily dive into those underwater caverns to place the bomb.

Chris, with whom I had shared dinner and sung karaoke.

Chris, who was dating Sidnee, a mermaid whom his family didn't approve of.

Chris, who had muddy-blond hair, just like Soapy.

I hadn't put it together earlier because I hadn't wanted to. I'd dismissed my vague concern without even consciously acknowledging it. I *liked* Chris, and Sidnee was well on the way to loving him. If he was using her to scope out the movements in the Nomo's office then all those calls of his weren't those of a concerned boyfriend but of a man who was using her.

I felt sick.

I checked my phone but no one had responded, not Gunnar, Sidnee, Connor or Stan. Fuck. I texted them my latest suspicions and, after a moment's thought, I also texted Patkotak. Then I headed to the fish plant to rescue Skylark.

Luckily I'd been to the fish plant before and knew something of its layout. I parked my car at the far end of the car park where there was a blind spot on the CCTV. Virginia Tide had parked Eric's truck there when she'd been trying to frame Stan. Keeping to the edge of the car park, I ran as fast as I could, digging deep into my supernatural speed and running far faster than I had the previous day. If I hadn't been petrified, it would have been exhilarating.

I ducked behind a crate and paused to assess the area. The warehouse door was wide open. I took a calculated risk, jogged to the loading-bay doors and slid carefully inside. The thing about risks ... is that they're risky.

As I slid into the warehouse, a cloud of hot-pink crystals was thrown into my face. *Deadly,* I thought.

And then I knew no more.

# Chapter 58

I woke up feeling sicker than I'd ever felt as a human. For the first time since I'd been turned, I craved blood – I *needed* it. It was all I could think about; I needed that hot liquid rolling down my throat, restoring me, saving me. My fangs flashed down and I bit my bottom lip. Iron liquid swelled in my mouth; it didn't banish the craving but it cleared my mind a little.

*Pink crystals.*

I tried to raise my arm because my hair had escaped its braid and was tickling my nose, but my arms wouldn't move. I jerked them but they were tied securely behind me, though my feet still felt free. I wrestled my eyes open and looked up. The world swam and the nausea amped up a notch. Fuck my life. This was fifty shades of not good.

Gunnar was tied up on the floor, unmoving. I was tied up on a chair, as were Sidnee, Soapy, and Sigrid – and yes, poor foolish Skylark. They were all conscious but bound and gagged.

I giggled. All their names started with an S. That had to be the freakiest coincidence in the world. S. S. S. S. I made the sound aloud, hissing like a snake before snickering to myself.

'She's awake,' Chris's voice said.

Oh shit. I should have pretended to be asleep, but really, the S sound was so much fun. I giggled again. I was high as a kite. *Let's go fly a kite, up to the highest height!*

The world swam around me. Calliope was tied to a chair too. Gunnar had been right: she wasn't involved. *Gunnar*. Worry for him helped slice through the giggling fog in my brain. Gunnar was down; he was down, and last time he'd virtually died. If we didn't get him medical attention fast, he'd be a goner not a Gunnar. Oh, fuckity-fuck-sticks. What could I do?

My arms were tied behind me. Chris was a fisherman, so no doubt he'd used knots that he was familiar with. I visualised a book my father had made me read once, a boy-scout book – Dad had always wanted a son. There had been a whole chapter on knots. I felt the one at my wrists and discovered it was a bowline knot. I visualised it in my head and started work undoing it.

Chris stalked over and gave me a smile. 'Wakey-wakey, Bunny. Rise and shine. Time to hop into action.'

I glared at him. 'Fuck you.'

'That's Sidnee's job,' he quipped.

A tear slid down Sidnee's cheek and I saw red. 'You're an absolute asshole.'

He glanced at her and the tiniest hint of guilt flashed across his face. It was there and gone in an instant, but it *had* been there. His jaw worked as he glared at me. 'I was hoping that the fisheye would kill you,' he said. 'But this is better. I'm not sure the Nomo is going to be helpful – I think I gave him too much.'

And maybe he didn't want to question Sidnee?

'What do you want?' I snarled.

'I want the product you took from us.'

I smiled. 'It's gone. You'll never get it back.'

He backhanded me across the face and my ears rang with the force of the blow. That hurt! He was incredibly strong. I'd been hit by my sire, Franklin, but this hurt twice as much. My jaw felt broken, not just dislocated, and my mouth was hanging open. I could feel saliva and blood dripping down my chin.

I tried to say something sassy, but I couldn't form words as my jaw tried to fix itself and use my blood to kickstart the healing. Chris took advantage of my silence to deliver a soliloquy. 'See, I know how protective our Nomo is. If he wakes up, I have his wife and his two assistants to convince him to play ball. It shouldn't be hard to get him to co-operate. If he doesn't, I have the same collateral for you. I know how you feel about your friend.'

My jaw snicked back into place and the ache faded. 'You love Sidnee. How could you do this to her?'

He laughed. 'Love? She was nothing but a mark, a way to keep tabs on the Nomo's office. She was fun and a good lay, but that was all.' I wondered if he knew that he was lying.

Fresh tears rolled down Sidnee's face and in that moment, I hated Chris even more. I fed the rage curling inside me and tried to reach out to the heat that I'd used to incinerate Virginia and Jim. Warmth coiled in my gut, but it wasn't the broiling heat I needed, and when I pushed out nothing happened. The fisheye had affected me more than I'd realised.

A man walked into the warehouse from the dockside door dressed in jeans and a rain jacket. I wracked my memory, but I definitely hadn't seen him before, not even in passing in town. Behind him were ten men dressed in army camouflage gear and carrying guns. They weren't taking any risks with the supernats.

'Ah, partner! I'd like you to meet the local law enforcement,' Chris said with mock joviality, as if this were a social event. 'This is Bunny Barrington, the Nomo's assistant. Bunny, this is General Samuel Thwaite.'

General? My stomach lurched. The fisheye – it *had* to be government manufactured. The lab physicist had encountered it before, and now we had a general strolling around. The government was trying to make a drug to affect the supernatural population – but to what end?

I took a shot. 'So you're trying out your poison on the supernaturals in Portlock?' I spat at the general.

He didn't answer; instead he turned to Chris and said, 'This one seems fairly intelligent.' He sounded surprised, as if he'd just heard a monkey talk. 'What is she?'

'Vampire.'

His eyes lit up and he appraised me with even more interest. 'How fascinating. All the vamps we've experimented on have died. We'll take this one with us for further analysis.'

Chris shrugged. 'She's all yours – *after* I've got answers about the location of our product. She's leverage.'

The general looked at the others. 'What else have you collected here? Anything else we can use?'

'Those three are shifters,' Chris said dismissively about Calliope, Soapy and Sidnee. 'I think you said you already had enough of those.'

His tone was casual and I wondered if he knew that he was trying to protect Sidnee from being taken, and probably Calliope as well. Calliope wasn't just a shifter, she was a rare Scylla; maybe he had retained some small vestige of loyalty to his kind after all.

Chris pointed at Sigrid. 'She's a witch. I'm not sure about him,' he nodded at Gunnar. 'There are lots of rumours about him, but I think he's a low-level magic user. I've only ever seen him open locks.'

I almost gasped: that's what I'd seen Gunnar do as well! Then I remembered the blast he'd used to temporarily heal the barrier. No, Gunnar was something more than a low-level magic user. Now I knew why he was so cagey about his skills: if no one knew what they were, he wouldn't flag up any interest.

'Only one interesting supernat in the bunch? That's disappointing.' The general paused a moment, stared at me then turned back to Chris. 'What about the shifter kid.'

Chris shrugged. 'Nothing special.'

'Still,' the general frowned, 'I haven't had the chance to work with a developing shifter yet, so we'll take him too.'

Chris didn't quite manage to stifle his grimace.

'Problem, lieutenant?' the general said dangerously.

He straightened. 'No, sir!'

The general stalked towards me. 'You're coming with me. We can make your incarceration pleasant or horrific. Tell me where the rest of the subdoid is.'

I blinked. 'The what?'

'Fisheye,' he said impatiently. 'Where is the cache you secured?'

I saw no reason to lie so I took some delight in telling him the truth, my little *fuck you*. 'It's been destroyed,' I smirked. 'You're never getting it back.'

His eyes narrowed. 'Well, that will be a problem, little rabbit. See, this village of yours is a testing ground. We need the product to go to all the supernatural groups so we can see how each one reacts. We'll have to import more.'

He spoke to Chris. 'You'll have to stay here and get more shared out. This many bodies or missing people is going to cause problems. Regrettable as it is, you'll have to use some amneiac on them. They'll forget even their own mother's names, but it'll be less hassle in the long run.'

He pulled out a thin case and opened it up to reveal a number of purple vials. 'You do it,' he ordered. 'Start with the women.' He nodded at Sidnee, Sigrid and Calliope.

Calliope's eyes were blazing with fury, Sidnee looked broken and Sigrid's eyes were locked on the too-still form of her husband. Chris approached them and I saw a moment's hesitation as he looked at Sidnee.

I'd been trying to buy time for Connor or Stan or Thomas to arrive – *someone* had to be on their way. But now I had to act; I couldn't let any of those women get their memories wiped. I'd picked the knots out and my hands were free but foolishly they had left my legs untied, presumably assuming that, as a vampire, I would drop dead anyway when they chucked fisheye in my face.

You know what they say about assumptions. Time for them to discover how much of an ass I could be.

# Chapter 59

I burst into action, leapt up from the chair and kicked the case out of Chris's hand.

'Don't shoot her!' the general barked to his men as ten rifles snapped towards me. 'We want her alive! Lieutenant, knock her out!'

All eyes focused on me, which may have been why they didn't notice one of their men collapse and slide out of view. The cavalry had arrived here: now it was one down and nine to go.

I needed to keep all eyes on me. 'You're a traitor – a disgrace!' I snarled at Chris as I threw a punch at him. He ducked out of its path easily, but while he was doing that I brought my heeled boot down on the vials. There was a satisfying crunch as the glass shattered and the purple amneiac liquid started to ooze out.

I saw a flicker of approval in Chris's eyes. I knew it! He hadn't wanted to wipe Sidnee's memories.

My hidden allies, whoever they were, got rid of two more of the armed men before the fourth guard called out and alerted the others. Then all hell broke loose.

Thomas, Stan, and Connor stormed into the room. Thomas had his tactical tomahawk in one hand and a handgun in the other; he shot two more guards and smacked one in the neck with his hatchet. Connor was a blur of motion as he took down two guards, then ran to Calliope to untie her. Stan let out an animalistic roar and flew towards Chris, rage in his eyes.

The general acted quickly, grabbing Gunnar and holding a gun to his temple. 'Stop,' he barked, 'or the Nomo gets it!'

Calliope exploded into action. Gone was the ethereal woman I'd often wondered about and in her place was the stuff of nightmares. Homer had not been exaggerating – Calliope was like Medusa on steroids. She had six serpentine heads and a body like a Great Dane dog, but bigger – much bigger. She thundered towards the nearest soldier and one of her heads flashed sharp, shark-like teeth before biting off his head, cutting him off mid-scream.

As we all stared at her, the general and Chris took advantage of the ruckus to slide away. 'They're escaping!' I shouted and dashed out of the door after them.

The general was fit and he ran fast for a human – but I wasn't human, I was the *wind*. I caught up to him as three of the guards leapt into a boat in front of him, and I grabbed his collar and yanked him back off his feet. His back hit the wooden dock with a sickening thud and he gave a loud, 'Oof!'

Someone started firing at me, but the boat was pulling away so the shots went wide. I heard a splash as Chris plunged into the water.

My fire magic still wasn't responding but my fangs were down. I *needed* blood so badly that I was shaking, and I did something I had sworn I would never do: I plunged my fangs into the general's throat and pierced his soft skin. Blood bubbled up and I sucked down the hot nectar. My body pulsed with strength and power, and the heat in my tummy coiled and snapped.

'Bunny,' Connor called to me from far, far away. 'Enough now, sweetheart. Enough. You don't want this. Look at me.' I didn't want to, but there was power in his voice. I looked up and met his stormy eyes.

'You're all done now,' he said softly, like he was talking to a child. He approached me cautiously. Some part of me wanted to plunge my teeth back into the general, because he was my *kill*, dammit. But – this was Connor. I could share the ruby liquid with him.

Beneath me, the general had stilled.

Connor reached out and touched me. An electric *zing* shot through me, and just like that my mind cleared.

I dropped the general. Eyes wide, I panicked. 'It's okay,' Connor soothed. 'He's not dead. You didn't kill him. You did so well coming back to me, such a good girl. Well done. Look at me now.'

His eyes were locked on mine, stormy blue like the sea; I could almost hear the crash of waves settling and soothing me. 'I'm okay,' I said weakly as the last hint of bloodlust left me.

'You're okay,' he agreed, taking me into his arms. I trembled, horror still lancing through me. I'd nearly killed the general – I'd *wanted* to kill the general. I'd felt like an animal, a predator.

I looked at the man on the deck; a trickle of blood flowed from the bites I'd made but they were small and clotted quickly. He was a bastard of the first order, but we needed answers. Connor released me and picked him up, effortlessly tossing him over his shoulder.

Back inside, Calliope was in her human form once more, dressed in nothing more than Soapy's huge shirt. An ambulance had arrived and was loading up Gunnar. I dashed over to him. Was it taking him to the morgue or the hospital?

'He's got a pulse,' Sigrid reassured me. 'He's tough as old boots and the hospital knows how to care for him this time. He'll be fine.' She gave me a quick hug. 'You're in charge of this mess, Officer Barrington.' She pulled Skylark into her arms and coaxed him into the ambulance, too. The doors slammed shut and the vehicle screamed off.

'Chris?' Sidnee asked me softly.

I crossed the distance and pulled her into my arms. 'He got away. I'm sorry.'

Her jaw worked. 'I hope the water dragon chomps him in half.'

Hard to disagree. I almost told her about all the clues I'd seen from Chris that showed he really did care for her, but now wasn't the time. I wasn't sure whether that would make it better or worse for her; either way, he'd betrayed her in the worst way possible.

Thomas and Connor had tied the general's arms and legs to the chair I'd been sitting on. 'Let's get some answers,' Thomas said grimly and backhanded him across the face as a gentle wakeup call.

'We need information, so don't kill him,' I cautioned.

Thomas shook his head. 'Oh, I'm not going to kill him. Not yet. He has a lot of suffering to go through for what he's done to this town. Bringing in drugs! Giving them to kids!' His lips curled back in a snarl.

Connor looked at me grimly. 'If we don't take care of it now, we'll have every black agency in the United

States government down here and he'll disappear forever.'

'He needs to pay,' Sidnee snarled. I squeezed her arm. I understood how she was feeling; I'd been inches away from killing the general in the heat of the moment. But this wasn't the heat of the moment.

Even so, I wasn't going to stop the men. They wanted information from the general, and so did I. We needed it to secure the town, and keeping Portlock safe was my job now. Gunnar had shown me time and time again that the rules were flexible, so I needed to use a little *flex*.

The general had come around and was staring at us blearily. 'What does fisheye do?' I asked him.

'I'm not answering anything.'

Thomas laughed. 'You will. You're in a town of supernaturals and, as the old saying goes, we have ways of making you talk.' He nodded at Connor, who went outside the warehouse on the street side. I watched curiously. A moment later he returned with Liv.

'You see, we don't need your permission or your co-operation,' Thomas explained. 'In fact, we don't need you to be alive at all. Liv is a necromancer and she raises the dead. That means all I have to do is slit your throat and she will reanimate you. All your secrets will be under her control.'

Liv smiled her creepiest smile and the feel of desert sands and hot sun washed over me. The general felt it too. He started to sweat and his face twisted with horror. 'You wouldn't dare!' he spluttered. 'I am a *general* in the United States army.'

Liv smirked. 'And I am a *necromancer* in Portlock.' With dramatic precision, she set out a salt circle and laid candles around it.

The general paled. 'I'll talk!'

'That's okay, we really don't need you to.' Thomas's face was expressionless.

The general squirmed and thrashed on his chair, but he wasn't going anywhere. Were they really going to kill and reanimate him? I remembered Liv saying it was rare that a spirit hung around long enough to be questioned, so killing him seemed risky to me, but what did I know? Maybe it was different if she killed him herself. That was something to have nightmares about later.

Liv continued to spread herbs and chant as she lit each candle.

'We were trying to make supernatural soldiers!' the general shouted.

Thomas ignored him. Liv continued.

'Why here?' Sidnee asked, arms folded.

The general swung his head to her. 'Stop them and I'll tell you everything.'

From behind the general's head, Thomas winked at Sidnee. She held up a hand, and Liv paused. 'I'm nearly ready,' she said huffily, as if she were annoyed at her preparations being interrupted.

Sidnee looked at me then tilted her head at the general; she wanted me to take over. I guessed I was bad cop. Given that I'd just drained a load of his blood, I doubted he'd have any difficultly believing my new role.

'We'll stop if you answer all of our questions,' I said. 'But if you hesitate, I'll have Liv do it the other way – the corpse way – are we clear?'

'Yes, yes, I understand.'

'Fine. Do you have records of what the drugs are and what they do?' He'd referenced amneiac as well as subdoid, so we had at least two supernatural-focused drugs bopping around.

'Yes.'

'We'll need that data.'

'Anything! I have an encrypted flash drive in my left pocket. It's all there!'

Thomas kept a knife to the general's throat as I searched his pockets. Sure enough, I retrieved a small flash drive. I put it in my own pocket. 'What's the password?' I asked.

The general rattled off a series of letters, symbols, and numbers, which I immediately memorised. 'How many supernatural communities are you experimenting in?' I asked.

'Five.'

I closed my eyes in horror. Five communities going through this? Just because the government wanted supernatural soldiers? 'What were you hoping the drug would do?' I demanded.

'We wanted supernaturals to be able to access their full powers on command, and if possible increase and enhance them.'

'That's not what we witnessed here,' I said angrily.

'We're still refining the substance. To do that, we need test subjects. Snatching too many supernats was raising suspicions, so we take a few from each community, release the drug to experiment on the rest and leave people around to collect the data.'

'I'm assuming you didn't ask for volunteers, or ask permission?'

He looked incredulous. 'No, of course not.'

'Why not?'

He actually looked confused. 'You're not human. We don't need your consent; in the same way we don't get a monkey to sign a waiver. Besides, we needed results fast and we didn't have time to go through normal channels. Checks and balances take time that we don't have.'

'You're saying that supernaturals are less than human to you.'

'You're nothing more than animals and monsters,' the general sneered. He grimaced after the words left his lips, as if he'd suddenly realised who he was dealing with. Calling me an animal or a monster might not be the wisest course of action.

'Bunny's not a monster,' Calliope said sweetly. 'But I am.' In a flash, she was in her Scylla form.

The general started to scream. 'No! Don't!'

One of her serpentine mouths, full of opalescent teeth all sharp as razors, opened wide. She swallowed the top half of the general's body while he screamed, then she snapped her jaw closed and cut his body in half.

Soapy pulled a shirt off one of the dead men and held it out to her but she shook her head. 'Let'sss go looking for Chrisss,' she hissed.

Soapy nodded. The two of them left the warehouse and dived into the water.

'Well,' Liv said. 'That was fun.' Her candles were scattered around. She ignored them, picked up her bag and strolled out, leaving the rest of us to sort out the mess.

And what a fucking mess it was.

# Chapter 60

It was all too clear that Thomas was intimately familiar with body disposal. He made a call and in minutes a team of humans rocked up with tarpaulins and shovels. The bodies were lugged into the back of the truck and Thomas's disposal team drove away again.

Stan headed to the hospital to check on Gunnar, and Thomas offered to drive Sidnee home. She accepted gratefully, looking worn and wounded. I hugged her goodbye. 'You'll get through this,' I promised as she clung to me.

She nodded against my shoulder. 'I've gotten through worse. But it hurts. Tonight it just hurts.'

'I'm sorry. You want me to come home with you?'

She pulled back, a real smile curving across her face. 'I appreciate the offer more than you can know, but tonight I just need to wallow.'

'I get it. I'm here if you need anything.'

'I know you are. Thank you.' She gave me one last squeeze and left with Thomas.

Connor wrapped an arm around my shoulder. 'Come on. Calliope and Soapy can deal with the rest of the clean-up. I'm taking you home.'

I couldn't do anything more than nod. Home sounded good, and I needed to see Fluffy and Shadow. Not to mention wash off the general's blood.

'Calliope just ate half of him,' I said dully.

Connor sighed, 'She does that. She's yet to come across a problem she can't eat away.'

That made me snicker. 'You're not supposed to eat your feelings.'

'Tell that to Calliope,' he replied drily.

When we got home, I snuggled my pets whilst Connor made me a cup of tea. He knew what I really needed.

Fluffy whined at me. 'I'm fine buddy. Just worn out.' I levelled him with a look. 'It was Chris that chained you up, huh?' He gave a bark.

That's why he hadn't wanted Sidnee to leave: he hadn't wanted her to go to Chris. I wanted to hit my head against the table. If only I'd watched him more, listened to his instincts. Well, it wouldn't happen again. From now on, if Fluffy barked I listened.

I drank my tea, sat on my sofa and let Connor wrap me in his arms. I lay against him for several minutes, my head resting against his chest, until I pushed up with a frown. 'I haven't felt one single heartbeat,' I protested.

His brow furrowed. 'No, of course not. I'm a vampire, Bunny. I'm undead like you.'

I sat up. 'I have a heartbeat. It's crazy slow, but it's there.'

He blinked and reached out to the pulse point on my neck. It took thirty seconds or so before my heart gave its ka-thunk. His eyes widened. 'I can feel it,' he said, 'but I can't *hear* it. Bunny – vampires don't have pulses. Not even slow ones.'

I swallowed hard. 'What does it mean?' I asked, anxiety swamping me.

He shook his head slowly. 'I don't know. But trust me, we're going to find out.' He licked his lips. 'Don't tell anyone else. If you have a heartbeat, you might not be as undead as we'd assumed.'

'So?'

'So the usual rules might not apply to you. Maybe you can be killed in ways other than being staked or decapitated.' He paled suddenly. 'God – when Virginia shot you, you lost so much blood. You were way more out of it than I would have expected. She could have killed you.'

I swallowed hard. 'Maybe I do still need to breathe,' I murmured. 'Juan said about vampires breathing, and how it's an affectation because they don't need to do it. But when I was in the water, my lungs were burning...'

'Hold your breath,' he suggested.

I took a deep breath, pinched my nostrils closed and held my hand over my mouth. I held it for as long as I could, and then I held it even longer. The world swam.

'Breathe!' Connor barked at me, ripping my hand away from my mouth. I gulped in a huge lungful of air gratefully.

Connor ran a hand through his dark curls. 'Well, you certainly need to breathe. This is ... unexpected.' He stood. 'I'll go home. I have books on vampire lore. I'll see what I can find about a vampire with a heartbeat who needs to breathe. You can't be the only one.'

His confidence was reassuring but I was freaking out. Why couldn't I do anything right, not even die?

Connor left without so much as goodbye kiss, and I hoped that my damned heartbeat hadn't stopped things between us before we'd even got started. I held onto the zing. Whatever else was going on, there was still something between us and I would hold him to it. I deserved that date, dammit.

Realistically, the date was the least of my problems. Portlock was on some sort of black government list, and the beast was back and trying to find a way in through the barrier. Gunnar was seriously ill and laid up in hospital, Sidnee was heartbroken, and Chris was still on the loose. Worst of all – my mother was coming to visit.

If I thought about it all like that, there was a real risk I'd run screaming into the sea. But the truth was that, despite all those disasters, I finally loved my life.

Whether I was undead, or not.

---

We hope you've loved this tale! If you can't quite wait for *The Vampire and the Case of the Baleful Banshee,* then never fear, we have a short story to tide you over! Hop into Connor MacKenzie's brain and see what happened when he met the MIB agent, Henderson.

Grab the free bonus scene by subscribing to Heather or Jill's newsletter, or going to https://dl.bookfunnel.com/hdq5027etl.

# About Heather

Heather is an urban fantasy writer and mum. She was born and raised near Windsor, which gave her the misguided impression that she was close to royalty in some way. She is not, though she once got a letter from Queen Elizabeth II's lady-in-waiting.

Heather went to university in Liverpool, where she took up skydiving and met her future husband. When she's not running around after her children, she's plotting her next book and daydreaming about vampires, dragons and kick-ass heroines.

Heather is a book lover who grew up reading Brian Jacques and Anne McCaffrey. She loves to travel and once spent a month in Thailand. She vows to return.

*Want to learn more about Heather? Subscribe to her newsletter for behind-the-scenes scoops, free bonus material and a cheeky peek into her world. Her subscribers will always get the heads up about the best deals on her books.*

*Subscribe to her Newsletter at her website www.heathergharris.com/subscribe.*

Too impatient to wait for Heather's next book? Join her (ever growing!) army of supportive patrons at Patreon.

## Heather's Patreon

Heather has started her very own Patreon page. What is Patreon? It's a subscription service that allows you to support Heather AND read her books way before anyone else! For a small monthly fee you could be reading Heather's next book, on a weekly chapter-by-chapter basis (in its roughest draft form!) in the next week or two. If you hit "Join the community" you can follow Heather along for FREE, though you won't get access to all the good stuff, like early release books, polls, live Q&A's, character art and more! You can even have a video call with Heather or have a character named after you! Heather's current patrons are getting to read a novella called House

Bound which isn't available anywhere else, not even to her newsletter subscribers!

If you're too impatient to wait until Heather's next release, then Patreon is made for you! Join Heather's patrons here.

## Heather's Shop and YouTube Channel

Heather now has her very own online shop! There you can buy oodles of glorious merchandise and audiobooks directly from her. Heather's audiobooks will still be on sale elsewhere, of course, but Heather pays her audiobook narrator *and* her cover designer - she makes the entire product - and then Audible pays her 25%. OUCH. Where possible, Heather would love it if you would buy her audiobooks directly from her, and then she can keep an amazing 90% of the money instead. Which she can reinvest in more books, in every form! But Audiobooks aren't all there is in the shop. You can get hoodies, t-shirts, mugs and more! Go and check her store out at: https://shop.heathergharris.com/

And if you don't have spare money to pay for audiobooks, Heather would still love you to experience Alyse Gibb's expert rendition of the books. You can listen to Heather's audiobooks for free on her YouTube Channel: https://www.youtube.com/@HeatherGHarrisAuthor

## Stay in Touch

Heather has been working hard on a bunch of cool things, including a new and shiny website which you'll love. Check it out at www.heathergharris.com.

*If you want to hear about all Heather's latest releases – subscribe to her newsletter for news, fun and freebies. Subscribe at Heather's website www.heathergharris.com/subscribe.*

Contact Info: www.heathergharris.com

Email: HeatherGHarrisAuthor@gmail.com

## Social Media

Heather can also be found on a host of social medias:

Facebook Page

Facebook Reader Group

Goodreads

Bookbub

Instagram

If you get a chance, please do follow Heather on Amazon!

# Reviews

Reviews feed Heather's soul. She'd really appreciate it if you could take a few moments to review her books on Amazon,

Bookbub, or Goodreads and say hello.

# About the Author - Jilleen

## About Jilleen

Jilleen Dolbeare writes urban fantasy and paranormal women's fiction. She loves stories with strong women, adventure, and humor, with a side helping of myth and folklore.

While living in the Arctic, she learned to keep her stakes sharp for the 67 days of night. She talks to the ravens that follow her when she takes long walks with her cats in their stroller, and she's learned how to keep the wolves at bay.

Jilleen lives with her husband and two hungry cats in Alaska where she also discovered her love and admiration of the Alaska Native peoples and their folklore.

## Stay in Touch

Jill can be reached through her website https://jilleendolbeareauthor.com/

Jill has also just joined Patreon! What is Patreon? It's a subscription service that allows you to support Jilleen AND read her books way before anyone else! For a small monthly fee you could be reading Jill's next book, on a weekly chapter-by-chapter basis (in its roughest draft form!) in the next week or two.

If you're too impatient to wait until Jilleen's next release, then Patreon is made for you! Join Jilleen's patrons here.

## Social Media

Jill can be found on a host of social media sites so track her down here.

# Other Works by Heather

**The *Portlock Paranormal Detective* Series with Jilleen Dolbeare**

The Vampire and the Case of her Dastardly Death - Book 0.5 (a prequel story),

The Vampire and the Case of the Wayward Werewolf – Book 1,

The Vampire and the Case of the Secretive Siren – Book 2,

The Vampire and the Case of the Baleful Banshee – Book 3.

The Vampire and the Case of the Cursed Canine – Book 4

# The *Other Realm* series

Glimmer of Dragons- Book 0.5 (a prequel story),

Glimmer of The Other- Book 1,

Glimmer of Hope- Book 2,

Glimmer of Christmas – Book 2.5 (a Christmas tale),

Glimmer of Death – Book 3,

Glimmer of Deception – Book 4,

It is recommended that you read *The Other Wolf series* before continuing with:

Challenge of the Court– Book 5,

Betrayal of the Court– Book 6; and

Revival of the Court– Book 7.

# The *Other Wolf* Series

Defender of The Pack– Book 0.5 (a prequel story),

Protection of the Pack– Book 1,

Guardians of the Pack– Book 2; and

Saviour of The Pack– Book 3.

# The *Other Witch* Series

Rune of the Witch – Book 0.5 (a prequel story),
Hex of the Witch– Book 1,
Coven of the Witch;– Book 2,
Familiar of the Witch– Book 3, and
Destiny of the Witch – Book 4.

# Other Works by Jilleen

## The *Paranormal Portlock Detective* Series with Heather G Harris

The Vampire and the Case of Her Dastardly Death: Book 0.5 (a prequel story), and

The Vampire and the Case of the Wayward Werewolf: Book 1,

The Vampire and the Case of the Secretive Siren: Book 2,

The Vampire and the Case of the Baleful Banshee: Book 3, and

The Vampire and the Case of the Cursed Canine: Book 4.

# The *Splintered Magic* Series:

Splintercat: Book 0.5 (a prequel story),
Splintered Magic: Book 1,
Splintered Veil: Book 2,
Splintered Fate: Book 3,
Splintered Haven: Book 4,
Splintered Secret: Book 5, and
Splintered Destiny: Book 6.

# The *Shadow Winged* Chronicles:

Shadow Lair: Book 0.5 (a prequel story),
Shadow Winged: Book 1,
Shadow Wolf: Book 1.5,
Shadow Strife: Book 2 ,
Shadow Witch: Book 2.5, and
Shadow War: Book 3.

# Review Request!

Wow! You finished the book. Go you!

Thanks for reading it. We appreciate it! Please, please, please consider leaving an honest review. Love it or hate it, authors can only sell books if they get reviews. If we don't sell books, Jill can't afford cat food. If Jill can't buy cat food, the little bastards will scavenge her sad, broken body. Then there will be no more books. Look at this terrifying, savage face. Jill's kitties have sunken cheeks and swollen tummies and can't wait to eat Jill. Please help by leaving that review! (Heather has a dog, so she probably won't be eaten, but she'd really like Jill to live, so... please review).

If you're a reviewer, you have our eternal gratitude.

Printed in Great Britain
by Amazon